Praise for Margot Early:

Margot Early's first Superromance novel,
The Third Christmas, won the Heart of Romance Award
and was a 1995 RITA Award finalist for Best First Book.

Her second, *The Keeper,* was a 1996 Janet Dailey Award
finalist.

"Hailed for her strikingly original style, gifted storyteller
Margot Early delivers another stellar achievement with
Nick's Kind of Woman.... [It] is the kind of intelligent and
emotionally satisfying romance that touches readers' hearts
and minds in a deep and lasting way. I can't get enough of
Margot Early's love stories."
—Laura DeVries aka Laura Gordon, author of
contemporary and historical romance

"In this deeply emotional story...two unlikely lovers battle
devastating odds to find themselves and each other.
[*Nick's Kind of Woman*] is a triumphant and satisfying tale!"
—Jean R. Ewing, award-winning author of *Scandal's Reward*

"Margot Early has given us a romantic masterpiece..."
—*Rendezvous* magazine on *Waiting for You*

"Margot Early delivers a powerful tale with *The Keeper....*
The title says it all about this heart-wrenching, emotional love
story."
—*Romantic Times*

"...an author whose talent will carry her to the top."
—*Affaire de Coeur*

Dear Reader,

I'm sometimes asked if I've actually participated in the kinds of activities I write about in my books: scuba diving, white-water rafting, tae kwon do, et cetera. The answer is yes, I have done some of those things—though never as well as the characters in my novels.

Day Sutter, who is indeed *Nick's Kind of Woman,* is close to my heart because of her struggles to excel as an athlete…when she isn't one. Like Day, I have pushed my mountain bike up the Moab Rim Trail, fought to make the crux of a 5.8 climb, and feared collapse while hiking under the weight of a sixty-pound pack. As Day does, I've found parts of myself through these battles (not always parts I liked, by the way).

Also, like Day, I have worked as Girl Friday of a river outfit in Moab, Utah. Actually, my employers—book lovers themselves—allowed me to write novels on their word processor while manning the phones. These lovely people do *not* appear in the pages of this book, but I thought of them often while writing *The Keeper* and this story, which is its spin-off. With these tales, I have enjoyed revisiting the never-dull world of wilderness outfitting. Through Day and Nick—and Grace and Zac, whom you may remember from *The Keeper*—I'm happy to bring this world and the Colorado Plateau, my home, to you…again.

Sincerely,

Margot Early

P.S. I love to hear from readers. Please write to me at P.O. Box 611, Montrose, CO 81402-0611.

NICK'S KIND OF WOMAN
Margot Early

Harlequin Books

TORONTO • NEW YORK • LONDON
AMSTERDAM • PARIS • SYDNEY • HAMBURG
STOCKHOLM • ATHENS • TOKYO • MILAN
MADRID • WARSAW • BUDAPEST • AUCKLAND

ISBN 0-373-70724-X

NICK'S KIND OF WOMAN

Researching for a novel can be an adventure—or a chore. I would like to thank each of the following people for sharing wisdom in their fields of expertise, making my research experience so enjoyable and helping this book come alive.

Gary Parker, Assistant Park Manager at the Edge of the Cedars State Park in Blanding, Utah, sent me a wealth of articles about pot hunting. Rooster Barnhart and Rusty George helped me with information about rock climbing. Margaret Brandenburg, R.N., and Maureen Matthews, my sister, read the manuscript for technical accuracy in medical matters. It's also worth mentioning that when I was a child Maureen taught me the rules of punctuation! My sisters Rosemary and Kathy also helped with this project. In addition, Rosemary was the person who first suggested I try writing romance, and Kathy always listened willingly to the stories I wrote as a teenager. None of the above begins to cover the love, nurturing and support I have felt from them as sisters and from *all* members of my family. Including my niece Chelsea, who told me the riddle about the birds.

To all of you, my heartfelt thanks. All errors in this fictional work are mine.

"The annals of former generations are lessons to the living: a man may look back upon the fortunes of his predecessors and be admonished; and contemplate the history of past ages and be purged of folly."
—*Tales from the Thousand and One Nights*
Translated by N. J. Dawood

"Ah, he wanders forth again;
We cannot keep him; now, as then,
There's a secret in his breast
Which will never let him rest."

—Alfred, Lord Tennyson
Idylls of the King

PROLOGUE

Colorado River corridor
Moab, Utah
Back in high school

HER FATHER had told her to stay away from him. "That boy's just like a dog who's been kicked his whole life. And a human who's been beat like that is much more dangerous than a wounded animal. You keep your distance, Day."

From her inflatable kayak, she lassoed a rock poking out of the riverbank and pulled herself to shore. A canoe was hidden in the tamarisk. *He* had stolen the canoe from Rapid Riggers River and Jeep Expeditions, but her dad knew it and hadn't done anything about it. And her dad owned Rapid Riggers.

When she got out of the boat, the mud in the shallows tried to pull her shoes off her feet. Day hated sand and silt. She'd never known anything else her whole life. They couldn't keep the sand out of the house or out of their clothes. Her cheerleading uniform was the only thing she managed to keep white and only by always hanging it in a plastic dry cleaner's bag.

Today she wore black baggy shorts and an oversize tie-dyed T-shirt. Her new high-top sneakers were ruined now. The rusty red of the Colorado would never come out.

As she lifted her knapsack out of the boat, the metal-and-air sound of a pop-top being pulled from a tin can made her jump. There he was, opening a beer.

Day didn't want to admit she was afraid.

His eyes were dark brown, and seeing them now, Day realized her father was right. Nick Colter knew things a kid shouldn't. Day could already smell him, and she remembered what had happened that morning, how the principal and the vice-principal had both restrained him because he wouldn't sit in the small windowless room between the two classrooms and work on his math. Her father had come down to the school, and at lunch Grace had told everyone that it was to find out about a PTA meeting. Later, when Day had called her on lying, her sister had said, "So, you want everyone in town to find out that Dad *likes* him? People are going to think he's our *brother*."

He couldn't be their brother. He didn't look anything like them.

The tall boy on the riverbank stayed where he was. Nothing about him invited Day to come closer.

Day told herself she was visiting out of kindness. It was a good samaritan act.

But she knew that wasn't the truth.

The truth was . . . he was cute.

And fascinating. A cave boy.

"Hi." Nervous, she explained, "I brought some books. English. I thought we could study together."

His eyes should have stopped her. They looked mean. As she waded out of the mud, Day said, "I thought, like, I could read the myth about Theseus and you could follow along."

Did the hardness of his eyes lessen? Difficult to tell.

Day felt silly in her expensive clothes that were supposed to look worn-out and comfortable. He was really poor. He didn't have good jeans, Levis or Ben Rogan designer jeans. His were part polyester, and his plain white T-shirt looked stained.

She trudged up the bank through the deep powder-fine red sand, the sand that would be in her socks forever. She'd better get back to the house before her dad came home from Rapid Riggers. But she had an hour till then. "Do you have another beer?"

He snorted. "No."

In other words, he wouldn't give her one.

Day said, "I drink."

"So what?"

They were neither of them within half a decade of legal drinking age. And what she'd said wasn't really true.

He, however, was draining his beer with ease. He crumpled the can and hurled it against the nearest sandstone wall, and it hit the crumbling red rock with a faint clink.

Day followed him to the mouth of the cave. Against one wall, beyond his blackened fire pit, she saw a roll of blankets, army surplus. Not very many, but it was spring, April.

"Didn't my dad give you a solar shower?"

He looked like she was speaking another language.

She knew her father had given him stuff. Her dad liked him. But none of the gifts was in sight. He didn't even have a cooler, and she knew he must be keeping the beer cold in the river.

A mosquito bit her arm. *It's so dirty and deserted here.* Day wondered how her dad had gotten the cave boy to come to school even once. He had to know everyone thought he was a freak, but he came every day.

"I could bring you some soap," she offered.

He headed down into the tamarisk and returned with two beers. He threw one to her; it was cold from the river. The water dripped down the front of her shorts and her bare legs. When she popped open the can, the foam poured all over her. Feeling adventurous and adult, Day put the can to her lips and drank the beer, which tasted pretty vile. She ought to be able to drink it; Grace was going to take her to a senior party that weekend, even though Grace was just a sophomore, not quite a year older than her.

Day asked him, "How old are you?"

"Fifteen. Almost."

"When's your birthday?"

"When's yours?" He drank his beer, and Day knew he was deliberately provoking her.

But he could be nice sometimes. Once he'd picked up her books when someone had bumped into her in the hall.

"I just had it." So there, thought Day, and so much for birthdays.

They sat in the sand outside the cave and leaned back against the red rocks. He smelled bad, like the homeless people she had seen when she visited Salt Lake City with her dad and Grace. As she opened her backpack to take out her school copy of Edith Hamilton's *Mythology,* Day tried to be helpful. "You should use that shower. I've used them on camping trips. They work pretty well, except for I always have to use two to wash my hair. Grace and my dad make fun of me."

He smiled a little at that. Then he touched her hair.

A strange shiver went through Day.

"Your hair's pretty," he said. "Mine's just brown."

It was almost black. Day wanted to touch his hair, too, but she was afraid of him. It occurred to her that he was a little drunk, and that she should leave. Instead, she opened the book and began to read about Theseus, the hero of Athens.

Her voice shook, but she kept to her plan, following the words on the page with her finger. He was silent, and when she glanced at him, he looked up from the page as if to say, *Why did you stop?*

While the sun lowered over the red canyon walls of the river gorge, she read to him.

Nick tried to make sense of the black shapes on the page. He couldn't. He watched her, instead.

She was so pretty. He'd never seen anyone that pretty.

Ashamed, he knew she was trying to teach him to read.

He tried to follow her finger on the page, tried to be smart. He understood stories, and this was a good story. About a monster in a maze. She read the whole thing, and he listened, trembling with wanting to touch her. Smelling how good she smelled.

"I can't stay much longer." Her voice was all shaky again, he noticed, as she took another book from her pack. "Grace and I have a contest with this book. We memorize it, and we try to say it fastest."

It was a little kid's book. The letters were big.

Nick wanted to shove her. Hit her.

She handed him the book, opened. "Okay, so here, start on this page, and see if I make any mistakes." Day began to recite *Fox in Socks*.

He felt himself smiling. Only when she reached over and turned the page did he recall what she was doing. That she knew he couldn't read.

He shut the book, mad. Why had she come, anyhow? She was like her father.

Recognizing his anger, Day put *Mythology* in her backpack. She nodded to the Dr. Seuss and said, "You can keep that. I have to go home."

"Stay awhile."

His hand on her shoulder hinted at a wiry strength. Day recalled the whole story of the canoe. After he'd stolen it, he'd paddled it down Cataract Canyon. Anyone that brave ought to be a good person, too.

But the world didn't always work that way.

She stood up, and so did Nick Colter. His eyes were murky and mean again, and she remembered how tall he was.

"Why'd you come here? You want to get—" The word he chose was not gentle or vague.

Day's throat ran dry, and her father's warning returned to her—belatedly.

She drew her shoulders up. "No."

"Maybe you wanted—"

She tried not to hear the rest, but she did. What he said was obscene. She hadn't heard all the expressions before, but she knew what they meant. It was time to leave. "Excuse me," she said. Walking toward the bank, she couldn't see his shadow. He was behind her, and the sun was the wrong way. He could be creeping up on her. As she climbed into the dinghy, a reflection moved on the water, and Day jumped, rocking the boat. She heard his laughter, but it was far behind her, and she didn't look back until she had shoved the dinghy away from shore.

He was standing beside the cave, smiling at her in a nasty way, as though he knew he had scared her and was glad.

CHAPTER ONE

Moab, Utah
The winter solstice
Fourteen years later

THERE ARE SACRED SECRETS. Day Sutter had one. She had kept the secret for almost a decade. Now she was twenty-seven years old, and the cause for secrecy occurred only once a year, always on this night, the night of the solstice. No other night mattered to her more.

New lights, shaped like toy rockets, hung on the fir tree in her living room. Her other ornamental light sets, strung throughout the house, included planets, cowboys and horses and covered wagons, bunny rabbits and carrots. For Day, Christmas was part of a pagan holiday season. She dated her new year from the winter solstice—the longest night that was always too short.

As usual she had decorated with holly and mistletoe and poinsettias. All real. It seemed important to bring nature indoors, to simulate the wilderness, though it never really worked. When he first showed up, he always seemed trapped and restless, like a person who'd arrived at an important business function only to remember that he'd left the coffeepot on at home. Or like a wild animal kept as a pet.

Through the patio doors, she noted the dimming of the desert colors, the gradual disappearance of light outside. He would come when the sun set.

Day crossed her freshly swept floors on high heels, lighting scented candles, checking the bulbs on the tree, re-arranging a gift-wrapped package beneath the lowest boughs—her gift for him. The yellow of her neighbor's house lights glowed between the slats of her backyard fence. By this time in the afternoon, she'd usually drawn curtains across the plate-glass windows beside her patio, on the French doors in her bedroom, on the windows facing Uranium Street. Tonight, she hadn't; she'd even left the windows and doors themselves open a crack, counting on the wood stove to warm the house.

At the end of the hall, she checked her reflection in her full-length beveled mirror, a yard-sale treasure. She looked pretty. Red-and-white herringbone-check straight skirt, white angora sweater, a string of real baroque pearls and matching earrings that had been a birthday gift from Grace and Zachary. Garters held up her stockings, translucent white silk stockings with seams up the back. She had purchased both stockings and garter belt from a mail-order outfit that recreated vintage clothing. She'd made the skirt.

Back in the living room, she glanced toward the windows. Darker. Now the glass reflected her lights.

A bottle of Courvoisier XO on top of the refrigerator beckoned, and Day considered taking a hit. But he would bring wine, and anyhow, what she really wanted was to step outside and smoke a cigarette. Unfortunately he hated the smell.

Dammit, why was she so nervous?

She knew why. Because of Shep. Shep, aka Elizabeth Shephard. Earth child, athlete, trust-fund brat.

Don't think about Shep. Shep is a passing fancy, a thing of the moment.

The question was whether or not the fancy had passed. If his latest girlfriend was a thing of *this* moment.

Day made for the bathroom and lined her lips with a lip pencil, her heart stopping and starting at the sound of a car passing on the street. She tried to feel happy, light of heart.

But the sadness was creeping in.

Her secret was sad. And getting sadder every year.

NICK COLTER RELAXED his fingers on the wheel of his blue '57 Chevy pickup and let the engine idle as he stared across Uranium Street at Day Sutter's one-story gray-and-stone house, a fixer-upper she'd bought years before, after it had lain vacant for two decades and been vandalized. Day had refurbished the place—or rather, hired someone to do it. *Hammer? What's that?*

Pink lights rimmed the windows, and white bulbs blinked in the trees outside, shimmering against the crust of snow on the lawn. A storm had dumped on Moab two days earlier, and bulldozers had pushed the snow to the middle of the street where it made a divider four feet high.

In the night shadows of a sprawling cottonwood tree's denuded branches, Nick considered a paper bag on the seat, the bottle of chianti. With a sigh, he switched off the ignition and rested his arms on the steering wheel.

Have to do it, he thought. *This is it.*

They couldn't go on like they had been, but he was tempted, anyway. What could it hurt? One more time. One more night. In her bed they could probably even reach some compromises about how to run Rapid Riggers.

No.

Disgusted with himself, he drew the key from the ignition and grabbed the wine. He'd leave it with her, to soften the blow. Nick didn't pretend that it wouldn't be a blow. About some things, they'd never had secrets.

DAY HEARD his footsteps on the walk and peered out the front window. Her heart pounded faster at the sight of his dark hair, which always looked overdue to be cut, the hair

that in the sunlight proved it wasn't quite black but a very
deep brown, with faint highlights of burnt sienna, like the
darkest rocks of the canyons. He was big, almost as tall as
her sister's husband, Zachary, and lean and powerful, like
an Indian hero on a paperback in the grocery store.

Day waited till he knocked before she opened the door
with a grin she hoped was effervescent, full of fun. They
had to have a good time. Each year should be better than
the year before.

Nick's hands were in the pockets of his parka, the bottle
of wine tucked under his arm. His shoe-black eyebrows
lifted slightly. "Hi."

"Hi." Nervousness poured through her again. Every
time it was the same. Fear that he might stand her up or
that something would go wrong between them. That he
would cease to care. She held the door wider, and he entered.

To Nick, her living room always smelled faintly of cigarettes, even now, despite the pungent evergreen. Shutting
the door behind himself, he saw the candles. The tree.

He shouldn't have let her do all this.

Should have picked another time to tell her.

Should have left her some pride.

She smelled good, and her platinum-and-dark-blond hair
looked frothy, shiny, like the hair of a 1940s movie star or
a Vargas girl. Her eyes were sky blue, and her mouth was
too big for her delicate face. There were dimple lines at the
corners of her lips, under her high cheekbones.

She was, bar none, the most beautiful woman he had
ever seen. In bed, no one could excite him more.

Out of bed, no one could be more frustrating.

Nick put his arm around her shoulders, hugged her, felt
her silky hair against his jaw.

Day closed her eyes, soothed. Everything was going to be
okay. They'd have some wine and relax and eventually wind
up on the floor in front of the wood stove or maybe go right

into the bedroom. They would know each other naked. And say the things that could only be said on the solstice.

Nick released her, and when she looked up, his eyes were on her face. She expected a joke, a flirtation. *I see you've worn something sensible.* Something he could have fun taking off her. Stockings. Garters. Nick was funny, lighthearted and easygoing. At work, he possessed a genius for winning over tourists, even those who spoke other languages.

Now he said in a strange dry voice, "How are you?"

"Good." Day smiled, hoping her lips didn't quaver.

She'd seen him just hours before, of course, at the office of their river outfit, now closed for the season. Rapid Riggers River and Jeep Expeditions, the oldest river outfit in Moab, Utah, had been founded by Day's father, Sam Sutter. Sam had been dead almost two years now, but only a few months had passed since Nick had bought half the business from Day's sister, Grace.

Day owned the other half of Rapid Riggers. As Day saw it, the fact that she and Nick were equal partners was a very good thing. A permanent thing. She hoped it would be a precursor to another permanent thing, once Nick reconciled himself to the big *M*. He was only twenty-eight. Not finished sowing his oats.

Blocking out a discouraging vision of an octogenarian Nick still unable to settle down, too wild to be tamed, still climbing mountains and rowing rivers and breaking hearts and unable to sleep with the doors and windows shut, Day reached for the wine. "Shall we open this?"

"Um..." Nick ran his tongue along his bottom lip. "Let's just sit down." He hadn't even unzipped his coat.

Day's breath stilled. Something was wrong. "Sure."

They moved over to the couch, a pale blue leather couch with cherry legs and rows of brass tacks at the edge of the upholstery. The couch was the color of her eyes.

He said, "I'm not staying."

Nightmare words. Day shifted on the couch and made herself look inquisitive. Interested.

Not afraid or heartbroken. Or shattered.

Nick thought, *I forgot how much class you have.*

She actually smiled. "Shep?"

It wasn't what he'd expected. His trachea felt as though it had a piece of gravel stuck in it. "Ah...no." He leaned forward, seeing a large glossy book on her coffee table. It was a book about rock climbing. Something he could spend hours paging through. *Yes. Have to stop this.*

Day wasn't a rock climber.

Day was just in love with him, and the book was there for him, to make things right for him, to hold his interest. He wanted to see *her* books, the evidence of things that were important to her. In her bedroom and her study were theater scripts and the sewing machine she used to make her own clothes; actually she'd made a lot for him, too. She had a decade's worth of costumes she'd designed and sewn for the Moab lip-sync contest, which she usually won. And there were the books she read to learn stories to retell at the library and the museum. Oral storytelling was her latest interest, but sometimes he wondered if that was because of him, too. Stories were something they'd shared from the first. Stories bound them, and Day made the most of that. Of anything that brought them together. And here, in this room, on this night, everything was carefully orchestrated, done for him.

Nick focused. *Shep.* "It doesn't have anything to do with Shep. I just realized it would be hard to see you at work tomorrow."

Day played that over. True, in the past he'd always done a disappearing act after the solstice. Shoestring river trips in South America, mountain-climbing expeditions. Nick was an EMT-I, an intermediate-level emergency medical technician, and a member of Moab's search-and-rescue team. Some winters he worked ski patrol in Park City or

Aspen and drifted into Moab only for the night of the solstice. Afterward, he left and never returned until spring, just before river-running season, to help teach annual classes in advanced first aid, wilderness medicine and river rescue.

But now he was an outfitter, a businessman, and his responsibilities in Moab extended into the off-season.

Day picked over some responses. *That's okay... But just for the record, it would be like usual.* Or, *Hard to see me how?*

The wine sat in its paper bag on the coffee table, still unwrapped, unopened. Nick wasn't going to stay.

She said, "Why is that?"

"What?" He jerked his chin up.

"Why would it be hard to see me?"

"Awkward." He could have said something more flattering—implied that he would be hot for her for the next three months, for the rest of his life.

It wasn't what he wanted to get across.

"This isn't going anywhere, Day."

Day smiled, hankering for a cigarette. Better wait—just in case. "We've always known that. That wasn't the point."

What is the point? he wanted to say. But he knew. He knew Day.

He wouldn't spare her pride or let her hope. This solstice he would give her back her life. He touched her, his right hand on her left arm as she faced him, and the electricity, the physical awareness he didn't want, arced between them. "We have two rules. No lies. No strings. We've never broken either."

No, thought Day, and we've made love and said, *I love you,* both of us.

No lies.

No strings.

Nick whispered, "I'm never going to marry you, Day."

Time for a cigarette. Day rose to get them from the top of the refrigerator, glad for a reason to keep her back to him.

On the couch, Nick put his hand over his forehead. The draft from the open window carried a memory—not fresh air, but stale. It made him think about himself and about Day, who understood. About windows.

In the kitchen Day lit a cigarette.

No lies.

She couldn't say, *What makes you think I want to marry you?*

Couldn't even say, *I never thought you'd marry me.*

Maybe she'd never thought it. But she had dreamed.

In the living room he was staring at her tree.

This isn't any fun for him, either.

Leaning against her breakfast bar with its 1950s-style soda-fountain stools, she said, "Okay."

Nick turned his head.

She smiled, telling herself she wasn't blinking too much. *Hang on. Just till he's gone.*

Nick thought, *Shit, Day, don't be a hero. Say something bitchy. Throw something.* He'd duck. He'd had lots of practice.

But she sucked on her cigarette, pretending her hand wasn't shaking.

Nick left the couch and came to the breakfast bar. He reached into one of the half-dozen or so pockets of his Patagonia guide shell, pulled out a small package and held it over the counter. "I got this for you."

The box was covered in brown paper and tied with red and green and gold bows. Professionally gift wrapped, wherever he'd bought it. Day knew what was inside. Basically.

"I don't want it."

A breath passed. He dropped the box back in his pocket. "I guess not." *Now* maybe she'd throw something.

Day tried to stop the emotions bubbling in her throat. *Be careful. Be careful.* Lightly she asked, "So this really is about Shep, isn't it?"

Her mouth was a natural line, deliberately relaxed. He knew she was trying not to be unpleasant. Trying too damn hard. "No," he said, "it really isn't." *Don't want to hurt you, Day.*

She didn't look hurt.

He knew she was.

"Then it's about Rapid Riggers, isn't it?"

"It is *not* about Rapid Riggers."

Oh, that got a little charge out of you, didn't it, Nick? "Truly?"

"You want to talk about new rafts, or you want to talk about us?"

"You just said it had to do with work. If this is about getting a loan—"

"It's *not.*" Her cigarette smoke stole too much air from the room, but he knew she was smoking because she was upset. Gently, ready to get away, he said, "I'll see you at work tomorrow, all right?"

Don't cling, Day warned herself.

"Sure." Her smile felt crooked. She drew on the cigarette as she walked to the door and opened it. "Want your wine?"

"I brought it for you." He lingered by the door, the heat rushing out with him.

"Thanks. See you tomorrow."

He wanted to lean toward her, to kiss her cheek before he left.

He liked her too much to do it.

"Bye."

Day watched his back as he went down the steps and blended with the colors of the night. When he reached his truck, she closed the door and stood listening till the engine started and he drove away.

Balancing on one foot, then the other, Day took off her shoes, red patent-leather high-heeled Mary Janes she'd ordered from New York. "Screw the wine." Ignoring the package under the tree—she'd figure out what to do with her gift for him when the idea didn't make her cry—she wandered back into the kitchen, took down the bottle of cognac, warmed a brandy snifter and filled it.

Minutes later she was ensconced on the couch with her cigarettes and her drink and the longest night of the year ahead of her.

"Shit," she said, and minutes passed before she thought to get up and close the blinds so that no one could see her crying. As an afterthought, she walked through the house shutting the windows and doors, because he wouldn't be staying there that night.

But Day would never be warm again. On the back of the couch was a throw with cowboys and Indians on it. She tugged it over herself and lay down against an embroidered pillow, to keep a vigil of misery.

She was too old to carry this torch. She had waited for him too long. She should never have loved him at all when she knew they were ill suited. She should never have accepted friendship for 364 days of the year and let it be enough that he loved her on the 365th.

Although the numbers weren't that strict. One time, his birthday gift to her had come with desperate I-need-you-right-now, I-miss-you-too-much birthday lovemaking. *That* was the real gift. Anyhow, things happened. For instance, two years ago, when her father had died . . . She'd learned more about Nick in those few weeks of loving and grieving than in their whole acquaintance.

Ten years they'd been lovers. Secret lovers. She threw off the afghan and went into her bedroom. The silver charm bracelet glistened in the top tray of her jewelry box. Nick had given her the bracelet the first year they'd made love— back during that spell when he was in love with her, too, when the only thing holding him back was her father. What he had called disloyalty to Sam Sutter. But even then, even then, he had known—and said—that the two of them were too different from each other. The bracelet had collected a charm that winter and every year since, always from Nick on the solstice.

Fingering the charms, Day started crying again. Why had she fallen in love with him? Nick could only break her heart. They both knew it, but they'd never wanted to give each other up completely. So they'd agreed to meet once a year, on the solstice.

But now...

Shep. It had to be Shep. He was probably with her right now. Nick and Elizabeth Shephard were probably lying in the snow under the stars drinking carrot juice, eating sprouted-bean bread and planning a mountain-bike expedition to Machu Picchu. Or maybe they were at Shep's house, which she shared with three other river guides, unemployed in the off-season.

Once, the previous summer, Shep had invited Day to her house for a potluck. Day had gone and felt like an alien beside the muscular suntanned women who rowed the river, who spent their free hours climbing cracks in Arches National Park or practicing rolling their kayaks on the section of the Colorado known as the Daily. In spectator pumps and a homemade copy of a Chanel dress, Day had studied the others in their woven Guatemalan fabrics and nylon-strap river sandals. Watching them compete with Nick and the other men, doing sets of fingertip pull-ups on the door frames, Day had felt envious and perplexed. Was this a mating ritual? She feared so.

After executing thirteen pull-ups, Shep had invited Day to go down the Grand Canyon with a group of guides when the commercial river-running season was over.

Nick had put in his two cents. *Day gets separation anxiety when she's apart from her hair dryer.*

She'd rolled her eyes. *Not to mention my stockings and garters.*

Perhaps feeling some separation anxiety of his own, Nick had immediately left the room. He knew why she wouldn't go down the river, and it wasn't as trivial as a lack of electricity. It was deeply ingrained fear, born of experience. But his dig had symbolized the greatest difference between them.

And it had hurt.

Though not like this.

In the past she'd always been able to tell herself that at least they had the solstice, that there was a part of him that belonged only to her.

Day downed her glass of Courvoisier and lit another cigarette. She'd read the books. The shelves in the spare room, her home office, were full of them. *Women Who Love Too Much. The Worst Mistakes Women Make.* She was a self-help junkie. Unfortunately her greatest addiction was Nick. What should she do now?

"Give up," she said aloud. "Get a life. Forget Nick Colter. He said it. He's never going to marry you."

Day burst into tears anew, hugging the pillow on the couch, wanting what could never be.

THERE WAS ICE on the river. Not a solid sheet, but big chunks of ice, shifting with the current in the starlight. In the Rapid Riggers parking lot, Nick sat in the cab of his truck watching the flow.

Usually, after breaking up with a woman, he felt emancipated, as though he'd just eluded a dire oppression. This was different.

He felt sick.

He considered ways to spend the night. He could stop by the Dry Gulch Saloon, see if Dirty Bob was around. They could drink 3.2 beer, weak Utah brew, and talk rivers and reincarnation over a game of pool. Or he could drive to Shep's . . .

No.

Feeling raw, he got out of the truck to go inside.

Day had talked him into stringing Christmas lights on the eaves of the two-story gray-shingled building that was the Rapid Riggers office. The bulbs provided plenty of light to find his key. As he slid it into the lock, the ghosts came.

He saw an old man's face. Blue eyes like Day's, but sharper. He remembered a coffin suspended above the torn lawn of the cemetery. Then those weeks in bed with Day. Telling her things, but avoiding what she'd wanted to discuss, the apologies she'd tried to make. For her father's will.

A more recent memory sprang at him. Tonight. Her hand jerking as she held her cigarette.

Now he'd committed the ultimate crime against Sam Sutter's memory. Hurting Day.

"So we're even, Sam." Nick let himself into the office and didn't bother with the lights. This was his home. Granted, he had another now, upstream on the river road—a trailer on a prime piece of real estate he'd bought for a song before mountain bikers discovered Moab and land prices skyrocketed. But the river office was where he'd grown up, where he'd learned which attitudes were acceptable and which weren't and what words to unteach his tongue. Things he would never have learned from the three sets of foster parents who'd kept him before he'd figured out he could survive on his own. In some ways, he'd always been on his own.

Till Sam Sutter entered his life.

He passed through the reception area and entered the inner office where Day worked. There he collapsed on the couch, on top of a layer of Ensulite camping pads they'd put down because of springs popping through the upholstery.

Outside, a siren wailed, and he sat up, curious. It was an ambulance, somewhere south. In town.

He could drop over to the hospital and see the guys after their call.

Nick reclined on the couch again. *Day*...

She made him *feel* like he hadn't had sex in a year.

He jumped up and slipped through a back door into his own office, the long narrow room he never used because it was dark—and had been Sam's domain. Now it was a memorial to unfinished arguments and apologies that could never be made. The keys to the Rapid Riggers Bronco, their twenty-year-old, oil-thirsty gofer vehicle, hung in the correct spot, the kind of detail Nick depended on—and Day often forgot. Nick plucked the key ring from its hook and left the room and the building, locking the door behind him.

No state troopers passing, and he was glad. Granted, as half owner of Rapid Riggers, he had a right to be there. But he hated being noticed by cops, the way he hated rooms without windows.

Climbing into the bed of his pickup, he unlocked the storage box and removed his backpack and, after a moment's reflection, his avalanche shovel. He dropped them down into the snow and mud, locked the box and jumped to the ground.

Minutes later, after loading his gear, he turned the Bronco south on the highway and drove across the bridge, over the ice-choked Colorado. Immediately after the bridge on the left was Highway 128, the river road, which led upstream toward his place. Ignoring the turnoff, Nick continued toward the lights of Moab and the vast expanse of public land that lay beyond.

Thoughts of Day came to populate the landscape as he drove toward his destination. Where he was going, what he might do there—one more good reason not to sleep with her. Soberly he mulled over other things, secrets he'd never told even her.

I've got a lot of reasons.

AT THREE IN THE MORNING, Day lay awake and lonely in her walnut four-poster bed. The pain would not stop.

There were too many memories. Naked beside him, telling and listening to stories. He'd never grown to enjoy reading, but he loved stories, and she had shared the tales *she* loved, of King Arthur's Round Table. He had told her his own stories, making them up for her. Or true stories, when they'd talked privately about things she knew Nick told no one else. Kissing. Making love with the muscular shape of his shoulders above her body, with the moonlight illuminating the ridges of his collarbone, shadowing the recesses around it. Sleeping in each other's arms and snuggling closer when they awoke and rediscovered each other. In the morning, his skin was dark as oak beside hers. They never had enough of each other's eyes, of each other's face. He had a way of cradling hers in his hands, touching before he kissed, drawing her spirit to his till she felt his unhappiness and need living alongside his confidence and adoration. Adoration of *her*. He'd told her what she needed to hear—and he'd needed to say. *I love you, Day. I love you so much.*

Was it all gone now?

Too hard to see her at work tomorrow. What had he meant?

Day knew what he meant. It was the same reason he never stuck around after the solstice.

Because they'd end up in bed again, in a frenzy of lovemaking, and after a few weeks the real problem would come up. High-risk sports. Nick would want to take off skiing or ice climbing or making a first descent of some Third World river, and she would be left behind. She didn't mind that, but he did. Nick wanted company, and he never had trouble getting it.

As far as Day knew, there was only one kind of woman more irresistible to Nick than those who could keep up with him in the wilderness.

Someone who needed to be rescued.

Day did not qualify.

I'm never going to marry you, Day.

The pillow caught her sob. "Nick," she whispered.

What he'd said and done tonight was only right, only decent. He knew how much she loved him, and he'd told her not to hope. That he wouldn't help her hope. She couldn't do the things he loved. She wasn't the kind of woman he wanted.

Closing her eyes, she imagined another world. She was pedaling a mountain bike up the Slickrock Bike Trail, up the treacherous section known as Testosterone Poisoning. She was trekking through a blizzard on Denali. She was kayaking Westwater Canyon...

Day shuddered.

Not the river. She'd never go down the river again. Not after what she liked to think of as the last river trip of her life.

But what about cycling? Cross-country skiing? An idea nudged her. *Come on, Day. You know what to do.*

She'd considered it before, of course. Not going on that Grand Canyon trip—there were limits—but...

Was there any chance she could learn to do the things Nick loved? She wasn't naturally athletic, and she hated being too cold or too hot or dirty or sweaty or too many miles from the nearest pack of cigarettes.

Cigarettes.

"Damn," she whispered softly into the sheets.

There was just one course open to her to bring the man she loved back to her side and keep him there forever, to make him renounce those words he'd said tonight. And say other words, instead.

She had to become Nick's kind of woman.

IN THE REMOTE Bureau of Land Management area known as the Back of Beyond, fifteen miles out of Moab, Nick squatted in the sand beside an Anasazi trash midden, picking through potsherds in the beam from his headlamp. The Anasazi, the Ancient Ones, had wandered the Four Corners area centuries earlier, leaving behind ceramics, basketry, worked wood and stone. Remnants of their civilization.

Farther south, other peoples had left their mark, too. Nick knew the work of the Hohokam and Mogollon. But this trash dump was Anasazi. The sherds showed indented construction coils, probably Dolores corrugated style. There was some black-on-white, too.

Even after fifteen years' hiking among the sandstone monoliths in the red-rock canyons, in the goblin desert that was his home, Nick was amazed by how broadly these craftsmen had spread their wares. And thanks to the Archaeological Resources Protection Act, which forbade disturbing such sites, much remained. Casual hikers who stumbled upon ruins might report them to the Bureau of Land Management or the park service, but they'd been educated and they seldom took anything.

Nick knew better, too.

He checked the glowing face of his wristwatch. Fourthirty. He should get back to Rapid Riggers. The fact that he had the Bronco wasn't a problem; his truck was two-wheel drive, so he often borrowed the Bronco to reach remote hiking or mountain-biking trails.

And he didn't have anything to hide—this time.

But his life sheltered silent crimes, and if he had to tell Day where he'd been, that he'd gone for a hike, it would feel like deception. Even if it was mostly the truth.

Nick donned his pack and started back to the Bronco, walking the road between his two lives. Behind him was a murky half-remembered past, a world of darkness eased only by the comforting candle of another child's presence, by the stories they'd invented for fortitude against pain and hunger. Against the things he'd told Day after her father died.

When he'd made love with her after those confessions, in the miracle of her acceptance, he had thought he would never be with another woman. Then spring had come, the snow had melted, the river had risen and called to him.

It was always easy to run when you were afraid.

Afraid of discovery, of being found out. That *wasn't* the reason he'd left tonight, the reason he'd broken it off. There was no single reason, but several.

He reached the Bronco just after five, stowed his pack behind the driver's seat, then thrust the key into the cold ignition and turned it. The idiot lights on the dash flashed on, and he watched them flicker out as he revved the engine.

But one remained red, glowing.

Bleary-eyed, Nick squinted at the panel of lights, realizing his error.

The Bronco had burned all its oil.

And it was a long walk home.

As he got out of the vehicle and reached behind the seat again for his parka and water bottle, the sleeve of his moss green fleece pullover caught on the door catch.

Afraid he'd torn it, he checked the fabric, and as he did so, he remembered. Not that Day had made the sweater; he never forgot that.

But that she must have made something else to give him tonight.

New Mexico

As THE DARKNESS lifted to morning, the woman known as Rory Abbot made her way around the alcove, shining her flashlight up on the mud-and-dab walls of a ruined cliff dwelling. She had already mapped the surface features on her computer, and the dig wouldn't start until March; there was no reason for her to be here now. In fact, she had to leave—return to the university for a meeting.

But the comfort she'd gained from spending the night here was worth the inconvenience. This project was personal, and she'd felt compelled to come down and see the place again, to make sure the pot hunter who'd dug a hole at the edge of the ruin did not return. To make sure no others came.

She'd participated in digs before, as an amateur archaeologist. But now she was well on her way to a master's degree in archaeology, and on the March dig at the site called Broken Sandal, she would be field supervisor, second in command to Dr. John Frazier, the expedition director. The site had been occupied during the Chaco era, and already human feces had been found, preserved.

Rory revered the clues of history. Her own past was part mystery. What she knew disturbed her. Yet she wanted—*needed*—to know the rest, and she dug diligently, keeping careful records, maintaining a mental grid of everything she discovered in her personal search. Unfortunately, like pot hunters, vandals who destroyed archaeological sites in their quests for artifacts, her parents had ravaged the historical record of her past. For different reasons. But the result was the same.

Squinting out the sadness, Rory followed the beam of her flashlight as she carefully surveyed the ruin. She acknowledged the need to dig. No matter what she might find.

CHAPTER TWO

DAY WAS SHAKY in the morning. Too little sleep. Too much hurt.

Last night, forming her plan, she had promised herself until the summer solstice. Six months. And if Nick showed no sign of making a permanent commitment, she would give up on him. For good. She'd tried in the past. This time she would succeed.

Carefully holding back the sleeves of her ivory silk lounging pajamas, Day built a fire in the wood stove, trying not to think of what it would have been like if Nick had stayed, had been with her before the sun rose. Sure, he would have built the fire, but it wasn't just that. In past years, those hours before sunrise had been the sweetest. The embraces always grew tighter, the emotions more intense, their lovemaking more ardent, as though they could touch enough, say enough, to sustain them for the rest of the year.

He really loved me. But did he still?

"'I'm never going to marry you,'" she said, trying to get used to the idea.

It didn't sound any better in the morning.

As she filled the espresso maker, she checked the weather on her five-inch-screen kitchen TV. It was six degrees out. A little cold for riding her mountain bike to work.

Oh, come on, Day. Would Nick's kind of woman let that stop her?

Suppressing a shiver, Day edged along the counter to tap a cigarette from a pack of Virginia Slims. Then she recalled her final vow of the evening.

Day collected the carton from the top of the refrigerator, and her hand held it over the trash can.

Let's not do anything drastic, Day.

Without releasing the carton, she withdrew her arm. In her pajamas, she climbed up on the counter and opened the doors of the cupboard above the sink. She shoved the cigarettes onto the top shelf, for an emergency.

Day hoped she wouldn't have one before, say, noon.

NICK MADE IT BACK to the office by eight-fifteen. After a six-mile hike to the highway, he had reached a truck stop and found a ride to the Moab City Market. From there, he'd hiked another four miles in the cold to Rapid Riggers.

There was no sign of Day's car, a ten-year-old red Porsche 928. Nick decided to wait for her, instead of going home. When she showed up, she could drive him out to the Bronco with a few quarts of oil.

Finishing a bowl of muesli—breakfast—at the reception counter, he heard the *tick-tick-tick* of a bicycle in the lot.

Shep?

But it was Day wheeling her Rockhopper up the steps to the porch. She wore black leggings, a long Icelandic sweater and a white hat that had a long tail with a pom-pom on the end. As she leaned her bicycle against the side of the building, she bent over, coughing.

Nick got the door for her. "If it isn't the nicotine queen." When she came in, carrying her backpack, he asked, "Where's your helmet?"

"I'm not sure." She drew off her hat, then her white wool gloves. "What does frostbite look like?"

Nick inspected her hands. "Nice manicure."

Without reply, Day marched to the rest room and shut the door behind her. The lock clicked. Grinning, Nick stepped outside and brought her bicycle into the office, then returned to the kitchen.

This time of year, Rapid Riggers offered no river trips and few four-wheel-drive tours. There wasn't much work. Just decisions about promotional materials for the up-coming season and routine bill paying. In the past two months, Nick had completed every maintenance chore imaginable. He'd even painted rafts, a task usually reserved for first-year boatmen. There was nothing left to do except what needed to be done most of all.

Buying new equipment.

He and Day were going to talk about that as soon as she came out of the bathroom.

Ages later, when she finally entered the kitchen, Nick saw what had kept her. "Now, *those* are cycling clothes. Who needs reflectors?"

Day wore high-heeled pumps that glittered with green, yellow, white and blue fake jewels. They matched her long-sleeved silk shirt—lime green and yellow with sparkling yellow buttons—and her yellow wool pants.

Pushing her fingers absently through her hair, freshly brushed into platinum waves, she said, "I just rode three miles in six-degree weather. My fingers feel like wood. You could at least be concerned."

"I'm always concerned when you ride your bike. Especially since you won't get training wheels."

"Ha ha." Day joined him near the coffeemaker and realized that he was wearing the same clothes he'd had on the night before and that he hadn't shaved or showered.

Her stomach rolled.

Shep. He spent the night with Shep. Shep lived in town. Nick wouldn't have bothered to go home. . . .

Trying to deal with the shock—it *was* a shock, even though she'd imagined them together the night before—she reached for the coffeepot. Her hand shook as she lifted the carafe, but she managed to stream the hot liquid into her porcelain cup. Instead of pouring it on him.

Don't say anything. Play it cool.

But she hated herself for it. This was not what her self-help books recommended. This was cruising for a bruising.

Casually she asked, "Sleep well?"

"Oh..." He should explain about the Bronco.

Her pants distracted him. Her body distracted him, and he had one of those frequent uninvited visions of screwing her in every room of the building. Against the kitchen wall, on the couch in the office, in the bathroom. He would carry her from room to room, her legs wrapped around him...

Day's apparently uninterested gaze bored holes in him.

Suddenly he caught on. Shep. Irked that Day could think another woman was the problem, he said, "Not a wink."

The lines around her mouth dropped almost imperceptibly. She turned away, fast.

Nick almost grabbed her shoulders to spin her back around and tell her he was teasing. "I went for a hike. Took the Bronco. The oil ran out, and I had to hitchhike home."

Day was still. She edged toward the counter and opened a drawer, then shut it.

Afraid he might touch her, Nick took his coffee out to the reception area. Her bicycle leaned against the wall. He'd lend her his helmet to ride home. It was on the enclosed back porch of the office, with his bike.

Day pushed through the kitchen doors, carrying a cup of coffee. Sipping it, she eyed him over the rim. "Want to go for a hike today? At lunchtime?"

A hike? "We might get frostbite."

She gazed at him like a queen who wanted his head.

Dragging his eyes away to some initials scratched into the reception counter, Nick said, "We have to go get that vehicle. It's in the Back of Beyond."

The phone on the counter rang, and Day lifted the receiver. "Rapid Riggers."

"Hi, Day. It's Grace."

The sound of her sister's voice comforted Day. Neither she nor Grace had ever known their mother, who died of a sudden illness when they were young. Day sometimes wondered if that absence in their lives was why she and Grace were so close.

Grace and her husband, Zachary, lived on River Inn Road, downstream from Rapid Riggers on river right. They were renovating the home where Grace and Day had grown up. In the early part of the century it had been an inn; through Grace and Zac it would be once more.

"Hi, Grace."

As Nick disappeared into the inner office, Grace asked, "Want to come to Grand Junction tomorrow? We're going to go get Pip at the airport."

Pip. Grace's brother-in-law. Zachary was English, the younger son of an earl. Upon His Lordship's death, the title and significant property would go to Pip. When Zac's family had visited the previous summer, Pip had glued himself to Day's side. It had been interesting.

After all, Zachary was a great guy. Her sister's husband had been a stage and film actor and a model until mental illness had interfered with his work, and he'd bowed out of professional acting because of the stress. Then he and Grace had decided to renovate the River Inn. Grace had trained as a chef in New York City, and they hoped the inn would become the home of Moab's finest restaurant—and its most elegant hotel. With the money Zac still raked in modeling Ben Rogan jeans, they would have no trouble getting the business off the ground.

Though Pip possessed only half his brother's good looks, he had the same Oxford education and charm. Plus, no mental-health problems, and he was already Viscount Someone-or-other.

But her few experiences kissing him last August...

Maybe it will be better this time.

Day had forgotten Pip was coming from Europe for the holidays. Christmas was just a few days off.

The airport. "Okay," she agreed. Then, loudly enough for Nick to hear, she asked, "Want to go hiking today, Grace?"

After several seconds, Grace said, "It's *cold*. What are you talking about? *You* want to go *hiking?*"

"Yes." Better not mention cycling to work; Grace would suggest counseling, even though it was the kind of thing she might do herself. When Grace had owned half of Rapid Riggers, she had been not just an outfitter but a river guide.

Day yearned for a cigarette from her desk drawer—her Rapid Riggers stash. She wasn't even going to make it twenty-four hours. "I just want some exercise."

Another puzzled silence.

"A hike," said Grace. "Just a minute.... Zac, do you want to go hiking later? It's Day."

Day couldn't make out her brother-in-law's answer.

Grace came back on the line. "We're supposed to meet some people at three-thirty for broomball in Courthouse Wash, and till then we're working on the floor in the Princess Room." The dining room at the River Inn. "We want to finish it for New Year's Eve."

Day chewed on her bottom lip. *Broomball.* Surely she didn't have to descend that far to become Nick's kind of woman. Why couldn't her friends play volleyball like other adults?

"Who's playing broomball?"

In the next room, the other line rang. Day heard Nick answer it.

"Nick and Bob and Susan are playing. And what's-her-name, your new guide?"

Not *my* new guide. Day answered, *"Arf."*

Grace giggled. "That's it. Shep. Well, you're welcome to join us."

"Thanks. I will."

Stunned silence met her words. Grace knew how she felt about broomball.

"I'll see you then, okay?" said Day, rushing. She'd kept her love for Nick from her sister for fourteen years; no reason to confess now. "Bye, Grace."

Hanging up the phone, she grimaced at the window. She hoped trying to become Nick's kind of woman wouldn't kill her.

WHEN NICK GOT OFF the other line—the 800 number—he returned to the reception area expecting to find that Day had gone outside for a cigarette. Instead, she was leaning against the reception counter swilling coffee.

"That was Yves, Paris Tours. He booked twelve people for Cataract Canyon in June. He's sending the deposit."

"Good."

Ready to talk about getting a bank loan? New equipment? Nick decided to wait until she was a captive audience—on the way to the Back of Beyond. "Let's go get the truck."

Day transferred her coffee to a plastic travel mug, and they set out to retrieve the Bronco. While Nick took the wheel of Suburban no. 2, known affectionately as the Red Sled, and headed south toward town, Day, in the passenger seat, gulped her coffee and wished it was something she could light and smoke.

They passed the A-Maze-Ing T-Shirt Shop on the left, Current Adventure Tours on the right. Nick said, "Carl Orson bought a dozen new Toyota Land Cruisers. He told me he's buying new rafts, too."

Day knew what was coming. "Carl Orson's silent partner is a millionaire," she pointed out.

"Sometimes *I* feel like a silent partner."

"I can't imagine when *that* would be." As he braked at a traffic light, Day squinted at him, suspicious.

He caught the look. "They're not related, Day. Don't think about it."

Business and his not wanting to be her lover, thought Day. Nick often read her mind. And a lot of times she knew his.

"Our rafts are unsafe. Look, Day. You know the books—I trust you on that. Trust *me* on this. We need to replace four of those rafts and about twenty-five life vests."

They'd had the same conversation before. So far, so good. "Okay," she said. "I already agreed that we should get four new rafts and twenty-five life vests."

The light changed and he pulled forward. "And since we have to get a loan, anyhow..."

"Nick, we have no place to put rental mountain bikes, and it won't bring in that much revenue."

"You'd be surprised. Come on, Day. Moab is the mountain-biking Mecca of the world. River Legends offers combination jet boat–mountain bike tours. They jet boat the passengers to—"

"Where are we going to put a fleet of rental bicycles?" Day asked. "There's no room in the office or on the porch."

"We'll hang them in the equipment shed."

"You know that's not practical. I don't want you to start renting mountain bikes, Nick. We're wilderness outfitters."

"And we could outfit multi-day bike trips on the White Rim trail. We're probably talking an extra five hundred dollars a day during the season. Maybe more."

"I'll believe that when I see it. Your riverboat plan makes more sense." Nick and Zachary shared a vision of building a Mississippi-style riverboat with a paddle wheel and running trips from Moab to Green River. It was a notion that had failed at the turn of the century, due to sandbars and variable water levels in the Colorado—obstacles that hadn't changed.

"I'm glad you're in favor of the riverboat, Day—"

"I didn't say I was in favor!"

"Want to talk about vehicles?"

Day faced the window. This was what it always came down to—a difference of about a hundred and fifty thousand dollars. She understood Nick perfectly. He'd spent more than a decade working under her father, carrying out Sam Sutter's every command and seeing his own perfectly sound ideas dismissed. Now, in his first six months at Rapid Riggers, he wanted to implement every scheme that occurred to him. Immediately. Total autonomy.

The result was constant friction.

"We have three working Suburbans, Nick. That's plenty."

"Two of them should be sold. And we should buy Land Cruisers, like Carl."

"They cost a fortune! You may as well get Range Rovers."

"They'll last forever, Day."

They left Moab, passed the ranches of Spanish Valley and the rodeo grounds, and drove into desert and snow-dappled slickrock. The pale winter morning glistened with sunlight.

This land owned Day. She had spent three months studying fashion design in Salt Lake City before discovering she missed the desert. She'd quit school and come home. Of course, the scenery wasn't the only draw. She'd never been able to stay away from Nick.

Beside her, Nick brooded. Day had to relinquish some control. But so far, he hadn't figured out how to make her do it—by noble means. Whenever he tried, the conversation turned ugly on both sides. They knew each other too well, knew what hurt the most.

Day's Achilles' heel was that she hadn't been on the river in ten years—and for a Sutter, avoiding white water was a disgrace.

His weaknesses . . .

Look, contrary to what you think, she'd told him months ago, *my father did know something about running a river outfit. Stop trying to change everything just to prove you can do it better.*

He'd wanted her just to shut up.

The four-wheel-drive road that led to the Back of Beyond was more than ten miles south of Moab. When Nick reached the turnoff and drove onto the deep red mud in the still, silent landscape, Day said, "I can't believe you came out here last night." On each side of the road, pinkish-beige sandstone humps rose in a grand-scale rock garden.

"Yeah, well, I did."

Day fell back into her thoughts. Maybe Nick really didn't care that she wasn't the earthy wilderness type. Maybe her changing would make no difference. What if she was giving up cigarettes—especially this morning, when a cigarette would really help—and it was all for nothing? Well, except maybe her health.

Later, when she was bawling her head off alone at the office, she told herself that needing a cigarette had made her ask.

"Nick?"

"Yeah." He avoided a chasmlike rut in the sandy road.

"Would it make any difference—with us—if I was more like the other women you date? If I was a rock climber or kayaker or something?"

"What?" He swerved around a large rock.

Fever feelings flooded her. "Forget it."

He couldn't. He knew what she meant. Nick pictured Day ice climbing.

His eyes left the road.

"Forget it," she repeated. Damn. She was going to have that cigarette the minute she got back to the office.

"Sure, it might be different." His voice startled her. "But you're you."

Nick knew he should shut up. He hadn't slept and hardly knew what he was saying. *Would it make any difference with us...* There were several things that could make a difference. The most serious weren't within his control—and definitely weren't within hers. He saw the Bronco ahead, pulled up behind it and switched off the engine.

Day's eyes had purple smudges beneath them and, under her makeup, her face was pale. Because of him.

"Don't do what you're doing, Day."

"What's that?"

He gave her a "What's that?" look, too. "Trying to fix it. Trying to make it work. It can't. I don't love you the way you want me to."

Her chin shook then, and she turned her face from him, putting her head back, hiding her tears.

Averting his eyes, Nick grabbed the yellow Pennzoil bottles and got out of the Suburban. "I'll see you back at the office." He slammed the door, hating himself.

HE DIDN'T COME BACK to Rapid Riggers, and Day almost made up her mind to forget the broomball game. There was no room for hope, so why torture herself?

"Because," she told her teary face in the scratched bathroom mirror of the river office, through the smoke of the single cigarette she'd promised herself, "you've never loved anyone else." It was worth six more months of her life to try. Nick had admitted it might be different—if she was different.

Right before he'd broken her heart.

It was after three, so when she'd savored every last millimeter of her cigarette, right down to the filter, she changed into the clothes she'd worn to ride her bike to work. She waited till almost three-thirty for Nick to return to the office.

He never showed up, so Day collected her broom, locked the door and trudged up the icy embankment and across the road to Arches National Park. Her nerves buzzed.

Broomball.

A violent game resembling hockey, broomball was played on ice, in boots rather than skates, with a broom and whatever ball was handy. One December afternoon two years before, Day had accepted Nick's invitation to join him and some friends for broomball. She had slipped on the ice and spent the evening in the emergency room having her chin sewn up.

No man is worth this.

The Rapid Riggers Bronco was parked in the turnout near Courthouse Wash, along with Zachary's faded Austin-Healey and a red Subaru station wagon with a boat rack on the roof. The last belonged to the Rapid Riggers boatman affectionately known as Dirty Bob. Just about everyone at the river outfit had some kind of nickname. Amazing Grace, Cute Nick...May-Day.

May-Day, to whom the boatmen ran after backing a vehicle into the river at the put-in or when they needed a cash advance...but whom they would never understand because she hated river rafting. She wasn't like them, wasn't one of them, and they knew it. Her father had known it, too.

As she approached the turnout, insecurity wrapped around her.

Elizabeth Shephard's car was absent. Either Shep wasn't there—or she had come with Nick.

A barbed-wire fence bordered the park, and Day had to climb over a pasture gate, then hike a short trail into the canyon, to the section of the wash that had frozen over. Sometimes children ice-skated there, but more often

Moab's seasonal employees and locals used it for off-season broomball.

They were already playing when Day arrived. She saw Zachary tearing across the ice to score a goal against Bob. Nick took the ball back up the wash. When Grace got in his way, he dodged her and passed the ball to Shep, who scored a goal.

That's a street-hockey ball, Day realized. Those things were hard.

As she wondered if it was too late to sneak away, Grace skidded toward her, light brown braid flying, cheeks flushed deep pink. Peering up to where Day stood on the bank above the wash, her sister said, "You came."

"Of course." Day tried not to sound as though she'd rather be back at the office working on the taxes or something really fun.

"Good, we need you," said Grace. "Zac and I are outnumbered."

Dirty Bob called, "Hey, look who's here!"

As the others waited for her to climb down to the ice, Zac tossed his brown hair out of his eyes and winked at Day. Grace's husband was so handsome it was hard to look at him without staring. Day liked him very much, liked how much he loved Grace. She smiled and waved to him and Bob as she tried to find the easiest way down the half-frozen sand-and-mud slope to the ice.

"Is Day going to play? All right!" exclaimed Shep. Reaching the bank, she held up a mittened hand. "Here. Hang on! It's slick."

Elizabeth Shephard was five foot four, stocky and fair, and ever since she'd arrived in Moab the men had been smitten. She seemed to hold an almost mystical sway over the opposite sex, in direct proportion to her ability to keep up with them on vertical mountain-bike trails and in class-V rapids. Shep was an expert spelunker, a kayaker and a pilot, and her father owned a chain of microbreweries.

Before coming to Moab in July, she'd spent a dangerous year on a college exchange program in Argentina, helping rural villagers install a sewage system.

Day hated her.

This was the first time in her recollection that Nick had been seeing anyone during the month of December. Surely Shep had something to do with his decision to end their solstice tradition.

"Thanks, Shep." Day thrust her broom into the enemy's outstretched hand, then turned backward to navigate the bank. As her boots touched the ice, they slipped, and she sat down so hard that everything in her stomach seemed to fly up to her head.

"Ow," said Shep. "Are you all right?"

Day tried to breathe normally. "Yes, perfectly."

Watching Zac help her up, Nick skated across the ice on his boots. What was Day doing here? She could get hurt. Day on ice was like a balloon in a cactus garden. Skidding to a stop where the others had gathered, he resisted tapping her bottom with the business end of his broom, but he couldn't help saying, "At least you don't need anything stitched up." He'd taken her to the emergency room when she'd sliced open her chin.

He looked more rested, Day noticed, and he'd changed his clothes. So he'd gone home.

Or to Shep's. Did he keep clothes there?

Dirty Bob scratched his curly brown beard. Steam billowed from his nose and mouth. "Maybe we should reassess teams."

In other words, *Who's going to take responsibility for this klutz?*

Nick said, "We'll take Day. You go with Grace and Zac."

"Great!" Shep exclaimed.

Day wondered if she could arrange a fatal accident.

The game resumed. As goalie, Day practiced skating on her boots while the others bashed brooms at the other end of the wash. Her rear end was sore and frozen, and the cold made her cough.

Suddenly Shep screamed, "Look out, Day! Look out!"

Dirty Bob smacked the ball toward the goal, and by some miracle Day hit it with her broom. It glanced off to the side, and Shep caught it and took it back down the wash with the others in pursuit.

Day positioned her broom against her body, took off a glove and gingerly touched her mouth. Had her lipstick worn off? Just then, the ball slammed between her legs, and Zachary raised both hands in the air. Goal.

Across the ice, Nick shook his head.

Wasting no time on regret, Shep retrieved the ball and sped away, a woman warrior out to defeat the enemy.

Day tried to put her glove back on. It was so damn cold.

Dirty Bob stole the ball and raced toward Day's goal. Overcoming an urge to get out of the way, Day positioned herself in front of the goal and skated toward the approaching ball.

Her right boot slipped to one side, she flew forward, and her body and face slammed against the ice.

"Day!" exclaimed Bob. "Are you all right?"

A familiar pair of worn boots slid to a perfect stop one foot from her nose. Day recognized them and the tattered cuffs of Nick's jeans as he crouched beside her.

Slowly she pushed herself up and saw blood on the ice. *Oh, great, Day.*

Bob said, "It might be indelicate to mention this, but I have the strongest case of déjà vu."

As she found a sitting position, the blood dripped. Her whole face hurt.

"You've got a nosebleed. Lean forward," Nick said, and no one argued. He was an EMT, and all of them but Zac had taken advanced first aid. If she swallowed blood, it could make her nauseous.

Day saw her sister above her.

"Here's a Kleenex." Handing her the tissue, Grace smoothly dropped to her knees beside Day. "Do you think she needs stitches on her lip, Nick?"

She'd bitten it. He carried disposable rubber gloves in his car and in one of the pockets of his parka, but neither were with him and he would have ignored universal precautions with Day, anyhow. Drawing the Gore-Tex glove from his left hand, he touched her mouth, pulling down her lower lip. "No, she'll be okay. Let's get you up off the ice, though. It's cold."

With Grace and Zachary following, he helped Day stand and led her across the wash and off the ice to a fallen tree trunk. He sat down, straddling the trunk beside her, and with his forefinger and the tissue, he pressed her upper nostril against her septum to stop the nosebleed.

Day... He wanted to shake her. To hold her. To kiss her. His groin was against her body. *Don't think about it.*

As Bob and Shep passed the ball back and forth on the ice, Day told the others, "You guys can go and play. I'm fine, Nick." She reached for the tissue.

"Just hold your horses, all right?"

Easier when his thigh wasn't against her back, she thought, when he wasn't sitting so close to her. When his callused hands with the dexterous fingers that sent magic swirling into her weren't touching her. At the moment she was what Nick found most irresistible—in need of rescue. The thought irritated her, but when Day met his eyes, ready to tell him she could deal with her own bloody nose, her stomach turned over. It was impossible not to remember making love with him. Deep love. Dragging it out. Shuddering closer and closer. Whispering and crying out.

Nick tore his gaze from her blue eyes, from the lip she'd bitten. Through the steam rising from his nose, he noticed Zachary eyeing him and Day curiously. *What are you looking at?*

Zac looked away.

"Hey, Nick," asked Grace, "you and Shep want to come to dinner Christmas Eve?"

Day trained her eyes on the ice. She would be a dinner guest that night as well, but she'd forgotten Nick was going to be around for Christmas this year. She couldn't remember a time he ever had been. He'd always left after the solstice.

Grace added, "Pip will be there. He's coming to help work on the inn."

Nick made a polite sound. Last summer, Zac's brother had followed Day around like a dog. No, not like a dog. Like a man who knew a good thing when he saw it.

Nick pictured Zac and Grace and Pip and Day making a foursome for Christmas Eve dinner. Grace *was* a good cook. "Thanks. I'll ask Shep." He carefully released the pressure on Day's nose. The bleeding had stopped.

She took the tissue from him and dabbed at one nostril. "Thank you."

"You're welcome." He had an unwise notion to kiss her bitten lip. Inching back from her to get up, Nick wished he was wearing his guide shell, which came below his fly.

As Day stood up, too, Shep appeared beside them. "Ready to play?"

Play? She was supposed to play again? But that was what Nick's kind of woman would do after a minor accident. It was what Shep would do.

Nick made a skeptical sound. "Let's not—"

"Great!" Day started back to the ice to pick up her broom.

New Mexico

IN THE APARTMENT she rented near the university, Rory Abbot booted up her computer, logged on the Internet and went to the web site for Birthright Reunions. It was a ritual, like calling up the bulletin board, reading the file names.

She had posted a message herself for several months, but seeing it had embarrassed her, reminded her of her shame, and she had deleted the file. The person she sought would not be surfing the Net searching for her, anyhow. She doubted he knew how to use a computer, doubted he had access to one. He'd never been lucky.

Like her, he had come from the bottom.

And Rory very much doubted he'd ever found anyone to lift him up.

CHAPTER THREE

DAY FOUND her bicycle helmet the next morning and wore it on the ride to work. Nick wasn't there when she reached the office. Day hadn't seen him since the broomball game; afterward, he'd left with Shep.

In the bathroom, she changed into a navy blue wool pinstriped shirt and trousers and navy spectator pumps. By the time she'd made a cup of coffee and sat down at her desk, it was eight-thirty. Zac and Grace would pick her up in half an hour, then go collect Pip at the airport. She could finish some work before then. Deposits for spring Cataract Canyon raft trips had arrived by mail the previous afternoon.

Hearing a vehicle outside, she glanced through the window. It was Nick's truck, the only navy blue '57 Chevy in town.

The bell rang as he opened the front door. Day heard him say, "I've applied for a Selway permit *five years in a row*. There's no permit in the country that's harder to get."

"Well, let's apply, anyhow. Both of us. Two chances are better than one. Maybe we'll get it."

Shep.

Swallowing envy, Day translated their conversation. On many rivers, private trips were regulated, and more people applied for permits to launch than received them. Permits were assigned by lottery. Apparently Shep was as eager as Nick to try the harrowing rapids of Idaho's Selway River.

Gingerly Day touched her bruised lip. *How can I compete with Shep when I'm afraid of white water?* Recollections dimmed after so many years, but a part of Day had changed back then, that afternoon in Cataract Canyon. Her father had said, *You just get back on the horse, Day. That's what you do.* Day had signed on for the next Cataract Canyon trip. But when she spent the night before the launch date vomiting, even Sam had said, *Maybe you should wait a bit.*

That was ten years ago. Day was still waiting.

"Whose bike?" asked Shep.

"Day's."

Nick looked in the door of the inner office. His hair was mussed, his suntanned skin flushed from the cold, the crevices in his cheeks deep and rugged and sexy. Bright dark eyes regarded her plainly, with no extra emotion, as though he and Day had never been anything but co-workers and business partners. Stepping inside, he tossed his head in the direction of the Colorado. "Guess what's happening on river left."

Day tried to think what he could mean. Tried to think at all. *So he slept with her again; it doesn't mean anything.*

"Carl Orson," said Nick. "New office. Why didn't we know about this?"

As Shep moseyed in, drinking from a plastic bottle of cabbage juice, Day fingered a rubber band on her desk. Carl Orson. Current Adventure Tours, the largest and glossiest river outfit in Moab. Carl was setting up a new office across from Rapid Riggers? "Someone else owned that land."

"They sold it." Nick threw himself on the couch, and Shep plopped down in close proximity. Her sunglasses dangled from a tie-dyed cotton knit keeper strap around her neck. It was a common sight, but one that, for the last ten years, had always evoked an unsettling reaction in Day. She shirked it off. Shep and Nick were touching.

I ought to be used to this. Although she knew Nick tried not to flaunt other relationships, occasionally Day ran into him when he was out with someone. In a town the size of Moab, it was inevitable. But it never felt good. *If I have to look at that nauseating little boatina another minute...* She gathered her blue alligator handbag, which lay beyond the bills. "Maybe I'll drive over and see what Carl has to say."

"I already talked to him. He looks forward to doing business together."

"We'll get his overflow," Day interpreted. In other words, when he had too many passengers for his boats, the rival outfitter would subcontract to Rapid Riggers. But that wouldn't be enough if he took the rest of their business.

Nick said, "Don't worry. We'll just keep trading on our image as the oldest river outfit in Moab, Utah." Shep handed him the bottle of cabbage juice they were sharing, and he drank some of it.

Day shuddered.

Nick saw—and licked his lips. "That hits the spot."

"That is disgusting." His swapping spit with Shep. *Dog* spit.

"It's very nutritious," said Shep.

Sharing mouths with Nick? Yes, it was the most nourishing thing in the world. Day could live on nothing else. She stood up, taking her purse. She needed a cigarette, an Almond Joy and a Mountain Dew; then she'd have some perspective. Self-help. "Um. I'm going out. If Zac and Grace show up, tell them I'll be right back. We're going to the airport to get Pip."

Pip. Nick tensed. *It's good for her to go get Pip,* he told himself. *Maybe she'll fall in love with Pip.* Struck by the profound generosity of the notion—he *did* want her to be happy; wasn't that love?—he watched her tall slender body leave the room. He listened to her go out, to her heels on the porch steps.

"You two have known each other a long time."

Nick started at Shep's voice. "Yes." He finished the juice and got up. "I should get to work." *Doing what?* The equipment shed was in order, everything from life vests to coolers already inventoried. He'd even built and painted a new sign for the roof peak of the office.

Shep stood, too. "Okay. Will I see you tonight?"

Nick wavered. He was still upset. Still not over Day. It was going to take him a little longer to feel right. "No. But we'll go to Grace's tomorrow night for dinner, all right?"

"Great." She grinned, carefree and young. Shep was twenty-one, and even her experiences in Argentina didn't make up for the years between them.

What are you doing, Nick? Why are you doing this again?

The reason never changed. He was trying to find someone... else.

In the reception area, Shep hugged him. "Have a good day."

Day. "You, too." He kissed her and tried not to think about the owner of the name she'd unconsciously invoked.

WHEN DAY LEFT with her sister and brother-in-law to meet Zac's brother, Nick took two books and a folder from his office out into the reception area. The books were *River Rescue* and *Advanced First Aid*. He would be teaching both courses in the spring, and he'd already prepared the handouts. There wasn't much else to do, and the side window distracted him. Across the river, construction was under way. Current Adventures would put Rapid Riggers under if he and Day didn't do something.

Day used to complain about her dad not spending money on the outfit. She wasn't as bad—at least she admitted they needed new rafts and life vests—but she wouldn't take risks. They'd been in business together five months, and Nick kept telling himself that when river-running season returned in the spring, everything would be fine. He'd have more to do and wouldn't feel like a useless figurehead.

He didn't believe himself.

Day was accustomed to being in charge of Rapid Riggers and to doing things as they'd always been done. It was the first domain where he'd ever known her to fight him so hard.

Nick *knew* how to win control.

It was no secret to him why she'd shown up to play broomball. Because he was playing. And if he told her it would make him love her more, she would let him do exactly as he wanted with Rapid Riggers. Day would do anything for him.

You love me too much, Day.

She loved him. And didn't really know him. Didn't have a clue why he'd gone to the Back of Beyond that night. Didn't know the other things he'd done. Didn't know about Kelly.

Her loving him and not knowing him was a bad combination for both of them.

She needed to get over him—*they needed to get over each other*—and it wasn't going to happen while they were business partners, while they saw each other every day and while he was so bored out of his mind that all he could think of was sex with her. They needed total separation, and there was only one way to manage that.

He had to find a way to buy her half of the business.

She wouldn't like the idea at all.

THE RIVER INN was a sprawling white building with a chaos of balconies, verandas and dormers. The Colorado flowed beside it—in high-water years, a little too close for comfort. Nick admired the architecture. The building, where Grace and Day had grown up, had many French doors which were propped open in the summer months. Nick liked the space and the light and, most of all, the ventilation.

He was less comfortable with the memories. Warmth, anger, other emotions, all jumbled together. Sam. Day. As teenagers, they'd messed around on her bed when no one was home. Slowly unwrapping the gift of sex. It had begun in the house, the house of other beginnings. Where the civilization of Nick had begun.

As he parked under the cottonwood trees outside the inn, Shep, in the passenger seat, said, "This place is awesome."

"Yes." The screened porch had been glassed in for winter, and the whole house was lit up like Disneyland, colored lights everywhere.

Zac's Siberian husky, Ninochka, pushed through a dog door in the porch as Nick and Shep got out of the truck. In her cotton dress, Argentinean sweater and hiking boots, Shep bent over to pet her.

Scanning the yard, Nick spotted the Austin-Healey and Grace's new Toyota 4Runner. The Porsche wasn't there yet, which troubled Nick. Riding with the Moab ambulance as an EMT, he had responded to many car accidents. All the roads along the river became icy in winter as the canyon walls locked them in unrelieved shade. Highway 128, the river road, the road out to his place, was the worst. Almost every year, someone drove into the Colorado and died. But River Inn Road could be just as bad, and Day drove about the way she played broomball.

Someone should go pick her up.

Shep straightened up from petting the dog. "What's wrong?"

There was no reason to feel guilty. He was concerned as a friend. "I think maybe we should go get Day. It's icy tonight."

Before Shep could answer, headlights cut across the mud and patches of snow in the yard, casting their glow far out onto the ice-clogged river. Nick recognized the low bullet shape of the red 928.

"Looks like she made it," said Shep.

Beyond the glass on the porch, the kitchen door opened, and Nick saw Zachary and another man come out. *Pip.* Both silhouettes were wearing dinner jackets. Though Nick owned a suit, one Day had helped him choose for a wedding, he hadn't thought to wear it.

When Zac opened the porch door, Ninochka trotted toward him, tail wagging. The other figure stepped outside. "Hello." Greeting Shep, he sounded more British than Zac. "I'm Pip."

Nick introduced Shep and managed some kind of smile as he shook Pip's hand. Neither he nor Pip said, *Good to see you again,* and at the first possible opportunity, Zachary's brother made a beeline for Day's car.

Nick followed Shep onto the porch.

The kitchen door opened again, releasing mouth-watering smells, and Grace peered out. "Hi, you guys. Come on in. Oh, there's Day. Good."

As Zac and Shep went inside ahead of him, Nick heard Day greet Pip. Tarrying on the porch, he watched the man and woman crossing the yard.

Day wore her white silky down jacket, the coat that always made Nick think she could get lost in the snow. With surprising dexterity, she navigated the slush in the yard in clear vinyl pumps with something glittery all over them and a skirt that probably made walking tricky.

Nick's breath grew shallow. *You make me hard, Day.*

Beside her, Pip was saying, "You look beautiful tonight. Have I told you that yet?"

Nick pushed open the door for them.

"Hi," Day said, smiling. "Thanks."

The Christmas lights stained her coat and her hair pale pink and green. When he saw her lips, Nick looked away, his blood rushing, his mind fogging.

"Ah, thank you," said Pip. "Still rowing boats, are you, Nick?"

Nick remembered how much he hated Zachary's brother. "Actually, in the winter I divide my time between cleaning outhouses and scavenging road kill. What about you?" Zac and Pip had both rowed crew at Eton and Oxford. Neither wanted anyone to forget it.

Pip didn't answer at once. "Not much, no. Oakhurst keeps me busy."

"Oh, right. The hotel." You had to find some way to pay the upkeep on those English manor houses.

An elbow jabbed his ribs. As Day continued innocently into the kitchen, Nick resisted sliding his hand to her delectable rear end.

Pip's expression was cool after the slur on his family home.

Salvaging civility, Nick said, "After you."

Inside, the first person Day noticed was Shep, in her cotton dress and hiking boots and barely twenty-one-year-old skin. Grace was at the stove. "Pretty dress, Grace." It was burgundy crushed velvet with an empire waist and calf-length skirt. Politely she added, "You, too, Shep."

"Oh, thanks. Salvation Army. I hate spending money on clothes."

Even Grace stared.

Was hating to spend money on clothes part of being Nick's kind of woman? It seemed to go hand in hand with cabbage juice and organic gardening. Day admitted, "I'm not that evolved."

Behind her, shutting the door, Nick said, "Day sews."

"Did you make that?" asked Shep.

The ankle-length clingy jacquard-silk skirt was a blush-coffee color, like her close-fitting blouse. "Yes. Polyester." Touching the blouse, she waited hopefully to see if Shep would break out in hives at the thought.

No such luck.

Pip offered, "Can I take your coat, Day?"

Shep had already hung up her sweater, Nick saw. Removing his own parka, he watched Pip take Day's from her. Her chunky gold earrings and the silky sheen of her clothing drew his eyes. He saw himself alone with her, felt her slender white fingers unbuttoning his jeans.

Cool it, Nick.

He hung his coat on the tree beside Day's. "Need any help, Grace?"

"No, thanks. I've got it covered."

Day opened her purse, a large cloth bag beaded with white seed pearls, and pulled out color brochures in two sizes. "Nick, these came today after you'd gone home."

Everyone crowded around, and Day handed several brochures to Grace and Zachary because they contained the offer of a package tour—four days on Cataract Canyon with a night before and a night afterward at the River Inn.

Nick unfolded a brochure, but his eyes drifted to Day's hands, then to her body. He *knew* what kind of underwear she had on. Stockings. Garters. See-through bra and panties. Through her clear vinyl shoes, he made out the sheer silk of her stockings.

Shep's Vasque hiking boots and dress blocked the view as she pointed to a picture on the brochure Day held. "That's Dirty Bob, isn't it?"

"Yes." Day sounded impatient. She let Shep take the brochure and backed away to eye Pip and Zachary. "You guys are wearing matching ties."

"Ah, yes, so glad you noticed," bantered Pip, straightening his knot. "We're—what do you say—power dressing."

"The old school tie," murmured Zac, still appraising the brochure. "Guaranteed to suffocate. This looks lovely." He caught Nick's eyes coming up from another sweep over Day. Zachary's smile was rueful, and Nick didn't know whether to be irritated or comforted a moment later when his friend handed him a glass of wine.

FOR DINNER, Grace had prepared lamb chops with nut crust, pasta with sun-dried tomatoes, mushrooms and artichoke hearts, bulgur with vegetables, currants and pine nuts, and River Inn bread. Nick sat between Grace, at one end of the candlelit dining-room table, and Shep. He was across from Pip.

While Grace was in the kitchen getting the dessert, Pip asked, "Nick, where is your family?"

He thought of Kelly. Child Kelly. Kelly who might never have reached womanhood, who could be anywhere, dead or alive. "I don't have any."

Cater-corner to him, Day reached toward one of the candlesticks on the table. "These are pretty. Where did you guys get these, Zac?"

As Zachary answered, Nick lifted his wineglass to his mouth and drank.

"Have you always lived in Utah?" Pip asked.

"Yes."

"Traveled?"

"Yes. So has Shep." Nick tried to transfer the attention. "She spent last year in Argentina."

"Now, that's an unusual destination. What were you doing there?"

While Shep replied, Nick kept his eyes off Day. She looked like a princess. She ought to marry at least an earl.

Nick remembered her legs squeezing him, her body holding the most intimate part of his. *Nick... I love you. I love you so much.*

He was going mad.

Maybe he could find a minute alone with her tonight to suggest she sell him her half of Rapid Riggers. Better yet, maybe he should mention it in front of Pip. If he was serious about Day, Pip would encourage her.

The wine grew sour in his mouth.
Generosity didn't feel good anymore.

AFTER DINNER they retired to the living room, where an enormous tree lit with white bulbs scraped the ceiling, and logs blazed in the hearth. Pip filled drink requests, and as Nick took a seat by the window in the path of a reassuring draft, Grace said, "Hey, Day, how about a story?"

The request both pleased and distressed Day. She loved telling stories. Her nature was theatrical; when, on a whim, she'd enrolled in a storytelling seminar at the local university extension that fall, it had been with the notion of broadening her dramatic range. But once she began, she saw that her life had guided her toward this art. And her fire and need were intimately bound with hot afternoons beside the river, with a dark and wounded boy turning into a man. A man whose body disappeared into a silence of concentrated listening whenever a story was told. Back then, it was how he learned, because he could not read. Even now, all her stories were for him.

Any truth so strong couldn't be hidden. He must know, and his knowing made Day vulnerable. Yet he was here. It was a golden chance to beguile him. And to give to the person she loved best. To tell him a story.

Perched on a striped wing chair, Day consulted the other faces in the room to see how everyone felt about Grace's suggestion. Nick was staring at the floor, alert. Listening. Waiting.

Seated on the end of the couch nearest him, Shep exclaimed, "Cool! I'd love to hear a story."

"Me, too." Zac loosened his tie.

"Do you have a Christmas story, Day?" asked Grace.

From a chair like Day's beside the hearth, Pip interjected, "I have to say, it fascinates me that Day enjoys storytelling. You know, through the ages, telling stories has been the perennial entertainment of the poor and the illiterate."

Illiterate. Day sat back, her internal reaction like that of a mother prepared to defend her young. Pip probably thought he was within a group of people who reserved that word for others, who had never known it applied to themselves. She stole a glance at Nick, and his black eyes were fixed on Pip. She could see his mind spinning.

"Which brings up the question," Pip continued, "of why this fad has emerged. In my opinion, it's a reversion to the—"

"Pip," said Zachary in a good-natured deadpan, "shut up and let Day tell her story, will you?"

His brother blushed with charm. "Yes, yes. Of course. I'll shut up. What story are you going to tell, Day?"

"Well, I don't have a Christmas story, per se," she said, "but I do know a story that begins at Christmas." Fingering her glass of cognac, she saw Nick still watching Pip the way a cat watches a mouse. "Sir Gawain and the Green Knight?"

Pip's smile was just polite. "How about one we don't know?"

In his chair Nick tensed. Beside him Shep said, "I don't know 'Sir Gawain and the Green Knight.' I'd love to hear it."

Good for you, thought Nick. He loved Day's stories about knights. In high school, she had always had her nose in medieval romances, from Arthurian legends to supermarket paperbacks. Nick remembered Sir Gawain from another story Day had once shared.

"Anyhow," Zachary pointed out, "part of the tradition of oral storytelling is repetition."

"Like on the river," said Grace. "How many times do we have to hear about the open canoe in Cataract, Nick?"

"Till the women get tired of it."

The three women pelted him with cocktail napkins. Zachary laughed.

Pip was talking again. "Now, this is fascinating to me. Where does storytelling still emerge? Among river guides."

Nick's eyes shot toward the ceiling.

Day could guess what he wanted to say. *Sure wish I'd learned to read.*

"Under primitive conditions, with no electricity," Pip went on, "mimicking the conditions of poverty *and* conditions under which it is difficult to read."

Oh, shut up, Day thought fiercely. Meeting Nick's eyes, she silently apologized for Pip.

He winked at her.

"Now, the interesting thing about repetition," Pip continued, "is that the stories change with different tellers."

"No kidding," Shep said. "Think of all the versions of what happened to Jim Antonio in Cataract."

Day stilled. Jim Antonio in Cataract... She'd been there. It was why she didn't go down the river. The experience had constrained and altered her forever.

It was a story she did not tell.

"Day?"

Nick's dark eyes reached out to Day. She found their expression as comforting as the heat from the blazing yule fire. He hadn't been on the river that afternoon—but he'd stood outside the bathroom when she was throwing up before the next trip, the trip she didn't take.

"Tell us about the Green Knight," he said.

At his words, Day seemed to come out of a trance, maybe a bad flashback of that Cataract Canyon trip. Nick watched her collect herself, smoothing her long elegant skirt, repositioning herself. Afraid his face might betray him, he gazed deliberately at the flames in the hearth.

"Well, it was the feast of Christmas," she told, in her husky alto, "and the knights of the Round Table were gathered for caroling and reveling. It was King Arthur's

custom never to begin a feast-day meal until he had wit-
nessed or heard of some wonder—''

Pip held up a hand, as welcome an interruption as the
phone ringing in the middle of sex. "Now, wait. It is worth
mentioning that many Arthurian legends begin in this way.
And this is what we were saying about repetition—''

Zac got up from the couch and stepped over the coffee
table, threatening to silence his brother with his Eton tie.

Go for it, Nick thought. We can lose the body in the
river.

Red-faced, Pip crossed his legs, folded his hands. He
smiled with embarrassment. "I'm very sorry, Day. I'll be
quiet now."

All eyes and ears returned to Day.

"As they were seated at the table..." Nick listened as she
described the Green Knight—even his horse was green. She
pantomimed Sir Gawain's decapitating the Green Knight
and the Green Knight picking up his own head.

"The lips moved, and the severed green head reminded
Gawain of his promise to meet him one year hence."

As Day described Gawain being outfitted for his adventure to meet the Green Knight, Shep moved from the couch
to the floor and joined Nick. He barely noticed.

"...Soon Gawain spied a grand moated castle atop a
rocky promontory. From the residents of this place, he
learned that the Green Chapel was just two miles away, and
the lord of the castle, Sir Bercilak, was delighted to have
Gawain as his guest. Such a friendship sprung up between
Gawain and his host that Bercilak trusted Sir Gawain to
remain at home with his wife while the lord went hunting.
Playfully he made a bargain—that every evening they
should exchange whatever they had won while they were
apart...."

Nick leaned forward as Day played the interchange that
occurred between Lady Bercilak and Gawain the next
morning, when the lady of the castle found him in his bed

and tried to seduce him. Lady Bercilak was determined to have Gawain, and Gawain was at his wits' end to fend her off without hurting her feelings.

Unwillingly Nick flashed on Day in the Red Sled, putting back her head to try to stop her tears. After his rejection.

He felt like shit.

"At last the lady said, 'I find it hard to believe you are really Sir Gawain, for a knight such as Gawain, who embodies courtliness, would not be in a lady's presence so long without asking for a kiss.' 'I bow to your command,' said Gawain, and kissed her, and when the lord came home from hunting that evening, Gawain gave the kiss to him and said, 'This is what I have won.' And the lord smiled with delight and asked, 'And how did you win that?'..."

The story spellbound Nick, reverberated through him. He admired Gawain's courage and honor. He knew his own lack.

When Day concluded the story, silence held the room. Then Pip stood up and burst into applause. "Well-done, well-done!"

Shep and Grace and Zac joined in the clapping, and Nick smiled at Day from the shadows, where he sat with his back to the wall and his arms resting on his knees.

Pip said, "Now, you notice that Bercilak did allow Gawain to kiss his wife, which would be considered a fairly liberal attitude even today. But actually the whole idea of courtly love transcended the idea of marriage. In the Middle Ages," he lectured, "it was acknowledged that marriages frequently occurred for political reasons rather than for love, and what was celebrated was not loyalty to the spouse but to the lover. Lancelot, for instance, on learning he'd been tricked into sleeping with Elaine of Corbenic, believing her to be Guinevere, nearly went mad. He was found wandering naked and starving in the forest, and..."

Nick swallowed, shutting his ears, peering between the translucent curtains framing the window. He tried to make out the glistening water and ice in the river beyond the screened porch. But Shep shifted beside him, grazing his thigh. And Day's reflection, from far away, shone in the glass.

Yes, he fell far short of the knightly ideal.

A man *should* go mad for sleeping with one woman when he loved another.

BY MIDNIGHT Shep was yawning, and Nick knew they should go. But Day showed no signs of leaving. Someone should follow her home and make sure she didn't drive into the river.

Nick tried not to wonder about the reasons for her delayed departure, but by twelve-thirty he had to. Maybe she planned to spend the night with Grace. The next day was Christmas.

Zachary's brother was staying at the River Inn, too.

Across the living room, Pip stretched his arm over the back of the couch, behind Day. On the rug by the hearth, Nick took a drink of apple cider. He'd switched from alcohol hours before, afraid he was spending too much time gazing at Day. And knowing he'd have to drive later.

When he caught Shep's eye, she covered a small yawn with her hand.

He got to his feet. "We're going to take off."

Day remained seated, and after good-nights, she was still talking with Pip and Grace while Zac got up to see Nick and Shep to the door.

As he and Shep left the living room, Nick's head brushed something. The culprit was a bough of mistletoe hanging from the door arch.

Mistletoe.

Wishing he hadn't seen it, Nick trailed Shep into the foyer. And hoped Day wouldn't kiss Pip the way she kissed him.

DAY WAS WRETCHED. Listening to Pip's voice and scrutinizing his green eyes and fair hair and the face that was just a little like his brother's, she found him handsome.

It didn't help.

She wanted Nick, who had said, *I don't love you the way you want me to.* And, *I'm never going to marry you.*

Pip said, "You know, Day, I was terribly rude earlier. I enjoyed your story so much. I talk a lot. I'm sorry."

The apology was obviously heartfelt, a true confession of weakness. This was a man with the propensity to change, to improve himself for someone else. The kind of man she should love.

"You know, if you ever came to England, we could go to Cornwall, visit Tintagel and Glastonbury," suggested Pip. "I think you'd enjoy it." He paused. "I know I would."

Glastonbury. Tintagel. The land of King Arthur and his knights. She could visit those places, visit a charming man who lived in a house that was practically a castle. *Maybe this is it. Maybe I'm meant to fall in love with Pip.*

Imagining Glastonbury, she actually *felt* a little bit in love.

He touched her face.

Day shied internally but did not retreat. They'd kissed last summer.

"I was going to lure you under the mistletoe, but I think it's more comfortable here." When she didn't object, Pip closed in and kissed her.

Day tried to kiss him back, but he wasn't Nick. In comparison to the five-course French meal and chocolate triple-layer something wonderful that was Nick, Zachary's brother was stale bread crust. As Pip's tongue slipped into her mouth, she pulled away.

"Are you all right?"

"Yes. Just tired." Cautiously Day met his eyes. "I think I should go home."

Silent communication passed between them, and Pip took it the way she hoped he would, that she just wasn't ready. It was true.

They stood up together.

"Let me get your coat and see you out. Are you all right to drive? Will you call me when you get home? I'll wait by the phone so it won't disturb Zachary and Grace."

Considerate. "Thank you. I will call."

She saw no reason to protest when he put his arm around her to guide her through the house to the kitchen, where her coat hung. Or later, when he kissed her again beside the car.

Just believe, Day. Believe you can love him.

She repeated it like a mantra all the way home, blotting out pictures of Nick making love to Shep.

NICK KNEW Shep expected him to go inside, to stay. But when he slowed his truck outside her house and shut off the engine, a fragment of a story lingered in his mind. Not Sir Gawain and the Green Knight.

It was what Pip had said. Lancelot and Guinevere. Nick knew Lancelot from Day's other stories. The queen was everything to him. He ran from their love, but love always brought him back. He forsook all others.

"I'm not going to stay." The same thing he'd told Day on the solstice.

How would Shep react? They'd been seeing each other five months.

She touched his hand and he flinched. Then looked at her guiltily.

She'd noticed nothing amiss. "Nick, I've always believed in that saying that, if you love something, you should set it free. If it comes back, it was yours forever. If it doesn't, it never was.

"I'm going to Park City tomorrow to see my folks. I know you don't want to come, so..." Her eyes raised a question.

"New Year's Eve. We'll go to Grace and Zac's party."

"Okay." She stretched over the bench seat and kissed his mouth. "I love you, Nick. Take all the space you need."

He always did.

It never made him free.

New Mexico

IN REGARD TO the circumstances of her coming to them, Rory's parents had done one thing right. They had kept her clothes. *This is what you were wearing that day.*

Filthy threadbare corduroys and a boy's striped polyester T-shirt.

Tonight, on Christmas Eve, Rory did not ask to see them. It would have upset her mother. But she knew where they were kept, and while her parents admired the tree the three of them had just trimmed at the far end of the house, Rory went to their bedroom and slid open their closet and worked the combination on the fire safe. The clothes were there, like an unforgiven sin.

She slipped them from the plastic Wal-Mart bag in which they'd been carefully wrapped. The pants were faded green—frayed hems, holes from seam to seam in both knees. The shirt was stained, the neck unraveling.

Through the corridors of the historic adobe ranch house, she heard carols playing. Andy Williams. The familiar record, one they played every year, invited her to forget the clothes, forget the child, forget the place from which she'd come.

But Rory could not forget, and she knew the haunting recollections would be with her in her sleep and at the dawn.

CHAPTER FOUR

"WHAT DOESN'T KILL US makes us strong," muttered Day, stumbling sleepily through her house the next morning.

It was the only good thing she could say about quitting smoking. And cigarettes *would* kill her, so... She abandoned the convoluted thoughts. Exercising willpower did make her feel strong. She'd gotten through the night. So Nick went home with Shep. What had she expected?

Not that he'd notice a change in her because she'd ridden her bike to work three times and shed her blood on the broomball rink. Today she would take a canyon hike. Alone. The compulsion went beyond pleasing Nick. Confronting the cold that made her cough had become personal. A challenge between her and the outdoors.

She wanted to win.

She dressed in black leggings, white silk turtleneck, an oversize ice blue fisherman-knit sweater and wool socks. As she laced her hiking boots, a vehicle drew up in front of her house.

Springing to her feet, Day ran and yanked open the front door. "Nick!"

He had his window down and was about to put something in her mailbox. Instead, he parked, turned off the engine and rolled up the window.

As Day went back inside, Nick stuffed the gift box into his pocket.

This wasn't supposed to happen.

He'd wanted her to have the charm. That was the *only* reason he'd driven by on Christmas morning.

No, you wanted to see if her car was in the driveway.

Her door was standing open, and he walked in, thinking that sometime he should return her spare house key. He'd had it so long he couldn't remember why she'd given it to him. He thought it was after her father had died, when he'd slept with her every night.

She was in the bathroom, and as he came down the hall, she dropped her cosmetics into a drawer, shut off the light and stepped out. "What's up?"

Her bedroom door was ajar. Nick could see the unmade bed. No sign of Pip. "Good morning."

Nick in her house on Christmas morning. Like a gift that might turn out to be her heart's desire—or crushing disappointment. Turning away from the bedroom, aching reminder of the past and what wasn't to be, Day headed out to the breakfast bar. "Want some coffee?" She could give him his solstice gift while he was here; she didn't know what else to do with it.

Nick took one of the soda-fountain stools at the counter. "Sure." They could talk about Rapid Riggers. His buying her half. *She's going to love that, Nick. Merry Christmas, Day.*

But this pain wasn't going to stop until their lives were truly apart.

While she got the coffee from the freezer and plugged in her espresso maker, he found her key on his key ring. Keeping his hands under the counter, hoping she wouldn't notice what he was doing, he removed the key.

"You caught me getting ready for a hike," she said. "I thought I'd go to the Ice Box Canyon."

"Alone?" Her back was turned, and he laid the key on the counter behind her television, in a spot where he hoped she'd find it much later. Maybe she'd even forgotten he had it....

Opening a carton of milk, she asked, "Want to come?"

Hiking? No. He wanted distance from her, not isolation with her. But that canyon was cold, full of frozen creeks and deep drifts. Day probably planned to walk to the end to see the icicles; that was the point of going.

She shouldn't go alone. "Sure."

But as soon as he spoke, he knew it was a mistake. Whatever happened, they had to go their separate ways. And it already hurt.

THE ICE BOX CANYON was on the river road. Nick drove slowly; it had snowed again during the night, then turned icy. High above the turnout at mile six, where he parked, the walls of the canyon squeezed together like the sides of a vice. Thick gray clouds covered the sky.

There was a cave in this canyon, carved out of a southern wall. In summer, it was completely shrouded by tamarisk, but still squatters found it, as a fourteen-year-old boy had found it years before. Nick had known all the caves. He had moved from one to another, and Sam Sutter had tracked him down every time. So had Day.

Now the tamarisk was stripped of its leaves, and ice dripped from the red sandstone walls. It was seven degrees Fahrenheit.

Day braced herself for the cold. But the minute she left the shelter of Nick's truck, the linings of her nose seemed to become thin brittle sheets of ice.

"Ready?" Nick zipped his parka.

"Yes."

The trail was six inches deep in snow. Day's boots were Vibram-soled, but she had no gaiters to keep the snow out of the tops, and her feet soon grew wet, then cold. No circulation. Holding her fingers loose inside her gloves, she told herself she was warm. As she hiked, she covered her mouth and coughed.

Nick, who had been walking ahead of her, stopped and came back. "Are you wearing a scarf, my little smoker?"

"No."

He unrolled the big turtleneck of her sweater so that it rose above her mouth and nose. "This will warm the air before you breathe it. It should help."

"I quit."

"What?"

She moved the turtleneck a little. "I quit smoking."

He stared. "When?"

"A few days ago."

Smoking. She'd stopped smoking. *Good. Stick with it, Day.* They stood close, and Nick's eyes fell to her lips. He couldn't remember the last time he'd really held her, really kissed her.

"Where's Shep today?"

"I don't know," he said, thinking of other things.

Breath lifted from his nose and mouth, forming soft puffs of gray in front of his dark hair. It didn't hide his eyes, his expression. Day knew the look; it jolted her to see it now. *He loves me. Dammit, he loves me.* They loved each other. What was wrong?

In bed he might tell her. Things came out.

Could she seduce him? The thought seemed wrongful. But if she made it seem lighthearted, festive, fun... Day smiled and called a mischievous light to her eyes. She was an actress. She could do this. "So, Cute Nick, how can I resist this opportunity when I'm alone in a remote canyon with such a famous river guide? I think I want my way with you."

Nick had not forgotten Sir Bercilak's wife, nor any detail of the story she'd told the night before. He understood the game she was inviting him to play. Day eased close to him and the curves of her body grazed him. Stirred him. In bed she always seemed so small and slender. Now her blue eyes, her high cheekbones, her white skin—all were before him, tempting him. He longed to put his lips to her face. To her mouth. He recalled what it was like.

Like they'd been made for each other.

Day watched his eyes. If he rejected her, it would kill her. "But you're not really Cute Nick, are you? Nick always kisses the ladies. This lady, anyhow."

"That's true." His hands threaded into her hair, hands that would not obey him, only her.

She lifted her mouth to his and they kissed, not as Nick wanted, but gently, warmly—and longer than was wise.

He pulled away. This was no courtly game.

This was torture.

Her head back, Day saw the pain in his eyes and was sick. At herself. *I shouldn't have done that.* Nick didn't want to hurt her. Feeling a stupid urge to comfort him, she said, "It's okay. I know it doesn't mean anything."

He turned and continued through the snow. Tracing his larger footsteps, Day tugged her turtleneck up around her mouth again. It did seem easier to breathe.

Nonetheless, she fell twice on the way into the canyon, once on the frozen creek. Nick helped her up, but each fall made her feel awkward and inept. And a little bit colder. *What if this actually works?* she wondered in a sobering moment. *What if this makes him want to marry me, and I have to spend the rest of my life doing things like this?*

Of course it wasn't going to work. It was just comforting to contemplate that the thing she so wanted and wasn't going to get might make her miserable even if she had it.

The end of the canyon was wrapped in ice, a great yawning cavern of gargantuan icicles, spectacular and hospitable as the North Pole.

As they stood amid the frigid splendor, Nick said, "Want to have a snowball fight?"

Was that what Nick's kind of woman would do? Visualizing herself in a hot bath, Day said, "Okay. But I demand that you have a handicap."

"Left-handed?"

She shook her head. "I throw all the snowballs. You try to get away."

"*You* get to throw all the snowballs?"

"Of course. You shouldn't throw snowballs at women."

"Okay. I agree to the terms."

Day bent down to pack a snowball and he walked twenty feet away.

"Bet you can't throw it this far."

She ran at him through the deep powder, her feet slipping, and Nick retreated beneath the giant icicles and stood there, breaking off the tips.

Day said, "Don't do that." What if they fell? He would die.

Grinning at her, he broke off another icicle.

Bastard.

She pursued him under the icicles, but the ground there was icy. He caught her arm before she could fall. Grateful, Day slammed the snowball into his neck.

"Ah, now you asked for it."

"You promised!" She tried to escape.

"No, no, Miss Lady of the Castle." In the blue glacier light beneath the tremendous wall of ice, he held her arm tightly as he scooped up some snow.

"Nick, no!"

"Never believe a boatman. You thought you had Sir Gawain on your hands, didn't you? But it was really just Nick the river guide, and you're going to pay." He held the snowball aloft, inches from her face, and released her arm to hold her waist.

She wrenched free and fled, and he chased her under the colossal frozen swords, easily catching her arm again. But he still didn't throw the snowball.

"Stop it!" When he brought the snow close to her face, she shrieked like a child who's afraid to be tickled but wants to play.

You're so pretty, he thought.

The breaking sound startled him. When he glanced up, Day tried to grab the snow from his hand, still fighting him.

Instinctively Nick grabbed her and carried her, plunging through the snow, as the cracking echoed through the canyon, and when he knew the explosion was imminent, he pushed her face first into the snow and flung himself on top of her.

The crash was deafening, and Day sensed slivers flying, though all she could feel was the snow smothering her, cold against her face, and Nick's body crushing her, his arms clasped around her head, so hard it hurt. "Nick." She squirmed beneath him, unable to breathe, and he shifted slightly but did not get up.

The ice was still settling, landing on his coat, and he waited for silence, the total silence after cataclysm, before he rolled off Day in the deep snow, gently turning her toward him. Her face was red and wet, her sweater and coat and hat covered with snow. Both of them gaped at the ice chunks scattered all around, from where the glacier had imploded on the canyon floor.

Day was still in his arms, too close, and it felt like the moments they'd had in bed, when he could live in her eyes, weak with love for her. But love couldn't make him *good.* And Day, who didn't know him, curbed her own spirit to make room for what she thought was his. He was bad for her, in every way. "Day."

She read his brown eyes. The yearning and the sorrow. *Dammit, talk to me.* "What is it, Nick?"

"It's too hard at work," he said. Lying there in the cold wet snow, he could be honest. "It's too hard for me. You want to be in charge. I'm...bored. I have no purpose there. You want to make all the decisions."

Day was surprised; he'd denied it before. And if that was all... "I can change." She shivered. The snow had seeped into her clothes.

"No. It wouldn't matter. What we're trying to do is impossible. We've been lovers, Day. We can't be business partners. It's insane."

"What do you mean?" She grew afraid.

"I want to buy your half of Rapid Riggers."

Stay calm, Day. Stay calm. She couldn't. He really wanted to end their relationship, and wanted to end their business partnership to ensure that it happened. "My half of Rapid Riggers is not for sale. That's my daddy's river outfit. It's not getting sold out of the Sutter family."

"Half of it already has been. Besides—" he tried to smile "—I'm like family."

Day's mouth dropped a little with a sleek glamorous disdain no other woman could manage so well—especially not while lying in a snowdrift. Her eyes accused him of hypocrisy.

He told her, "I've said it nice."

Day sat up, then stood, shaking off snow. *I hate you. I hate you. How can you hurt me this way?* "If that's how you feel," she said, "I'll buy you out, and you can start your own outfit, like you planned before Grace offered to sell you her half." She hoped he wouldn't call her bluff. Before he'd bought into Rapid Riggers, Nick had been their best guide and more. Indispensable. She wasn't sure she could run Rapid Riggers without him.

His words echoed in her ears. *I've said it nice.* And what he'd said was that it was over. He was killing her, and her tears paid no attention when she told them to stay in her eyes.

Nick got up. "Don't, Day. Please." But she was crying, crying hard, and he grabbed her, his throat choked. "Stop. Please stop." *Please stop, because I can't stand hurting you. Please stop...*

"I can't!" She screamed it at him, sobbing. "I love you. I have more love for you than for...anybody. And you love me, too."

And he'd thought she was going to let him go easily. He had thought there would be no tears from this woman who loved him best in the world. Hugging her tightly, absorbing the convulsions of her body, he whispered, "I know. I know. Shh... Stop. Please, stop. *Please stop.*"

She clutched his arms and screamed at him. "Why are you doing this? Can you pretend to me you make love to anyone else the way you make love to me? And if you say you do, I'm going to kill you!"

"Stop! Just accept it." He wished he could cry, too, from the months of tension, the pain of being with her and not having her, of knowing he shouldn't make love to her anymore, shouldn't encourage her love and her dreams and her prayers.

"Tell me *why.*"

"I've told you why! Stop doing this to me. You and I are on different planets. I want you to fall in love with someone else. I want you to marry someone and have babies." The thought made him bite his lip. He could see her in a garden, pushing children on a swing. He could feel her, quaking and gasping in his arms.

"I want to have *your* babies."

His chest constricted, and he didn't know how tightly he was holding her. "Don't," he begged. "I'm not like that."

"You're twenty-eight years old—" Day stopped the words. It was all falling down around her. She had done it. She had lost control, said all the things she shouldn't. It was really over. It was really over.

The world swam around her. She didn't feel the cold, only his arms crushing her and the knowledge that he wouldn't hold her like this again. A sob welled inside her, but she bit it down, tried to push away from him, not knowing she was still crying.

Nick thought, *I want to be dead so I don't have to feel this. So I don't have to know I did this. So I don't have to remember what it feels like to have you in my arms, Day.*

He made his voice work. "I'm going to go away for a while. When I get back, we can figure out what to do about Rapid Riggers. I might do what you said."

Sell. In the easing circle of his arms, she tried to wipe at her eyes, at the tears freezing on her face. "I think that would be best." If he left. If they never had to see each other.

Later she couldn't remember the walk back to the car. On the way home, neither of them talked, and she knew that he was sorry for hurting her. As sorry as the depth with which he'd loved her.

When he pulled up beside her mailbox, he said, "I'm not going to walk you to the door. I'll be back by New Year's, and we can . . . settle things."

Day nodded. She let herself out of the pickup and walked sickly toward her house.

NICK DROVE HOME, back along the river road, trying to keep his speed down, trying to care that he didn't sail off one of the low red-rock banks and into the river. The miles passed.

At the new Dewey Bridge, the highway turned left, crossing the river, but before that, dead ahead, near the ghostly frame of the old bridge, the two narrow mud tracks of his driveway led away from the pavement, cutting through a bramble of tamarisk. With relief he followed them, slowing the Chevy as he spotted the aluminum fifth-wheel, an Airstream that had been missing one side when he bought it. He had built onto it, and the result looked like poverty, but he didn't care.

He parked and was home. He walked under the forest of bald cottonwoods to the river, where he stared at the ice and the steam.

The box was still in his pocket. Nick took it out and fumbled off the ties and reclaimed the piece of silver inside. The charm was a primitive figure of a woman's head and torso.

It was a goddess.

Like her.

He hurled it far down the river, halfway to the distant bridge, then reassembled the box and winged it like a flying saucer. Hurt welled inside him.

Tell her, Nick. You could just tell her everything.

But there were some things he could never tell. He wasn't that brave or that stupid. Just for instance, if Day ever found out how he'd paid for this land and how, ultimately, he'd bought half of Rapid Riggers, if she ever discovered how he'd earned most of what was his, she would never respect him again.

And there was no one whose respect he needed more.

New Mexico

RORY ABBOT AWOKE Christmas morning in the room most familiar to her. She'd chosen the floral wallpaper when she was seven, when she'd first come here. Right away, she had loved the arched windows that went along two walls, and even now she never pulled the drapes, never used more than the translucent chiffon curtains. She had always loved the room, but for many nights when she'd first slept there she had cried.

Even now she could recall clearly what he was like, the person she'd missed when she'd come here. Him. She had slept curled up with him at night, against his skinny body that was just a little larger than hers. He'd made her feel safe. Without him, she was scared, and she'd missed him and cried until the man who called himself her father—her new father—said he would find him, he would bring him to live with them. It didn't work out that way.

Her father had gone out, and when he returned he told Rory that she must stop thinking of the person she missed, that she must never mention his name. *It might be best if you'd just forget him.* When she'd cried, so had he, her new father. *I'm sorry. I'm sorry, honey.*

As snow fell outside the window, Rory listened to the house and heard water heating in the kitchen, the kettle rattling on the range as the water boiled. Her parents must be up. Rory wasn't ready to face them. This year was different. Everything had been different for months, ever since she'd confronted them in March. *Who am I? Where did I come from? How did you get me?*

They'd told her all they knew.

It was horrifying. And appallingly little. She'd asked too late. Uncle Levi, the doctor who'd arranged it all, was dead.

What she had were her own memories.

She had not followed her father's advice. She'd been unable to forget.

That *he* had told her stories.

And taken care of her.

She knew why he had done what he did. He'd promised to take her away where it wouldn't happen again.

It.

She bound It inside. It never came out.

But on Christmas morning, she did what she did every morning, asked for a miracle—that she would find him again. Because the sickness and fear, the primal grotesqueness of that world, were not all she recalled. She remembered his goodness. And she would never in her life forget his name, the name of her brother.

She said it, and it was her prayer.

CHAPTER FIVE

NICK LOADED his pack and his truck and drove to Rapid Riggers to borrow the Bronco. Trying to forget what had to happen, that he was going to have to leave the river outfit for good, he moved his gear to the company vehicle and headed south on the highway toward Mexican Hat and Bluff, under a gray Christmas sky, through the snow-spackled desert. His thoughts consumed the miles, and a familiar claustrophobia descended on him as he neared Blanding and the town of Covenant.

He fought it, fought thinking about things that were done and could never be undone, fought the paralyzing remorse of one error so grave that for him it had become a mortal sin. Fought the questions that never ceased. *Where are you? Please tell me you're all right.* He fought so hard, became so absent, that the desert swallowed him, and he didn't notice when he reached the Navajo reservation.

Nick loved and hated the reservation. Indian blood ran in his veins, from his mother's side and maybe from his father's, too, but he'd never known what kind. His mother had worn her hair in a ponytail and had spoken to him in her own tongue when his father wasn't around to hear. Nick couldn't recall a word of that language now. During his childhood, she'd been away from home often, working, and she'd disappeared altogether when he was eight. Died, though he hadn't learned that until he was an adult and had looked up the records. He still missed her.

To camp on Navajo land required permission, but Nick disregarded that. He didn't want to see anyone, didn't want to utter a word to another human. Didn't want to say his own name.

He paid cash when he filled the Bronco's tank in Tuba City. Then he took a four-wheel-drive road into nowhere, into a place called Tanner's Wash, and he left the vehicle under some cottonwoods. He drew his heavy pack onto his back and began to walk, knowing he would walk every hour of daylight and into the dark, until he could no longer feel.

DAY CALLED GRACE and told her she wasn't feeling well but she'd try to make it for dinner if she could. Somehow, she would fill the hours till then. She was making cookies and getting drunk when her doorbell rang.

Fast Susan, a Rapid Riggers guide and a friend of Day's, stood on the doormat. Susan was six feet tall, with a blond Mohawk and a heart as big as the river. She'd given up a child for adoption when she was seventeen.

"Merry Christmas!" She held out a poinsettia. "The Dry Gulch was getting rid of these, so I thought I'd bring you one." Susan worked as a waitress at the Dry Gulch Saloon during the off-season.

"Thanks." Day embraced her and accepted the plant. "Come on in." Her body weak from what had happened with Nick, from the finality of it, she walked ahead of Susan into the kitchen to set down the pot and take her cookies out of the oven. She lifted the bottle of cognac on the counter. "Want some?"

Susan eyed a nonexistent watch on her wrist, then shrugged dramatically. "Why not? How are you, Day?"

"Fine." She blinked, smiled at Susan. "What about you?"

"So-so. It's not the greatest day, you know?"

"Jennifer?"

Shedding her black-and-white cowhide jacket, Susan nodded.

Day knew she had listed on a register to be reunited with her daughter if Jennifer should ever look for her. It hadn't happened yet.

Susan helped herself to a glass from the cupboard. She squinted at Day. "You don't look so good."

"I'm fine." Day quaffed some cognac.

"No, fess up. What is it? A man? Oh, no, let me guess—"

"It's nothing." She never talked about Nick with girl-friends, with Grace, with anyone. Nick had never shared their secret, either.

Susan picked up her jacket and fished in the pocket for a pack of cigarettes. "Mind if I smoke?"

"No." *One Christmas cigarette. What could it hurt?* Day wasn't sure what made her resist, except the certainty that the deprivation was making her stronger. She set an ash-tray on the bar and regarded the sugar cookies. "I was go-ing to take these to Grace's tonight. What do you say we eat them all, instead?"

"A woman after my own heart." Susan winked at her. "Hey, let's talk about the lip-sync contest. Have you got anything planned?"

Day tried to summon enthusiasm for the upcoming Moab event, the biggest party of the winter. But a lump formed in her throat when she remembered other lip-sync years, other routines. She and Nick had put something to-gether a few times, always humorous. They'd always placed. Afraid her face showed what she was feeling, she turned to dig through her cupboard for a bowl to mix ic-ing.

Behind her, Susan said, "Would another time be better, Day?"

Day shook her head, grabbed a paper napkin from a holder on the counter, tried to hold back the tears.

"That son of a bitch," Susan muttered, clearly meaning someone in particular.

Day wiped her eyes and blew her nose. "I've just had a bad morning."

Without comment, Susan lit her cigarette and poured herself some cognac. "So, the lip-sync," she said after a moment. "Let's brainstorm."

Grateful for her friend's presence, Day gave herself to the conversation. It couldn't take away the pain but could help the time pass.

FOUR DAYS after Christmas, Nick stumbled on a cave among the slickrock monoliths crowding the mesa near Tanner's Wash. Ducking inside, he found that pictographs, paintings, covered the walls. In one place there were dozens of handprints, like a community record.

Nick adjusted his headlamp and ventured farther into the darkness. The cavern was dry, clean with the smell of dirt. As the ceiling grew lower and he had to crouch, he spotted a gap in the rock. Leaving his pack, Nick wedged through the slot into another room. Bats slept on the ceiling. He made his way onto a rock ledge and shone his headlamp at the floor six feet below. A pictograph on the wall showed a man lying on his back. He was painted white. Dead? Was this a burial cave?

Nick's heartbeat accelerated. He'd vowed not to do this anymore. Buying Rapid Riggers had been a turning point. But the recent days had been without peace or joy. In contrast, this was a fine moment. Swiftly he edged back to the main part of the cave and went out into the dusky afternoon sunlight to look around. The cave mouth was beside a wash and partially hidden by scrub oaks and cottonwoods. No one around for miles. But he waited, listening.

Nothing.

Back in the cave, he collected the avalanche shovel from his pack and returned to the burial room. With a quick glance at the bats, he plunged the spade into the earth, not caring about anything except the moment, this obsession he'd first learned as a twelve-year-old foster kid wanting to make money to buy a basketball. His foster father—his *second* foster father, an unemployed miner—had said, "I'll show you how to earn you some money. You come with me." He'd paid Nick a dollar for his first find—a black-on-white olla.

Back then the pot had probably sold for five hundred dollars on the black market. Today Nick could get much more. It had taken him sixteen years to learn how not to get screwed.

His shovel struck something and he stopped. Cloth. Bone.

"I bet they didn't bury you all by yourself." Picking another spot directly over the skeleton, he dug in again and heard and felt a splintering crack.

The shovel handle. Broken.

He'd meant to replace it—back in November. Now he was fifteen miles from the Bronco, much farther from town. He could hike out, go buy another. But he'd promised Shep he'd take her to the New Year's Eve party at the River Inn. He'd told Day he'd be home by New Year's.

That world. That other world, where no one really knew him.

Staring at the broken shovel, he came back to himself. *What are you doing? You weren't going to do this anymore.*

The primitive picture of the white figure sleeping attracted him. A shaman? Probably. Whoever it was, his life was over, and his children and grandchildren were dead and gone, too. Nobody cared about this man. He sure wasn't anyone's beloved relative anymore.

But this was the ugliest part of pot hunting. Disturbing the dead. It was why pot hunters were called "moki" diggers. Nick had dug a burial cave once before and sold his finds for twenty thousand dollars.

So what had changed?

Day, sobbing, grabbing his arms and screaming at him, telling him he didn't make love to anyone else like he did to her.

You're shit, Nick, he thought. *From shit you came, and to shit you will return.*

The bone exposed by his shovel seemed obscene.

Sometimes he wondered if Kelly lay in some shallow grave like this.

Who would want a seven-year-old girl with a messed-up face? Why would *good* people take that kind of risk?

The night he'd told Day things, told her about his childhood, he'd said Kelly had been taken to a different foster home. A lie.

He knelt and used his hands to scoop the dirt back into the hole he'd made, smoothing the loose dust. In the sandy soil, he touched something cool and smooth like stone.

Too small for a pot. The wrong shape for a rock.

Nick pulled out the object. It was a ceramic dog. A coyote?

An effigy.

He'd never held one in his life. Never even seen one, except in books. Not even in a museum. They were rare.

They were worth a fortune, but it wasn't money that made him hold the dusty figurine, the ancient thing someone had carved. It wasn't money that made him stand up and take it from the burial cave.

I won't take anything else.

He was quitting. This was the end.

But he would keep one souvenir.

THAT NIGHT he hiked till dark, ate cold refried beans from a can and slept under the stars. At dawn he was up, and by noon he'd reached the Bronco.

A white Blazer was parked in the wash behind it.

There was a bar of lights on the roof.

Nick's mouth dried up and immediately he thought of the effigy. *Why had he taken it?* Suddenly it seemed meaningless. Worse than meaningless. Just stupid. If he'd wanted souvenirs, he had three at home, three artifacts hidden in a box in his trailer, pieces he'd liked too much to sell.

Now, he'd given in to temptation—the one time it mattered.

The guy can't know you've got it.

Nick walked tall and straight toward the Bronco as a uniform of the Navajo tribal police climbed from the Blazer. The officer's gut hung over his belt, but his manner was relaxed.

"Hello," he said. "This your vehicle?"

"Yes, sir." Nick filled his mind with nonincriminating images. Refried beans. Climbing harness. Anything but the object in his pack.

The cop pushed his sunglasses up on his nose. "It's been here two days. Doing some backpacking?"

Shit. "Yes."

"Can I see your permit?"

"Permit?"

The cop backed up a step, eyed the almost completely faded letters on the side of the Bronco. Rapid Riggers River and Jeep Expeditions.

Nick's stomach rolled.

"May I see your driver's license?"

Carefully Nick released the hip strap of his pack, slid it off his shoulders. The guy couldn't ask to search his pack. The effigy was carefully wrapped in a long undershirt in the top pocket. *If only he hadn't taken it.* From a side compartment, he produced his wallet and removed his driver's license, glad his boatman's license was out of sight in another slot.

The cop examined the license. "What do you do in Moab, Nicholas?"

Did he have to answer?

This guy looked like he could wait for the second coming.

"I'm an outfitter."

The tribal policeman's face showed no reaction. None was needed. Outfitters knew about permits. "Would you please wait in your vehicle?"

"Yes, sir." Knowing he wasn't going to leave with anything worse than a ticket and his own shame, Nick retrieved his keys and unlocked the Bronco while the cop walked back to his cruiser.

Nick tossed his pack onto the rear seat, got behind the wheel and waited, listening to the distant crackle of the police radio. He closed his eyes.

Eventually the officer returned with a small clipboard. He handed Nick his license. "I'm going to cite you, Nicholas, for camping without..."

Nick listened to the spiel and signed the ticket.

He couldn't see the officer's eyes behind his sunglasses as the man said, "Don't visit us again."

He nodded.

The policeman returned to his vehicle, and Nick started the Bronco. There was nothing else to do. The cop was watching.

He drove away with a stolen artifact, wishing he could put it back.

New Year's Eve

ELLA FITZGERALD CROONED "Love Is Here to Stay" through the stereo system, while a mirrored globe revolved near the ceiling of the Princess Room, the magnificent dining room of the River Inn. Though the room had not yet been fully restored, the hardwood floor was refinished; it was a perfect place for Moab locals to dance in formal wear and toast the new year and Zac and Grace's venture.

Day had purchased her gown at a vintage-clothing store in Salt Lake that summer. Mandarin collar, long-sleeved, fitted down its entire length except for a slit up one side. The dress was pale gold and covered with black velveteen leaves and vines. When she'd bought it, she'd eagerly anticipated wearing it during the holidays. Now she hardly cared.

Pip never left her side. As they danced, Day occasionally glimpsed Nick in the crowd. He must have come home that day; tonight was the first she'd seen him, when she spotted him across the room with Shep.

"Day, would you have dinner with me tomorrow night?" asked Pip. "For the new year? Grace tells me there's a place that's very good."

It shouldn't have been a difficult question. Pip really cared about her. Twice now he'd mentioned her visiting England. She should be thrilled by his interest—a chance to get over Nick. But her emotions weren't working, except for the sheer agony she felt whenever she recalled Christmas morning in the Ice Box Canyon.

Dinner with Pip. "I'm not very good company right now, Pip. Thank you very much for asking, but I think I'd rather not."

His brow crimped in concern over his expressive green eyes. "Can I help?"

"You are. I'm enjoying dancing."

He replied with a remark she couldn't hear but knew was charming and flattering, and she smiled up at him, pretending her heart wasn't torn in pieces.

FROM THE REFRESHMENT table, where he was drinking punch with Dirty Bob, Nick watched Day and Pip dancing. As the couple spun out of sight behind some other people, Nick moved a foot to one side, trying to see them.

Bob murmured, "She's an adventurous spirit."

"What?" Distracted, Nick saw where his friend was looking—fortunately not at him but at Shep. Nick had practically forgotten that his date stood several feet away, talking class-V rapids with a River Legends guide named Harry.

"I want to do the Upper Animas," she shouted to Harry over the music. "We should get a trip together this spring."

"She talks about rivers like they're men she wants to screw." As soon as he'd said it, Nick wished he hadn't. Shep had been his lover. And wasn't her "adventurous spirit" what had attracted him in the first place?

"One should be more reverent about rivers," Bob agreed.

The ironic comment was vintage Dirty Bob. He meant, *One should be more reverent about one's sexual partners, but we're river guides so we love the river more than people. Rivers are what we hold in reverence, but, God, aren't we messed up?*

"If you'd like me to take her off your hands..." his friend volunteered.

Nick didn't answer.

The music switched to the Indigo Girls. "All right!" said Bob. "This is my favorite song. They've got it down. We're all overcoming past-life baggage. You and I were Sahara princes in our last lives. That's why we're river rats in this one." Reincarnation was one of Bob's favorite topics. Preparing to expound, he ladled himself another glass of punch and stiffened it with vodka from a fifth he'd brought. With drunken generosity, he added some to Nick's glass without asking.

Nick frowned at the drink.

"Sorry. Forgot you don't drink that much. Here, let me pour you another."

"No, it's fine." Tasting it experimentally, Nick said, "I'm going outside." Where he didn't have to see Day.

DAY WANTED to leave before midnight. She wouldn't be able to stand all the kissing. When the last notes of Bonnie Raitt's ''Have a Heart'' faded away, she excused herself to Pip and searched for Grace among the bodies on the dance floor to say goodbye.

Her sister was nowhere in sight, so she decided to look in the kitchen—always a likely place to find Grace.

As she left the dance floor, Dirty Bob wrapped an arm around her shoulders and breathed alcohol on her. ''Hi, May-Day. How're you?''

''Great.'' She hoped he would stay the night at the Inn rather than drive home. Grace and Zac had invited people to bring sleeping bags or use the beds upstairs; there was plenty of room.

''You look beautiful this evening,'' he said gallantly. ''You can be on my broomball team anytime.''

Day laughed and squeezed his arm. ''Take it easy, Bob. I'm going to find Grace.''

The boatman lifted his glass in cheerful salute, and Day continued toward the kitchen.

Only one light glowed, over Grace's restaurant range, and her sister was just coming down the hall from her bedroom. Grace was dressed all in white, a Ben Rogan dress that had been a gift from Zachary. Adjusting a large white earring, she said, ''Hey, sis, how's it going?''

''Good. I was going to head home.''

Grace paused at the junction of the hallway and the kitchen. ''Is everything all right?''

''Sure.'' Her sister would never love a man who hurt her. Grace had even left Zac once, and he had come after her. *She's strong,* thought Day. *Not like me.*

''Is everything okay at Rapid Riggers?'' Though she'd sold her half of the outfit, Grace maintained an almost proprietary interest.

''Everything's fine. I'm tired, that's all. The holidays.'' To stanch her sister's questions, Day added, ''Let's get together soon and work up something for the lip-sync contest. With Susan.''

"Great.'' Smiling at the mention of something in Day's normal routine, Grace kissed her. "Let's find your coat. You're not drunk, are you?''

"No, I'm fine.''

"Do you want me to have Zac take you home?''

"No, no.''

They wandered down the hall to where the coats lay on the couch in the parlor. Two Current Adventures river guides lounged by the hearth drinking beer and talking to Zachary. He helped Day on with her black cashmere coat, and she said good-night to him and Grace and went back through the hall and into the kitchen.

As she reached for the door handle, the door opened and almost banged her face.

"Excuse me.''

That deep voice. Day retreated as Nick stepped inside. He was alone, and she slipped past him to go out.

Nick held the door, the last of any good feelings he might have had for the night gone. *You look beautiful.* He wanted to ask if she was safe to drive, but she never looked back, just left the screened porch and faded into the night, all but her bright hair.

He couldn't take care of her anymore.

Someday soon they were going to have to talk about Rapid Riggers, but he wasn't ready yet. A good solution would be to get out of town again. For longer. He'd call her in the morning.

He shut the kitchen door but stood against it as the Porsche's engine and then its lights came on. He said a prayer she'd get home safely.

IT WAS ALMOST ONE-THIRTY when Nick and Shep returned to her house. The lights were off, and Shep said in an overly happy, overly optimistic voice, "Nobody's home. Just us.''

She knew what he was going to say, Nick could tell.

He told himself it wasn't going to be bad like it had been with Day. Nothing could be that bad. "Shep, I've got to... I can't..." Somehow he found the words to tell her that she was too nice a woman for a man like him.

DRIVING HOME on the river road, he was numb. Shep had cried. Guess she'd thought that when she "set him free" he'd come back. Had he been born to make women cry? Why did they even like him?

Because they don't know. He tried to slough off the feeling that clung to his skin like dirt, the smell of human waste in the air. He'd told Day about the shack and the cellar and the springhouse. She'd held him while he said it and made love to him afterward. It had felt good. It had felt so good.

Day, you don't know everything. You don't know how bad I am.

How disgusting.

He kept his pace slow, watched the curves of sandstone illuminated by his headlights. The road seemed monotonous, and he thought about leaving Moab. Maybe when he returned, things would be the same as they'd been before.

But Nick knew not to expect that kind of magic. Ever since he'd bought Grace's half of Rapid Riggers—maybe since even before then, when Sam Sutter had died—his life had been changing. He couldn't change back to the person he'd been before he was rejected by the man he'd depended on.

He couldn't become again the person he'd been before he'd hurt Day in that canyon, before he'd made her break down and cry so hard in front of him.

He slowed for the familiar bend in the road after mile fourteen, the last curving red-rock corridor before Castle Valley. Just around the first curve, a red Subaru with a boat rack on the roof stuck out of the tamarisk; it stood at an angle, on the river side of the road, its tailgate over the blacktop.

Nick braked. Then, slowly, pulled over to the shoulder. What was Bob doing?

But he knew. Bob hadn't parked the car that way, with the tail in the road.

Broken glass winked at him from the asphalt.

He's walking around here somewhere.

His mind suddenly keen, utterly clear, Nick grabbed his headlamp from the glove box. Rubber gloves and a disposable face shield. A voice inside him kept asking questions he didn't want to hear, questions that argued with the lies he was trying to tell his instincts.

Why didn't he put on his flashers if he had to leave the car here?

Nick flicked on the Chevy's flashers, got out, closed the door, and calmly crossed the road.

There won't be anyone there. Someone picked him up. He's drunk, so he forgot the flashers.

The pavement under his boots was icy. From the still automobile, music played. Reggae. Loud.

He's in there. Dammit, he's in there.

Far away down the river corridor, headlights panned a field of white over the Navajo sandstone walls, then went away. Nick lit his headlamp and shone it at the Subaru through the back window.

A figure was slumped over the wheel.

He almost slipped on the ice, moving too fast. The front end of the car was crunched, the windshield broken, and he couldn't open the door or see through the shattered driver's window. The stereo blasted Bob Marley. "Lively Up Yourself."

He circled the back of the car, past the familiar bumper stickers—FRANKLY, MY DEAR, I DON'T WANT A DAM and INDIGO GIRLS—and through the mud and leafless tammies. The passenger door worked.

The car smelled like blood, and he saw it spurting red against the windshield.

"Bob? Are you okay?" As he shouted over the stereo, he drew on his face shield and gloves.

No answer, no motion from the figure. *Shit, Bob, it's not time for that next life.* "Bob!"

Adjusting his headlamp, he crawled into the car. Bob was breathing, in labored raspy breaths. Nick put direct pressure on the spurting wound. Compound fracture of the femur. Blood sprayed around his hand, and he repositioned it and found the pressure point in the femoral artery with his other hand as the music blared in his ear. He checked to make sure he was controlling the bleeding. There was so much blood it was hard to tell, and he couldn't let go, couldn't even spare a hand to turn off the music. He should have brought bandages, should have brought his whole kit.

Was Bob bleeding anywhere else? Through the red splotches on his mask, Nick surveyed Bob's body. His left leg was broken, too, and his head was bloody. His ear seemed to glisten. Trying to see, Nick knocked his mask against Bob's shoulder and dislodged his headlamp, too. It fell to the seat behind him, but now he could see. There was pink fluid coming out of Bob's right ear.

He peered through the bloody windshield toward the road, begging for headlights, listening to the wailing pulsing song.

CHAPTER SIX

DAY WAS ENJOYING a breakfast of leftover Christmas cookies at nine the next morning when her doorbell rang.

It's not him. Stop thinking that way.

With a cookie in hand, she unfastened her chain and opened the door.

Fast Susan stood on the other side. "Can I come in?"

"What is it?" Susan's Mohawk was still blue from the New Year's Eve party the night before, but it was flat, as though she hadn't bothered to gel it up. She looked like she'd been crying, and Day imagined terrifying possibilities. Grace? Zac?

Nick?

She shut the door behind Susan.

"Bob was in an accident last night. They flew him to Grand Junction. He had head injuries and internal injuries and two broken legs, and they're still operating on him."

"Bob?" Everything around her assumed an unreal quality, as though she'd just heard someone had died. But Bob wasn't dead.

Instinctively she latched onto Susan's arm. Like old women helping each other across a street, they made their way to the breakfast bar. "How did you find out?"

Susan sank onto a stool, and Day found her an ashtray. "I saw the accident scene on the way home. It was on the river road."

Susan lived in Castle Valley, a community fifteen miles from Moab on the way to Nick's place.

"He hit a wall right before the Valley turnout. Nick found him. He was the first one on the scene. After that, a cop came and they got an ambulance."

Dry horrible sensations crawled up Day's throat. Susan looked like she hadn't slept. Trying to think, she said, "What can we do? Where's his family?" Then she remembered that Bob really didn't have any.

We're it. Rapid Riggers. The outfit her dad had made into a family. She was mother, now, to her guides.

"Nick went up to Grand Junction," said Susan. "I asked him to call me this morning, and he did. I think he's been up all night."

Not my problem. Whatever he's feeling now is not my problem.

While Susan tapped a cigarette out of a pack, Day measured coffee into her French press and filled the kettle with water. Suddenly she gasped. "Does Grace know?"

"I haven't told her, Day."

Day breathed unevenly. Bob had been coming from Grace and Zac's party. He'd drunk too much. *Oh, Gracie.* "I've got to go over there, Susan."

"Afterward, will you drive me to Grand Junction? My car doesn't work."

"They won't let us see him."

"I want to go, anyhow." She dabbed at a mascara-blackened eye, crying. "I'm sorry. I can't seem to stop this. I haven't been to bed."

And Bob was her good friend. Day hurried over and hugged Susan, who had lost so much already. The baby she'd given up. "I'll take you. After I tell Grace."

The kettle whistled, and Day tried to remember why she'd wanted the water. Her half-eaten cookie lay beside the sink.

They drove the Porsche to the River Inn. Several cars still sat outside, cars of friends who had spent the night after the party.

Bob hadn't stayed and should have.

How was she going to tell Grace?

Day went inside, and Zac was in the kitchen, and she chose the coward's way out. She told him first.

GRACE SUTTER took little on her shoulders that didn't belong there. Bob's accident, reason told her, was Bob's fault. He was thirty-two years old and knew better than to drink and drive.

It didn't help.

In her kitchen, the old kitchen she and Zac hoped to phase out as soon as possible and replace with a new restaurant kitchen off the Princess Room, she accepted her sister's attempts to console her, but felt as though her dreams were crumbling.

What if this upset Zac and his mental illness returned? So far, he seemed okay. He and Pip were in the Princess Room cleaning up from the party.

"I'm so *mad,* Day."

Seated on the edge of the kitchen counter, smoking another cigarette, Fast Susan said, "So am I. I told him he should stay. He wanted to get up and go skiing early in the morning. He had that streak—*has* that streak . . . What am I saying? You couldn't tell him what to do when he was set on getting out in his kayak or on skis or whatever."

Like Nick, Day said to herself. But Nick was different.

Grace saw her sister's sadness. Upset about Bob, of course. But Day had been acting so weird lately. Riding her bicycle to work. She'd been unhappy even before this accident.

Zac and Pip came into the kitchen, and Zachary said, "Grace, Pip says he can stay longer. We called the airline."

"Oh, good." Zac could use the emotional support. And maybe Pip and Day... It was a dream close to Grace's heart—not exactly that her sister would fall in love with Pip, but... *I wish she'd find someone who makes her as happy as Zachary makes me.*

Bob and tragedy returned to the forefront. "I'd like to go to the hospital," Grace said.

Zachary threw glances at Day and Susan. "I'm not sure that's a good idea. Is his family there? They might not want to see you, Grace."

So he felt the guilt, too.

Day spoke up. "We're his family. I think it will be okay, Zac."

But she knew, from what Susan had said, that Bob might not even be alive when they reached Grand Junction.

THE THREE WOMEN drove the two hours to Colorado in Grace's Toyota 4Runner. Day took the wheel, while Grace sat in the back and let Susan have the passenger seat. As they crossed miles of snowy desert, Susan said, "I just can't stand this. And poor Nick. He said he could have done more for him sooner if he'd had oxygen and an IV kit. And another pair of hands."

Day clutched the steering wheel, trying not to care how Nick was feeling. He was closer to Bob than any of them. They'd spent a winter in Chile together with two other guys, climbing friends of Nick's from Wyoming.

As Day pulled into the visitor lot beside the six-story sandstone-colored hospital building, Grace said, "I really hate this place."

Their father had died here. And Zachary had been locked in the psychiatric ward here after going mad in Cataract Canyon. Nick had been on that river trip. It was, Day admitted reluctantly, the fact that he was here that made the hospital less dreadful to her.

Nick had always been there when she needed him.

He was in the waiting area outside surgery, sleeping sitting up, still wearing the clothes he'd worn the night before, jeans and a charcoal gray pile sweater. They had dried stains of blood on them, in patches big as place mats.

No wonder I love you, thought Day. *You're the only knight I know.*

He opened his eyes and saw them, and Grace and Susan were immediately on either side of him, hugging him.

Day kept her distance. Two weeks ago she would have given herself, laid down her body and heart and let him use her as he liked, anything to give him comfort. Two weeks ago he might have taken it. Something like this would have brought them closer.

But Christmas in the Ice Box Canyon had changed everything.

After a moment, feeling isolated, Day approached the others. Nick was saying, "They probably won't be done till two or three."

Susan lifted her eyes to Day's. "Brain surgery."

They settled in to wait, Day and Grace side by side in two chairs against the adjacent wall, Susan with her head on Nick's shoulder. River buddies.

Day wished she could be part of that circle.

She never would be. She wasn't like Nick. She couldn't witness a hideous accident and just...go on. Jim Antonio's death had changed her forever. She hated white water.

Across Susan's head, Nick observed Day. Her baby blue leggings and long sweater looked thrown on in a hurry. No makeup.

But she wasn't crying. She was being the pillar her sister could lean on. She'd done the same thing when Zachary went mad and before that when Grace and Zac were split up. And for him, when her own father died.

So strong. Everyone knew it but her.

Nick realized she was staring back at him, and he closed his eyes. He needed to talk to her. During the night he'd made some decisions. About himself. About what mattered.

Bob... It had taken Bob's accident, seeing Bob that way, to show him.

There was only this life.

AT LUNCHTIME, Grace and Susan went down to the cafeteria, but Day did not. Across the room from Nick, she pretended to read a magazine. When he came to her, sat beside her, Day smelled the sweat on him and the blood. She didn't look at him. She already knew how he looked. Unshaven and exhausted and a year older than he had yesterday. She could tell herself anything about his experience with highway accidents, his ability to cope with emergencies. But he was only human, and he was wearing this one. Literally. It was Bob's blood on his pants.

Nick didn't bother to ask how she was. He'd broken her heart. Now this had happened, and she was watching the clock like the rest of them.

"I've decided to go to Salt Lake till the season starts," he said. "You don't need me till then, and my time could be better spent there."

She didn't reply. Didn't say she needed him.

He hadn't expected she would.

"Are you still thinking of selling me your half of the outfit?" she asked.

Her voice was too high. Strained.

"Thinking about it." He shrugged. "If your dad had wanted me there, he would have made a place for me himself."

Day turned her head. Without mascara, her lashes were long and the color of dark ale. "What a load of crap. Excuse me, but he spent about twelve years of his life making a place for you."

One could not gracefully argue.

Seeing his expression, Day regretted her words.

After all, there *had* been one other person who knew about her and Nick. The man who knew them both best. And Day had never stopped wondering if that was why her father had left Nick out of his will. By Sam Sutter's standards—and probably by the standards of most decent men—Nick had not treated her right.

But it was how she'd let herself be treated.

Nick dropped the subject. "So for now, let's do things your way. Borrow fifteen grand and get the rafts and life vests. I'll help you with that, and then I'm leaving. I'll be back in April."

Leaving. Day was disquieted. She had never run Rapid Riggers completely alone, even in winter. There had been her father—then Grace. But this was what she and Nick had agreed would be best. *Be brave, Day.* Hard, when even the first-year boatmen knew her for a coward. "What are you going to do in Salt Lake?"

"I want to be a paramedic. I'm most of the way there. I need two classes."

A paramedic. He'd been an EMT-I for years, breaking up volunteer time on rescue teams with less emotionally demanding work. But whatever he did, whether running raft trips or patrolling ski runs, it always involved taking care of people. He did it with kindness, compassion and understanding.

Proud of him, glad of his goal, Day groped for his hand. His fingers wove through hers, and peace came.

Everything's going to be all right.

It was the first time she'd felt that way since the solstice. Or maybe ever in her life.

"You won't go till you find out how Bob's going to be."

I know how Bob's going to be. Nick didn't say it. He said, with more optimism than he felt, "It could be months before we know that. Anyhow, I need to be at school on the tenth."

Day withdrew her hand, got up for some coffee. When she returned, she asked, "Where's Shep?"

The question jarred him. He'd forgotten Shep's existence, forgotten that he'd made her cry right before he found Bob. What he'd told Shep the night before was true—she'd never deserved someone like him. Nick wished he could undo his whole relationship with her. It hadn't been worth hurting her. She was a good woman.

But not the woman he wanted.

Knowing he'd have to call Shep, tell her about Bob, he said, "That's over."

"Breaking hearts full-time now?" Day murmured.

He leapt up and strode away, angry, but not at her. At himself, for not being able to do enough for his friend.

When he looked back, Day had picked up the magazine again.

BOB CAME THROUGH neurosurgery, and for the next three days he lay in a coma, under the protective guard of the ICU staff. The nurses allowed brief visits, and Day and Susan and Nick and Grace and Zac took turns seeing their friend. Even Shep drove up to see him on the way to Telluride, where she planned to spend the rest of the winter skiing; no one expected her back in the spring. They all lied and said they were family members. Susan engaged herself to Bob. Day and Grace and Shep were his sisters.

The nurses knew they were lying. And also that they were his only family. Nick practically lived at the hospital for those too-short moments with his friend, returning to Moab only once, for clean clothes.

But on January fourth, he came home, and he and Day went to the bank and were promptly granted the loan. When they left the bank in fifteen-degree weather, a dead bird lay on the asphalt beside the passenger door of the truck. Day had seen it earlier. Opening her door, Nick said, "Yum."

Ignoring him, Day got in the car. All morning, he had been excessively cheerful, like some dark caricature of his usual self. She knew it was his coping mechanism, that it was because of Bob.

Sliding behind the wheel, he asked, "What did the deer say after he went through the windshield of the hunter's car?"

"I don't want to know. Tell me where you're going to get those rafts."

He started the engine. "There's a place in Colorado. In Glenwood Springs. Want to come? We can go see Bob first. You know, while he's in a coma maybe we should give him a Mohawk. He always kind of wanted one."

Day felt stretched. About four years earlier Nick had helped retrieve the body of a mountain biker who had gone off the Portal Trail, the narrow trail that wound hundreds of feet above the river portal. The week afterward he had made everyone around him tired and edgy with his cease-less humor. He'd spent the nights with Day, making silent love to her. On the fifth night he'd told her what he'd seen on that treacherous talus slope, the condition of the body after the force of that fall, and the following morning he had taken off to climb some peak in Colorado.

Her father had told her, *You make your bed, and you lie in it.*

I like my bed just fine.

Nick had returned from Colorado with a new friend, a kayak champion named Tess.

Remembering her heartbreak and humiliation, she barely heard him say, "We need a new Cataract boatman to fill Bob's vacancy. No pun intended. God, you know what he was listening to? 'Lively Up Yourself.'"

Day's nails bit into her palms. She wanted to help.

"And here we are in Santa Fe." Nick beamed at Carl Orson's new building. "If he hangs some Navajo blankets in the windows, maybe people will thinks it's a gallery."

They crossed the Colorado.

I will not go to Glenwood Springs with him.

As Nick drove into the Rapid Riggers parking lot, Day spotted Zachary's Austin-Healey. The front door of the office opened, and Pip came out.

"I thought I told Susan to keep the riffraff away."

"Nick."

He parked the truck, glanced at her.

The words stuck in her throat. She pulled them out. "Can you cry?"

Nick shook his head and opened the door. "There's nothing to cry about." *I saved his life, kept him from bleeding to death. It's good to have a life, Day, even if you spend it in a coma.*

He told himself not to be morbid and jaded. It was early. The nurses had said so, and he knew they weren't lying. Anything could happen.

Pip waited on the porch steps for Day. His herringbone overcoat belonged in *GQ*. *What future earls are wearing this season,* thought Nick. "Hi, Pip."

When he continued inside and the door shut behind him, Day almost breathed a sigh of relief.

"You look tired," Pip said. "I stopped by to see if I could persuade you to have lunch with me."

It sounded restful. "Let's go."

PIP TOOK HER to the Moenkopi Café, the best restaurant in town. He was solicitous about Bob. He talked about Zachary's mental illness.

"I think the hardest thing about being sick that way must be letting someone else take care of you. Zac was captain of the Oppidan Wall at Eton. He's very macho really. Grace has a good balance with him. But you know, Zac told me he can't stand thinking of that Cataract Canyon trip. Of cracking up when he needed to be strong."

Day said sincerely, "He's a wonderful man. My sister is very lucky."

"So is my brother. By the way, Zac and I have started gutting the space for the new kitchen. Why don't you come over tonight and see it?"

"Thanks. I will." *I feel better,* Day realized. *I'm making it.*

Pip raised his glass. "To Grace and Zachary's River Inn."

When he dropped her back at the office in Zachary's Austin-Healey, Nick's truck was still there, but Susan's Volkswagen bus was gone.

"Shall I pick you up at eight o'clock?" Pip asked.

"Fine."

Pip lifted his chin in the direction of Nick's truck. "Please tell me if I'm overstepping myself, but is there anything between you two?"

Day hesitated. Her secret with Nick no longer seemed to matter. Remembering how Susan had reacted when she'd found her crying at Christmas, Day wondered if it even *was* the secret she'd always thought. "There has been. I really— I'm not a very good bet right now, Pip." *I never have been. I fell in love with him when I was a kid. We lost our virginity together.* "But thank you for all your kindness."

"Thank you for your honesty. I'll still look forward to seeing you tonight. I can always hope."

So can I.

Pale sunshine lightened the gray clouds over the river as Day made her way up the muddy steps to the office. She entered quietly and listened for Nick. Nothing. Maybe he'd gone somewhere on his bike.

Shivering, she turned toward the inner office and stopped short when she reached the door. He was asleep on the couch with both window sashes raised halfway. He didn't stir when she slipped off her shoes, crossed the room and quietly closed the windows, leaving them cracked at the bottom.

Day hurried silently through the reception area and the kitchen to the storage closet where the sleeping bags were kept. She grabbed one, pulled it out of its stuff sack and unzipped it as she brought it back to the office.

He was wearing blue jeans and a pile pullover, the moss green fleece shirt she'd made him. As Day started to lay the sleeping bag over him, she saw his right hand half-open at his side, against the back of the couch. There was something in his palm, a small black clay figurine, like an effigy, the kind of thing sold at trading posts and galleries.

Day wondered why he had it. Nick wasn't much for trinkets. Maybe it was a talisman. Carefully she spread the sleeping bag over him. He turned his head slightly but didn't awake. Wanting to leave before he did, Day went into the bathroom to change clothes for the bike ride home.

Back at her house, after the daily ride that now gave her a sense of accomplishment, she left her helmet in the laundry room and switched on the kitchen TV. Planning to catch the news while she had a snack, Day pivoted the set to a better angle.

Nick's key winked up at her from the counter.

The doorbell rang, inopportunely, ten minutes later.

Quieting her sobs, Day hid in the kitchen. She wouldn't answer.

But the doorknob turned and Grace looked in. "Day? Oh, there you are. Oh, Day, what is it? Has something happened? Bob?" She flew toward her.

"No." Day grabbed a couple of tissues from a box on the breakfast bar.

"What's wrong?" Grace put an arm around her. "Tell me."

Hadn't she just convinced herself that the secret didn't matter anymore? Nonetheless, she'd kept it so long it was hard to give up. But maybe telling the secret was part of getting over him.

Day squared her shoulders. "I'm in love with Nick, and he doesn't love me."

Dead silence.

Tell the secret. Break its spell. "We've been lovers. Off and on for years."

The pink hues left her sister's face. "You and Nick?"

Oh, God, she had broken their promise now. *Over,* Day told herself again. *This is part of it. You tell your sister, your girlfriends. You say how you can't stop loving him, how you don't think you'll ever love anyone else. They tell you he's not worth it.*

Grace whispered, "You jest."

"We have to break up our business partnership. We haven't figured out how. He's going to Salt Lake to become a paramedic."

"What about Rapid Riggers?"

"He's bored, Grace. It's winter. There's nothing going on. You know how he is. He needs something to do. For the past four months, I've had to deal with him rearranging every file in the office, every dish in the kitchen. I have to set down the checkbook in exactly the same place every time." She closed her eyes. "Anyhow, we can't keep working together. We just can't. I'll never get over him. Either one of us will have to become a silent partner, or one of us will have to sell."

"But you can't be silent partners!" Grace knew the way things worked at Rapid Riggers. "He needs you for the things you do in the office. And you can't do what he does in the yard."

Day spread her hands helplessly. "So I get a yard dog." A yard dog was a maintenance person, lowest on the totem pole at a river outfit.

"Day, are you sure...?"

"What?"

"Well, are you— I mean, it would be perfect if you two could just get married. Oh, stop, I didn't mean to make you cry. Shit, I'm sorry." Grace hugged her, while Day held a tissue to her mouth. "Oh, Day. What's happened? What did he say? I can't believe what you're telling me. I mean, there were one or two times I wondered, but— You're so... different from him."

Day wiped her eyes and tried to stop crying. *I can live through this. I can live through this.* "He doesn't want to marry me. He said so. 'I'm never going to marry you, Day.' For a little while, I fooled myself that maybe if I took up some of the things he likes... He's why I quit smoking, why I've been riding my bike to work. I was going to give myself six months to try to get him to make a commitment. Then, on Christmas, he said he wanted to buy my half of Rapid Riggers. And that's not all he said. He wasn't vague, Grace. He's said it two or three times in different ways, all of them clear. It's over between us. He doesn't want me the way I want him."

Grace held her. "Shh... Oh, Day, it's all right. It's all right."

"I'm fine." Day rubbed the shredded tissues across her face again. "I mean, poor Bob. He's got real problems. This is trivial."

Grace's eyes said she didn't think a man making her sister cry was trivial. "Well, what about Pip?"

"Pip. Now that's an idea." Day escaped her sister's embrace and took a pitcher of juice from the fridge. "That would be great. It would be great if I wanted any man in the world except Nick. Grace, *for ten years* I've wanted no one else. It's not healthy. It's not right. But I can't seem to change." She grimaced. "I *have* to change."

In her blue jeans and an Oxford sweatshirt of Zachary's, Grace straddled one of the stools at the breakfast bar. "I know you, Day, and I can't believe you've loved him for ten years without any encouragement. In fact, I've *seen* him encourage you. He always remembers your birthday. And never notices mine."

Day grimaced. The birthdays hadn't all been sweet.

Grace hit her forehead. "I feel so stupid not to have known this. Why didn't you tell me? We don't have secrets."

"Nick and I had one. We have a pact. I just broke it. See? It's really over. Want some juice or an English muffin, Grace?"

"No, thanks. I've got groceries in the car. I was just stopping by to ask you to dinner." Grace looked as though she didn't want to pry. "I mean, was this, like, a one-night stand, or—"

"Get real."

"Oh."

"Let's talk about something else. Let's talk about the lipsync."

After a heartbeat Grace went with the change. "Sure. You know, Susan had an idea that we should make the lipsync contest a benefit for Bob. It won't be a lot of money, but we're going to put jars in all the stores and banks, too, to help pay his hospital bills."

"Good."

Grace's brow furrowed. "What's going to happen to Rapid Riggers, Day?"

"We'll work it out," said Day, feigning confidence.

She wasn't ready to tell Grace that the outfit might be losing Nick.

New Mexico

THE HOLIDAYS DEMANDED action from her. Christmas and New Year's had first appeared in her life when she was seven, with the shock of toys. Presents. She'd always wanted to share her gifts with him. But he was never there.

The letdown this January was no different. Part of the cycle. The season had come and gone without him, and she wondered if he was even alive. He'd been mistreated worse than her and for longer. He had protected her, doing everything he could to deflect attention from her and take it on himself. The kind of attention no child wanted. And in the end . . .

She had begged, *Don't go back. He'll hurt you.*

Her brother had promised he wouldn't. But he was only a child. Where had he gone, instead?

She had to do something.

As soon as she reached her apartment, before her pride could stop her, Rory booted up her computer, went to the Birthright web site and pulled down the menu on the bulletin board to choose POST MESSAGE.

Her shame overcome by a stronger need, she typed, "Dear Nick: I am looking for you. If you read this, please write back. Kelly."

CHAPTER SEVEN

WHEN DAY ARRIVED at Grace's house for dinner, Zac was at the kitchen table, cuddling the ugliest animal she had ever seen. Grace was sliding a tray of rolls into the oven when her sister came in. "Hi, Day."

Day's answering smile was wan, a contrast to Pip's cheerful "Hello, hello," as he appeared from the dining room and took her coat.

While Day thanked him, Zac set the animal he'd been holding—some kind of dog—on the floor. Ninochka, who'd been sitting beside him eagerly watching, gazed down at the newcomer and gave a low whine.

"Eat it, Nina," Grace suggested. "It'll taste good."

The Siberian lay down in front of the smaller dog and began to wash it with her tongue.

"See how well they get along!" exclaimed Zac.

Day guessed where the dog had come from. "Stray?"

"Yes," replied her sister. "Want a dog?"

Day knew Grace wouldn't really let anyone take the stray dog from Zachary. With a smile that said the same thing, Pip invited, "Come see the new kitchen, Day. Or rather, the gutted walls."

He led her out of the room, and Grace turned to Zachary, remembering what she'd meant to tell him the minute she came home, before she met the *thing*. "Guess who my sister loves."

Zachary repositioned his chair so he could pet his new dog. "She loves Nick Colter. Are they getting married?"

"Ahh!" Grace cried. "No, they're not getting married. How did you know? How come everyone knows these things but me?"

"Because you're...pragmatic. For instance, you look at this animal and see an undesirable stray. And I look—"

"Don't get back on that. Tell me what you know."

"I don't *know* anything, except that they spend a great deal of time gazing into each other's eyes. That's a usual symptom of being in love. You and I do it quite a bit." He got up from the table to hold his wife and look down into her eyes. "Can I really keep him?"

Grace found it very difficult to refuse Zac anything, even a wheezing, one-eared mutt with a pushed-in face. "I said you could. For a coupon." In fact, it was the first thing she'd said when she saw the animal. *If you want to keep it...*

She and Zac exchanged coupons for gifts on birthdays and Christmas and other special occasions. Coupons good for housework or back rubs or...strays.

"Done," said Zac, as Grace had feared. Releasing her, he hurried down the hall toward their bedroom to get a coupon. When he returned and handed her a coupon good for ANYTHING, he said, "That's what I'm going to call him. Coupon."

Grace collected the ticket and stuffed it into her pocket. Speaking low, because her sister and Pip were somewhere about, though out of earshot, she said, "Well, Day says he doesn't love her. She says she's even thought of trying to take up the things he likes. Rock climbing, mountain biking—"

"That's not the answer."

Grace wished she knew the answer. On Nick's lower back was a long striped scar. Grace had seen it on the river and in the boat yard every summer. Her father had told her and Day that he'd been beaten. But Nick never said what his life had been like before he came to Moab and started living in caves on the river like Huckleberry Finn. Any other woman she would have warned away from Nick. But Day was strong enough.

Or *could be* strong enough. Grace had seen a long line of women take turns with Nick Colter. Day shouldn't have put up with that. "I think she's right, Zac. Nick always picks girlfriends who share his love of the wilderness. It might be the thing standing between them."

"I very much doubt it. Let them work it out themselves, Grace."

"But what about Rapid Riggers?"

"Grace," Zachary suggested, crouching beside the dogs. "Keep out of it."

"He's going to Salt Lake and leaving Day alone all winter."

"Hmm. Imagine deserting the second-most beautiful woman in Moab." He winked at his wife as he scooped up Coupon and brought the smelly thing over to Grace. "Look at these eyes. How can you not love an animal with eyes like this? Now, this is Grace, Coupon, and she's in charge of everything here."

Grace surrendered to his silliness, but she couldn't stop thinking about Nick and Day. It was much better than contemplating Dirty Bob lying in a coma in Grand Junction.

THE NEXT MORNING Nick reached the river office before Day. When she wheeled her bicycle inside at seven-thirty, he said, "Let's go to Glenwood Springs and buy rafts."

Standing the mountain bike against the wall, Day hung her helmet on the handlebars. "I don't want to go."

"Day, if I leave this place, you'll need to know your equipment."

He was offering to teach her. "All right. Shall we stop and see Bob?"

Nick suppressed a wisecrack. Part of him knew that humor was his defense against the pain of what had happened to Bob. But it wasn't a good reaction. "We can't. He had some seizures last night, and they sedated him and said no visitors."

"Seizures? What does that mean?"

Nature—reflex—won. "Picture...Sacco and Vanzetti in the electric chair?"

"God, Nick. Just don't, all right?"

She saw too much, knew him too well. But the compassion in her eyes, and her insistence that he sober up, helped him do so. When he did, waves of pain came through. Fighting the hurt and fear, he answered her original question more seriously. "I don't know what it means. But they're doing all they can for him. You and I can't do anything."

He was right. "Okay. Let me change, and we'll go."

"You're dressed better for Colorado now."

Black wool leggings, blue fisherman-knit sweater and her down coat. She shrugged. What did it matter what she wore?

They gassed up the Red Sled and left immediately, since Glenwood Springs was four hours away.

Nick sang to himself as they drove between burgundy red formations and past the visitor center of Arches National Park. Then the song faded away. "Feel like telling stories?"

Day had been reading some new stories to present at the museum. Practicing their telling would pass the time—and maybe help take Nick's mind off Bob. "All right. Who goes first?"

"You."

She began the Hopi legend of Tiyo, who had gone down the Far Far Below River in the hollowed-out trunk of a cottonwood tree. They were almost to the state line by the time she finished. It had started to snow.

Nick said, "Thanks. I liked that. I like his boat."

Day could believe it. At fourteen, Nick had braved Cataract Canyon in a canoe. Perhaps that was why she always pictured Tiyo like Nick. She said, "Tell me a river story. Tell me about the canoe in Cataract."

He did. She'd heard it before, but he embellished freely, drawing out the section where he'd swamped the canoe in Mile Long Rapid and it had almost sunk, making up an episode with Little Niagara, the massive hole in Satan's Seat. As they passed Grand Junction on I-70, avoiding the business loop but both thinking of Bob in the hospital, Nick told her about reaching the calm of Lake Powell, known to river guides as Lake Foul, the reservoir that had drowned the best rapids of Cataract Canyon and swallowed forever the beauty of Glen Canyon. End of story.

Silence fell on the car for so long he was startled when Day spoke.

"How did you get back to Moab?"

"Hitchhiked."

"With a canoe?"

Nick didn't answer at once. "Actually, when I was paddling in Lake Powell, your dad came up behind me in a J-rig."

Day stared. "*That's* when he caught you with the canoe. How come you never told me?"

"It's embarrassing. Still." He held the steering wheel lightly, watching the road. "I didn't know who he was. He had a bunch of passengers, and he asked if I'd like a tow to the marina, a ride back to Moab."

Nick wanted to abbreviate, to leave things out. Because it was Day, he told it as it had happened. There was safety in the role of storyteller, as though he was talking about some other person, some made-up story boy.

"He put the canoe on the roof of the Suburban he was using to haul the J-rig, and then he said, 'That's my canoe, son. Now, you must know where you got it, because it disappeared from my yard Friday night.'"

Hearing her father, Day smiled.

"Then he said, 'Now, right here on the side of this J-rig, it says 'Rapid Riggers River and Jeep Expeditions,' and there's a big sign outside my outfit that says the same thing. And you look like a smart observant boy, so I can only guess you can't read.'"

Day laughed. "I wonder if he really knew. I mean, he used to say that to everybody. 'Can't you read?'"

"Yeah, right. I don't know when he figured it out. I ran away, and he caught me behind the trading post." Nick had been certain he would be hit. "He said, 'You want that canoe?' and I did, but I didn't trust him. He asked me who I was and where were my parents, and I told him I was eighteen."

To her giggle, Nick said, "Yeah, he laughed, too. He asked where I'd run away from, and he tried to get me to ride back to Moab with him, but I was afraid, and he didn't make me. He just let me go."

Day waited a long time for him to continue. "So you hitchhiked to Moab?"

"The next day."

"How did you hook up with my dad again?"

"I got hungry. You were right, what you said in the hospital. He did everything for me."

"He loved you."

"Sure."

He said it like it didn't matter. Day knew her father had taken Nick for his own. Her father had *had* to love someone who would steal a canoe and take it down Cataract and not wreck the boat. He'd kept a careful distant watch on Nick, following him from cave to cave, checking on him. They'd had a deal; Nick had told her about it after her dad died. Nick could keep the canoe—if he went to school.

They'd both honored the bargain.

Day missed her father cruelly. Even that mixture of compassion and disappointed resignation with which he'd viewed her fear of the river. It felt almost as though the only part of him she still had was Nick.

But that wasn't true. She had Rapid Riggers. She had his outfit.

Refusing to pine for what she could *not* have, she said, "So tell me about rafts."

IT TOOK THREE HOURS to choose boats and life vests. The new innovations in equipment surprised Day. The Rapid Riggers boats really were outdated.

They bought two eighteen-foot and two sixteen-foot self-bailing rafts, two dozen new oars and thirty life jackets. All would be delivered to Rapid Riggers in the following weeks.

By then, it was dark, and they were hungry. Lunch had been the salad bar at a City Market. They went out for dinner at an Italian restaurant below street level. Neither of them wanted anything alcoholic with the meal, and Nick seemed indifferent to the idea of an appetizer. Day ordered bruschetta, anyhow, and ate it all herself, while he shifted in his seat and occasionally drank some water.

Even when their food came, he barely touched his.

"Nick, are you all right?"

"Sure."

"Shall we try to see Bob on the way home? Maybe they'll let us in now."

"Maybe." At the moment Nick wasn't eager to see more of Bob in a coma. He talked to him whenever he visited, told him jokes and river stories, trying to wake him up. But he never moved, and it made Nick want to hit things.

Day yearned to reach across the table and stroke his hair back from his face. *It's Bob,* she realized. *That's why he's not eating.* "Did you go through one of those debriefing sessions after Bob's accident?"

Critical Incident Stress Debriefing. He'd told her about the sessions for emergency-medical-services personnel. "No. It wasn't that bad." If he'd been on the ambulance team, though, they would have made him talk to someone, just because Bob was a close friend.

Restless, he sat back in his chair and glanced toward the stairs that led up to the street.

Day followed his gaze. *Oh, God*. It hadn't even occurred to her when she'd suggested the restaurant. They were underground, in a room without windows.

Nick guessed her thoughts. "I'm fine, Day. I'm just not hungry."

She hurried, anyhow.

While she scraped up the last of her manicotti, Nick brooded. He needed to do something. He diffused stress with activity. There was a full moon tonight, and they were in Colorado, surrounded by mountains. If he had his skis... But Day didn't ski.

When they emerged on the sidewalk, it was 8:00 p.m. Nick caught Day's arm before she could start toward the car. "Day, do you want to have an adventure?"

His eyes were hopeful, like those of a child who wants someone to play.

But Nick played hard.

"Like what?"

"Surprise?"

It had to be some outdoor thing. "Is it something I can do?"

"I think so."

Obviously he didn't want to go to the hospital. And they were together, anyhow; what further damage could his adventure do? "Okay."

His smile was boyish, excited. "Let's go up the street."

Downtown Glenwood Springs was still decorated for the holidays. As Nick and Day headed up the sidewalk, cars drove by with skis on their roofs, coming down from Aspen.

Nick led her into a mountaineering store and asked the clerk if they rented snowshoes.

"I've never been on snowshoes, Nick."

"Easy as walking."

There was a rack of those fabric keeper straps for sunglasses on the counter. They caught Day's eye, triggering memory. While she relived a private drama, Nick requested two snowshoe rentals with ski poles and, after deliberation, chose some climbing equipment and a headlamp. Pointing to three ropes on the wall, all eleven-millimeter UIAA-approved, fifty meters long, he woke Day from her reverie. "Pick a color."

They were beautiful. Turquoise, shocking pink, neon yellow—all interwoven with threads of contrasting colors. "Blue."

It was what he would have chosen. He asked the clerk to get it down, then talked him into lending them a second rope and a climbing pack.

"What are we going to do?" asked Day, half laughing. He was crazy. "It's nighttime."

"You're going to have the best night of your life."

Their eyes met and held for too long, trapped in memory. His eyelids dropped, shielding his thoughts, and Day turned away and pretended interest in skis and snowboards. All the best nights of her life had been with Nick. But this couldn't be one of them.

THEY STOPPED at the grocery store for fruit and trail mix and Power Bars, plus hot water and herbal teabags to fill the two thermoses. Although Nick wasn't hungry, he knew Day would be before they were done. Out in the Red Sled, he removed one pair of rental snowshoes from the storage pack they'd come with. "Put the food in here."

He started the engine while Day dealt with the groceries.

As he drove south, the moon lit up the silvery snow and the Victorian buildings. He headed west at Carbondale onto another highway, and they passed a motel and a school and some small ranches with corrals. The road narrowed to two lanes and wound into the mountains.

"I take it we're not going back to the desert."

"Not right now. Relax. We've got a little drive." He adjusted the heat in the car. "You can go to sleep if you want."

"No. That's all right." She was wide awake, watching the curves, the shadows of the trees.

They had left ski country, moved into closed-up snow country. More twists. Past the town of Redstone, with its row of historic coke ovens for processing coal, they entered evergreen forest. There were no other cars. As Nick turned onto a new road, Day read the highway sign. "Marble. Is that where we're going?"

"Yes." Feeling the intimacy of what they were doing, Nick reminded himself why he'd ended their relationship. All the whys. When he'd awoken in the office the day before with the effigy in his lap and the sleeping bag covering him, he'd been worried. But if Day had seen the object, she apparently hadn't thought anything of it.

It was a big lie between them. His life was one big lie.

"It's really dead up here," she said. The cabins they passed were all dark.

"Especially this time of year. It's inaccessible. One of the least-discovered places in Colorado." He'd asked about avalanche conditions. They were good, the snow as stable as it got. He was more concerned about Day. *She'll be okay.* She'd quit smoking. She'd been riding her bike.

Eventually they reached the town of Marble, shut tight for the winter. Outside a restaurant that wouldn't open again till spring, Nick parked the Suburban. The road leading off to the right, to the quarry, was not plowed. "We're here."

The valley was dark, the mountains surrounding it so high and steep that the moon had not risen above them. Instead, it cast a glowing white outline around the ridges. As soon as she got out of the car, the cold sank into Day's bones, but she ignored it. At least she was dressed right. She pulled on her hat with the long tail.

Coming around the side of the car, Nick said, "Give me that thing." He took it from her and tied the tail in a knot.

"What are you doing?"

"Don't want it to get caught on the rope."

Rope. Because she was with Nick, the prospect didn't make her nervous. She trusted him and put on the silly hat.

Nick loaded the climbing gear into the borrowed pack and gave Day the smaller snowshoe pack, which held the food. "Okay, these snowshoes are easy." They were aluminum, and he showed her how the bindings worked, with three nylon straps and buckles to fit around her boots. He stabbed the ski poles into the snow beside her. "These help you walk in deep snow."

Enduring the cold on her bare hands, Day snugged the snowshoes over her boots while he put on the other, larger pair. As she pulled on her gloves, he checked that they had everything they needed from the Suburban and locked it.

Day grasped the ski poles and experimentally raised one foot, then moved it forward. The snowshoe sank a few inches into the snow. She picked up the other foot. "I can do this."

"Of course." Nick felt no urge to tease her now. He just wanted her to make it to the top. "Let's go. You set the pace."

They started along the road, heading toward the nearest ridge, past a sign that said Marble Quarry.

"Is that where we're going? To the quarry?"

"Right."

It sounded interesting, and the snowshoes weren't bad at all. The cold left her body. Even her fingers and toes grew warm from the exertion of poling and of lifting the shoes in the powder. "I like this. I'm warm."

"Good."

The squeaking crunch, the gentle clinking of the levered bindings, made a reassuring rhythm in the still night. As the path began to rise, winding up onto the mountain, Day's breath came hard. She coughed some, then pulled up her turtleneck around her face.

Nick paid careful attention to her. *She's going to be tired.* But he would turn around if she seemed in danger of exhaustion.

When they had climbed for some time, she stopped. "I just want to catch my breath."

"Sure." While she rested, he opened her pack to get the trail mix. Removing one of his gloves, he untied the twist and offered her the food.

Day peeled off her gloves to eat and to drink hot tea from the thermos. Moonlight shone on Nick's hand holding the bag, and she looked up and saw the bright disk rising over the far ridge. It illuminated the valley, the trees and a frozen creek below. Till then, she hadn't even noticed that they'd crossed a bridge. "It's beautiful."

Seeing the keenness with which she was studying the view, thinking how beautiful *she* was, Nick felt free. *This is the best thing I've ever done.*

It was because she was there.

He put the food and the thermos away. "It'll probably take us an hour and a half to get up to the quarry. It's faster in summer. I'm going to walk in front of you and break trail, but I won't go too far ahead."

"Okay."

Nick was the perfect companion. Without looking back, he seemed to know her speed, slowing his steps so that he was never more than about ten feet in front of her. Day alternated between walking in the prints he made in the deep powder and cutting through it on her own. But even though she was sweating in her clothes, she felt her muscles and her body growing stronger, her lungs cleaner as she coughed the phlegm out of them.

Whenever she stopped to rest, Nick offered her the thermos and something to eat. She grew used to the sight of his face and his dark eyes in the moonlight, to seeing his hair against his ski headband. His eyes tilted at the corners when he smiled at her, and in his expression she saw a part of him she hadn't known before. He was at peace.

Now I understand why you do these things.

It was especially good to see him like this—calm—after his edginess since Bob's accident. She'd longed to help him relax and hadn't known how. In the past, after he'd been through a crisis like retrieving the mountain biker's body, even making love to him hadn't really worked.

She realized she'd never known him before tonight. Shep had never met the lover that Day had. But undoubtedly Shep and many other women had seen this side of Nick.

No point in trying to guard her heart from emotion; she could not. On this mountain every wave of love seemed safe and right, like in the hospital, when they'd held hands after he'd told her he was going back to school to become a paramedic.

"This is fun, Nick."

"I'm glad you think so." *I'm glad you're with me.* He paused, waiting for her, but she kept going, each rise and fall of her breath audible. He sensed the deep flush on her cheeks.

He felt himself falling more deeply in love with her.

It's okay. Just enjoy this night. Enjoy her friendship.

Eventually he spotted the first of the pieces of quarry equipment, draped in snow. "See the waterfall?"

It was up ahead, iced over, glittering under the moon. The wall beside them was steep, straight up and down, the mountain cut away to make the quarry road. But they were at the end of the road, and it changed to a narrower path up through the trees, alongside the frozen creek falls.

"This trail is going to be tricky, so we'll stay close together. Just take it slow and use your poles." He broke the trail for her, taking care that his steps weren't too long for her legs. He picked out the stairs, avoided boulders.

Day struggled, deliberately putting her feet exactly where his had been.

"We're almost there."

"Almost there" turned out to be a long quarter of a mile, but when the trail ended, they were on level snow.

"This way."

Nick led her alongside another sheered-off wall of rock to a giant overhanging mouth in the mountainside, the gaping manmade entrance to the quarry. The snow beneath it tapered off to ice and then to nothing.

"Stay here, Day."

He ventured across the snow and ice toward the edge of the quarry. Eventually the ice stopped, leaving cold concrete. Nick took off his snowshoes. A four-inch diameter pipe protruded from the ground, a sling and a carabiner already around it. He crouched and examined them, then removed his pack to get the headlamp.

When he returned to Day, she was gazing up at the roof of the entrance, thirty feet overhead. "This place is incredible." She met his eyes. "I take it we're going in."

"Game?"

Day regarded the monstrous hole with only blackness beyond. "Okay." She shivered. Now that she'd stopped moving, she was cold.

In the pack, Nick found a length of one-inch tubular webbing he'd bought at the climbing store. "I'm going to tie a harness for you. It was cheaper than buying one, and it works just as well as long as you do it right." Directing the headlamp where he needed it, he wrapped the webbing briefly around her thigh, checking her size. "Go ahead and

take off your snowshoes, but stay over here, off the ice."
His eyes teased. "Since you're so graceful."

Day listened attentively as he explained knots and
watched his hands as he expertly tied them. When she
stepped into the harness he'd made, he adjusted it, then
secured it with two other knots. The knots all looked perfect. "Comfortable?"

She picked up her legs, felt the webbing around them.
"It's snug."

He slipped his fingers inside the webbing, against her
wool leggings.

Oh, God. Just a little higher, Nick.

"It fits." Satisfied, he withdrew his hand and used another length of webbing to make himself a harness, taking
the same care he had with Day's. He noticed her shivering
and took the thermos out of her pack. "Drink some tea."

He went to set up the anchor. The pipe was solid, em-
bedded deeply in concrete, but he added a new sling to the
one already in place. After anchoring the rope he'd bought,
he went back to Day. He loaded their extra gear, including
the snowshoes, into the two packs. "I'm going to lower
these after you go down. You'll have to take them off the
rope."

"Okay."

"Hang on to me. It's icy." Giving her one arm, he used
the other to carry the gear over to the anchor. While she
waited, he set up a belay with the second rope and tied in.
"Here. This is a locking carabiner." He fastened it through
all the layers of webbing on the front of her harness, both
waist and leg loops, so that her weight would be evenly
distributed. "It's important to lock the gate. You screw it
like this. It's supposed to be as fool-safe as two regular
carabiners with the gates opposed. But because you're
you," he said, knowing he was on the verge of saying what
he wanted, saying more than was wise, saying *because I love
you so much,* "we're going to use an extra one, anyhow,

and oppose the gates. Now, this is a belay plate." He fed a loop of rope through the plate, then through the gate of each biner and closed and locked each gate.

Day listened carefully to everything he said. Brake hand. Friction, which he said would keep her descent as slow as she wanted.

"When you start, you say, 'On rappel,' and I know you're going down. When you get to the bottom *and* you're off the rope, you're going to yell, 'Rappel off.' On rappel. Rappel off. You use the words in different order to avoid miscommunication. What do you say when you start?"

"On rappel."

"When you're off the rope."

"Off rappel."

"Rappel off."

"Rappel off."

He gave her the headlamp and adjusted the band tightly over her hat. "At the bottom, there's plenty of room to walk around. But don't go anywhere. There's a lot of ice and a lot of water."

Regarding the impenetrable darkness of the quarry entrance, Day choked back a laugh. "You think I'm going to wander around in there?"

He wanted badly to kiss some part of her face before she went down. Any part. He couldn't, so he just grinned at her. "Okay, balance." He demonstrated how she should hold her legs. "The hardest part is right at the top, going backward over the edge. Keep your feet high and your legs at a ninety-degree angle to the wall, parallel to the ground. Like walking down it. Backward. If you let your feet get too low, you'll fall against the wall."

A swarm of butterflies launched in her stomach.

Nick checked her harness and his, the anchor, all the knots, the ropes. He fastened her gloved brake hand around the turquoise rope and threw the coiled end over the ledge and down into the quarry.

Cautiously Day crept toward the edge, bent her head so that the light from the lamp shone down. She saw streaked walls of marble, white and yellow and gray. The rock had been cut away in slabs, and the remaining wall showed the cuts. An ancient ladder stretched hundreds of feet up the nearest face. Ledges running the length of each wall cut into the marble approximately every eight feet, creating a reverse shingle effect and disappearing below the light shed by her lamp. She couldn't see the bottom. "Is the rope long enough?"

"Yes."

Nervously she turned her back on the chasm and faced Nick, clutching the rope tightly in her brake hand. "On rappel."

CHAPTER EIGHT

SHE COULDN'T BRING herself to move.

"Just lean back. Trust the rope. This is the scariest part."

The shape of his body in the moonlight reassured her. Nick wouldn't put her in danger. Day leaned back into the rope, letting some of it out. Abruptly, with the stomach-flying sensation of a roller-coaster ride, she was upside down, her feet up by the ledge, her head and shoulders in blackness, the wall cold against her back. Day hung in the dark, her heart racing.

Nick's voice came from above her. "Are you okay?"

"I'm upside down." Since she wasn't going anywhere, it actually felt fun, but she was sure it wasn't supposed to happen.

"I know. The Austrians do it that way. See if you can bring your feet down the wall."

Soon she was in the right position, leaning back in space with her feet on the wall. The beam of her headlamp shot white light over the marble wall of the quarry. Letting some rope slide through her brake hand, she descended a few steps, walking down. It worked just as Nick had said. Easy to stop.

Adrenaline raced through her as she lowered herself farther into the black vault, moving out over a ledge where marble had been removed. She watched her boots in the circle of light from her headlamp, then trained it below. The ground was less than a hundred feet down.

Lord, what a rush. *No wonder Nick likes doing things like this.* This time she was with him. As many other women had been before—and would be again.

Depressing reality crept over her.

Too soon she reached the ground.

Day touched one foot down, then the other, on sand and marble talus. Getting her bearings, she discovered that the ground extended twenty feet or more from the wall, running the length of the entrance. Beyond lay water, giant slabs of marble and wooden catwalks.

It was a wondrous place, a giant's cathedral of stone.

She remembered Nick.

Directing the beam onto her harness, she unscrewed the gates on the carabiners and freed the rope. The belay plate fell to the ground and she picked it up and tied it to the end of the rope, knotting the cord twice.

"On rappel," she whispered. "Rappel off." She yelled it. "Rappel off!"

Her voice echoed through the quarry.

The rope went up, slowly at first, then rapidly.

After a moment, she saw Nick's silhouette far above her, looking over the ledge.

He said, "Are you okay?" More echoes.

"Great. How do we get out?"

"There's a shaft. We'll walk to it. I'm going to lower our packs."

He lowered the packs and ski poles, which she untied. Then he rappelled down and stood beside her. "Hi."

"Hi."

Nick unfastened the rope from his harness. "Was that fun?"

"Yes."

Her eyes were shining. But as soon as they met his, she looked away, down, and he could only see her lashes against her cheek.

Emotion avalanched through him.

"Stand back. I'm going to pull the ropes down." He'd rappelled using both tied together with a Flemish bend, so that he could slide the length out of the anchor at the top.

They backed away from the wall, and he pulled on one end of the tied ropes. The other half came free at the top and snaked down, falling in a heap on the ground, sending soft echoes through the quarry. While he untied and coiled the ropes, Day asked, "How many times have you been here?"

"Five or six. They took the marble for the Lincoln Memorial and for the Tomb of the Unknown Soldier out of this quarry."

Day had never seen either monument. The farthest she'd ever been from Moab was the Grand Canyon.

Nick packed their gear and took off his harness. Even without her gloves, Day had trouble with the knots in hers. Her hands grew cold.

"Here." He helped. "Put your gloves back on." She did, her stomach hot. *Nick*... Day closed her eyes, aching. *I love him so much. How can I ever get over him?*

Nick put on his own gloves, stowed all the equipment and helped her with her pack. Carrying all four ski poles in his left hand, he reached for hers with his right. "This way. Be careful."

His hand swallowed hers as he led her over a narrow wooden catwalk with a wire railing.

"Hold on to the wire."

She did. Alongside the narrow plank, ice floated in the water, water cold enough to die in. Day clung hard to his hand, followed the bobbing light beam and his tall form until they rounded a corner of marble, and moonlight shone down a wide slanted shaft littered with marble talus and boulders. When she saw the path out of the quarry, Day released a breath.

Nick squeezed her hand and drew an extra breath himself. *Why did I bring her here? Why did I do this to both of us?*

The shaft opened out onto a snowy plateau, a parking area for quarry trucks. Slipping off her pack to put on her snowshoes, Day admitted, "You know, I was a little nervous we were going to be trapped in there."

"Don't trust me?"

Day recognized the question's undercurrents. He didn't believe she trusted him to make decisions at Rapid Riggers. "There's no one I trust more, Nick."

Nick fastened on his own snowshoes, chastened by her answer. He didn't deserve her trust.

THE RENTALS and borrowed climbing rope had to be returned in the morning, so they stopped in Redstone and got a cabin for the night.

There were two rooms. Nick took the couch, Day the bed, and when she had stripped down to her camisole and panties and slipped between the sheets, she listened to him running water in the bathroom. Walking around. Cracking a window.

From the other side of the door, she imagined his body. She knew his wildness, his absolute virility. She knew the scope of what he had to give. How would another man, an ordinary man, be enough after Nick?

She tried talking to herself as a friend—or a therapist— might. *It will happen. Just trust, Day. He's hurt you. He's used you. What he's given you is crumbs, and you deserve a banquet.*

It didn't help.

She could remember sleeping next to him, even the first time, on a river trip when she was seventeen. She'd snuck into his tent, and after they'd made all they could of the waking hours, he'd turned her back to his chest and whispered, *Sleep with me this way. It feels good.*

Bundling the sheet against her lips, Day shut her eyes, shut out the world, trying to keep from crying. The truth was in her heart. *He never used me. It never was crumbs. It never was cheap. It was always love, and it was beautiful.*

It was also over.

WHEN THEY REACHED Grand Junction the next day at noon, Bob was in surgery. He'd had another seizure and stopped breathing, and the surgeons had gone back in to take pressure off his brain. Nick and Day sat down to wait.

At about three, weary of the strain of being with Nick and yet not with him, Day found a pay phone and called Grace to tell her where she was and what she'd been doing.

"You rappelled into the Marble Quarry at night? In winter?"

Taken aback, Day said, "It was wonderful."

"It's dangerous! That's incredibly dangerous. Nick knows better than to do something like that."

A lump swelled in Day's throat. *It was special. It's all I have, Grace. That and seeing him first thing in the morning and remembering when we were lovers.* She wiped at a tear on her cheek. "I had fun."

"Good." Day heard her sister catch her breath. "I'm glad you're all right." Grace paused. "Are things better with Nick?"

"No. Nothing's changed. It's not going to. He's leaving for Salt Lake tomorrow."

Grace said, "I'm sorry."

Day said, "I'm not."

THEY LEFT GRAND JUNCTION at five, after Bob had been out of surgery for an hour and they'd been allowed to see him. Still in a coma.

Nick drove Day to her house, though her bicycle was still at Rapid Riggers. When he stopped the Suburban beside her mailbox, she said, "Thank you, Nick. For taking me to the quarry."

"You're welcome." He couldn't stand thinking about it. Or about how she'd looked in the morning when he'd peeked into her room. Day in bed.

She was opening her door. "Have a safe trip, Nick."

"Thanks."

They parted without an embrace. Without the word goodbye.

NICK RETURNED to Grand Junction the next morning to see Bob again before heading for Salt Lake. He sat with his friend as often as the staff would allow and told Bob's unconscious body about rappelling into the quarry with Day. "She did good. You would've been amazed. She leans back to rappel, and all of a sudden I'm looking at the soles of her boots." Nick laughed, remembering, then frowned at Bob's motionless face with the ventilator mask over his mouth and nose.

As he listened to the rhythmic whooshing of the breathing machine, Bob stirred, rotating his head a few degrees.

Nick's heartbeat sped as he rose slowly from the chair. "Bob, it's Nick. Come on."

Bob's eyelids fluttered. As he moved one arm, the alarm on the ventilator went off, beeping loudly. Nurses rushed in, and Nick stepped back as they worked, listened as they spoke to Bob, explained where he was, what had happened to him.

NICK SPENT THE night camped at Colorado National Monument. When he returned to the hospital in the morning, they were extubating Bob, taking him off the ventilator. After that, he could talk, with great difficulty. He spoke little, in a laryngitis voice, and he couldn't remember who he was, who Nick was. He was terribly confused, and at the first sign the patient was tiring, a nurse banished Nick from the room.

When she came out later, Nick said, "He can't remember stuff. Things I said two minutes before."

"It's posttraumatic amnesia. This is the next stage."

"How long does it last?"

She lifted her shoulders. "That's always the question."

Susan and Grace arrived at the hospital soon afterward, saying that Day was busy at the office.

Right. We all know it's the height of the season.

Nick didn't blame her for avoiding him. He was relieved she had.

Leaving Bob to other hands and hearts, he headed for Salt Lake. He had already contacted friends there and located a place to live, a house with two other EMTs, both ambulance attendants who spent every free hour skiing. He had his own tiny room, but there was also a screened gazebo in the backyard, and the two lovers of the outdoors did not find it unusual that he often chose to sleep there.

He studied intensively, medical terminology and pathology for paramedics, and he volunteered on a city ambulance, earning training hours. There were coeds all over campus and a few pretty women in his classes, but he declined invitations to study over coffee, to grab a beer after class.

Shep had been his last casual relationship. Bob's accident had changed him, changed his priorities. What if it had been him, instead of Bob? What if he died suddenly? He didn't want his tombstone to read, HERE LIES NICK COLTER, WHO CLIMBED MOUNTAINS, ROWED RIVERS AND MADE MANY WOMEN CRY.

He drove to Grand Junction to see Bob two weekends in a row. His friend had left the stage called posttraumatic amnesia—apparently a good sign. But as far as Nick was concerned, Bob was still a complete mess, having difficulty with the most basic functions, with eating, with speech. On both visits, Nick ran into Fast Susan. In the hospital cafeteria after one brief visit, she poured her worries into his ears.

"What if he can't work again? What's going to happen to him? Who'll pay for his care?" Susan had moved Bob's things out of the place he rented, taken them to her house. No one knew when he would be able to live alone again.

Nick told her, "We'll work it out, Susan."

He'd pay Bob's bills, bring him to live with him, if it came to that. Bob was a good friend. On one memorable day in Chile, they'd reached five different summits together. Nick didn't plan to abandon him on this mountain. Anyhow, if he had to leave Rapid Riggers, had to leave Moab, it would be good to take one friend with him.

But no matter how he tried, Nick couldn't imagine leaving Moab forever.

When he had been in Salt Lake for a month, Grace called. His roommate Jack summoned him to the phone.

After greetings Grace said, "I wanted to let you know that the lip-sync contest is the Saturday night of Presidents' Weekend. It's a benefit for Bob, for his hospital bills."

"Thanks for telling me. I'll try to be there."

"Also, Zac and I are getting together some people for a backpacking trip in March. We're going to the Maze. Think you could get away?"

Nick hesitated. He had a break then. But Grace was Day's sister. Too close. "I'll let you know." He heard a British-accented voice in the background. It didn't sound like Zac. "Is Pip still there?"

"Actually yes. He'll be here for another week or so, and I think he'll be back in the spring for the grand opening."

Nick's housemates were drinking beer in the living room, just feet away, so he schooled his features. "Well, maybe I'll see you at the lip-sync."

When he'd hung up the phone, he wondered whether or not to go, whether it was too soon to see Day. She would be on that stage. She always was.

And she *almost* always won.

Nick edged around the kitchen counter to see the calendar beside the phone. The lip-sync contest was one of the best parties in Moab. But it was more fun to be a participant than just a spectator. Impulsively he picked up the telephone receiver and dialed the River Inn.

"Hey, Grace. It's Nick again. Is Zac around?"

WHILE HE WAS in Salt Lake, Day kept busy.

She visited Bob in Grand Junction at least once a week and cycled to work daily. Saturdays she told stories at the library, Tuesday afternoons at the museum. By the second week in February, Day tried to convince herself she was healed, almost over Nick. If she could just meet the right man, she'd be completely cured.

Unfortunately the right man hadn't yet materialized. And Rapid Riggers worried her. She lacked Nick's physical strength, and she couldn't do his job. When the new rafts and life vests had arrived, she'd had to call Zac, and he and Pip had driven over and helped her move everything to the equipment shed.

Pip was back in England now, and Day was glad. Whoever waited in the wings to cure her of Nick Colter, it wasn't Zachary's brother.

The Friday evening before the lip-sync contest, an Anasazi pottery exhibition opened at the Moab museum. Archaeologists were scheduled to present a slide show and lecture, and Day had been asked to tell a Native American myth.

For the evening she selected a Southwestern-style outfit, a blanket jacket with silver conches on it, boots, suede pants, and silver and turquoise jewelry. She reached the museum early and had time for a coffee with Verna, one of the museum volunteers, in the gift shop. Verna was flipping pages in a new collection of Navajo myths, with Day reading over her shoulder, when Zac and Grace arrived. They waved to Day as they headed for the refreshment table.

Verna shut the book. "It's a nice one, don't you think?"

"Yes. I'd like to buy a copy. Will you hold one for me, Verna?"

Leaving her friend, Day slipped out into the main section of the museum. The stunning brick building was just a few years old. Indoors, the architecture was modern, with cream-colored walls and displays and a curving staircase leading up to a mezzanine. Rows of chairs arced in a semicircle in the back of the main room, facing a lectern and slide screen.

When Day joined them, Grace and Zachary were peering into a display case at an Anasazi basket found by some local children. With her jeans and denim vest, Grace wore hand-tooled red cowboy boots identical to Day's.

"Geared up for tomorrow night, cowgirl?" Day asked her sister.

Zachary winked at Day. "I like those costumes."

"Why haven't we seen *yours?*"

Grace's eyes slid toward Zac's, and she smothered a smile. "You will."

"Is this a solo act?" asked Day.

"No, as a matter of fact," Zac said. "You'll just have to wait till tomorrow night to find out more."

The lip-sync contest would be held at the Dry Gulch Saloon. Dress rehearsal was at three the next day.

"Hi, guys." Fast Susan stirred some powdered creamer into coffee in a plastic-foam cup. "I just saw Bob at his new place, the rehab center."

"How is he?" Day had seen him Wednesday at the hospital. She still hadn't gotten used to the change in Bob, that someone who had once been so vital and sharp could now have so much trouble just speaking.

Susan sighed. "Not too good. And as if he's not having enough problems, he's worried about money and work."

"He'll always have a place at Rapid Riggers," said Day.

Everyone was sober. No one knew if Bob would ever row boats again.

They sat in the third row, and the program director introduced an archaeologist from the University of Utah.

"We're going to start our presentation," the archaeologist said, "with an educational film on pot hunting, which should also help to explain the value of a professional dig." The sound track began with a somber flute melody, and a female narrator's resonant voice set the tone, hinting at history buried in the land, talking about the Ancient Ones who had made their homes in the Four Corners centuries before, then mysteriously vanished. Why did they leave? The answers lay in the land. The history belonged to all, but it was being stolen....

The film panned over an Anasazi ruin that had been plundered with a backhoe. Day was sickened by the sight. Unfortunately pot hunters were, at least in part, the product of twenty-percent unemployment in some of the southern counties. And many pot hunters had been born into families who'd always dug for artifacts. Even Day's father had amassed an arrowhead collection of his own, which she and Grace had donated to the museum after his death. Removing artifacts from public lands had been illegal since the turn of the century, but it was only recently that the public had begun to respect the issue.

Nothing in the film was news to Day. As an outfitter, it was part of her obligation to see that passengers on trips were taught to respect the natural resources of the area. That included archaeological sites.

When the lights went on, the archaeologist discussed possible explanations for the disappearance of the Anasazi. It was the oldest question of the Four Corners, and Day was bored until he said, "Findings of New Mexico archaeologists suggest that during the period from A.D. 900 to 1200, the Anasazi may have practiced ritual cannibalism."

He explained that recent excavations had uncovered burned human bones, the ends polished from hours of simmering in a cook pot and bones scored with fine cut marks. They had been processed the same way the Anasazi butchered and cooked antelope and prairie dog.

Beside Day, Grace whispered, "Wow. This changes a person's picture of the Old Ones, doesn't it?"

When the program director introduced Day, she took her place in front of the podium, where she could use her hands and her body in the telling of the tale. Facing her audience, she panned the faces.

Nick was in the back row.

He winked at her.

Day forced her eyes to move on. *Nick.* Had he come back to Moab to attend the lip-sync contest, for Bob? Why had he come *here?* He wasn't interested in archaeology.

He came to hear my story.

She told it for him.

With a smile she introduced the Pueblo folktale "The Man Who Married the Moon."

"Now, Na-chu-rú-chu, whose name means 'the bluish light of dawn,' had no parents. The Trues themselves created him, and his powers were second only to theirs. He was a weaver, and he possessed remarkable gifts of healing, but besides all this, he was tall and strong and handsome, and the girls of the village thought it a great pity that he didn't take a wife...."

Nick listened with reverence. When Grace and Zac had told him what was happening tonight, he couldn't stay away; he'd wanted to hear her story. He hadn't planned to see a film defaming pot hunting.

The story helped take the film and the slide-show images from his mind.

"The most determined of Na-chu-rú-chu's admirers were the Yellow Corn Maidens. The Corn Maidens possessed every gift of grace and beauty—and magical powers, as well. But they used their magic for evil. They were witches...."

As she told the tale, Day addressed all the listeners. But the one who really mattered to her was Nick. His arms were folded across his chest, his eyes closed, and he seemed as peaceful as he had the night they'd rappelled into the Marble Quarry.

Why did you come? Why did you come?

The moment her story ended he got up and left, and the fact of his presence and abrupt departure played a cruel trick on her.

It made her hope.

THE RIVER ROAD took him home along the Far Far Below River, past the campgrounds on the shore, past the wall of red rock Bob had hit to the sandy track leading to his land, his spot at the edge of the Colorado.

He turned down that path with a sore heart. He'd always dreamed of building a home here where the trailer sat. A place with lots of windows. Now it shamed him that he had bought this land with money from stealing pots.

Everyone at the museum tonight had been in accord with the archaeologists. As a child in Covenant in southern Utah, Nick had understood something different—that public lands belonged to the public. Pot hunting wasn't stealing; it was taking what was yours.

His second foster father had told him that. Nick could barely remember the first. He'd been with that family only days, and he must have done something that disturbed them, but no one ever told him what. The second family took in foster kids for the money. They never said so, but

Nick could tell. He had run away in the end, after more than a year, and there were gaps in his memory. He didn't know why he'd left or who had found him. In the third home, the man had taken off his belt once, and that was enough.

It wasn't until he met Sam Sutter that Nick knew he'd been taught wrong, about a lot of things. He hadn't agreed with Sam about the pots. There were times in childhood he'd never had a cup or a spoon, and the Old Ones had left dishes everywhere. Nick loved the primitive people who had been so civilized. He liked their houses and the things they made. That they stored food. They might have been his own ancestors, and the treasures he found had seemed like gifts to him.

Till recently.

The trailer smelled stale and enclosed, so he decided to sleep outside. He took logs from the lean-to beside the trailer and arranged them in the fire pit and returned inside for kindling and matches. Crouching in the dirt, he touched the match flame to newspaper and watched the sparks fly.

As he let the blaze heat his body against the frosty night, he remembered Day's story of Na-chu-rú-chu and the Moon, whom he took for his wife. After the wedding, the jealous Yellow Corn Maidens drowned her and buried her. But Na-chu-rú-chu picked a flower from the earth over her grave where she lay and set it between two mantas he had woven. Singing to her and shaking his gourd, he made her body grow from the single blossom and brought her back to life.

More pleasant than doing CPR on the dead.

Nick liked the magic in stories. The enchantments of Arthurian legends. The magic of Day's Pueblo weaver. If Nick had known magic like Na-chu-rú-chu, things would have been different with Kelly. In the firelight he saw fuzzy memory, her little face with her flattened nose and mal-formed lip, the kind of lip people had named for a rabbit.

Did anyone ever fix it, Kelly? Or did he lie to me?

Later, when he laid out his ground cloth and mattress and sleeping bag, it was Day's face that came into his mind. Nick let himself imagine her slim white body and her laughter, her clothes that were all the colors of daylight, of the world outside, like a garden of flowers. Her arms around him, stroking his hair. Caressing his scars. She'd done that the first time, when they were teenagers figuring out sex together. She'd touched him with her hands and with her lips. Nervous, he'd said, *What are you doing?*

Unhurting you.

He shut his eyes, missing her.

THE BACK ROOM of the Dry Gulch Saloon was the women's dressing room for the lip-sync contest. Beside shelves lined with empty kegs and cases of beer, Day readjusted her chaps over the suede bikini she wore, being careful not to smear her blue body paint.

In the bar the Talking Heads played. It was Bess Gordon's act. She was a fifth-grade teacher whose lip-sync group, the Benders, always participated in the annual competition.

Fast Susan cracked her bullwhip experimentally, and Shelley Gonzalez, a seasonal ranger at Dead Horse Point, said, "Yahoo!"

Grace peered out the door. "It's packed out there."

Day wasn't surprised. Though the cover charge of six dollars was a little steep, everybody knew it was for Bob and wanted to help. Day had seen people putting twenties in the hat.

She wondered where Nick was. The hope she'd felt the night before had turned to frustration when he hadn't even stopped in at Rapid Riggers all day. When she'd arrived at the Dry Gulch with Grace and Susan earlier that evening, she'd spotted his truck in a far corner of the lot, but she hadn't laid eyes on him.

"So, Grace," said Susan, "why wasn't Zac at the dress rehearsal? Doesn't he have an act?"

"He has a *secret,* and I may as well warn you, my husband does not like to lose. They're going to give us a real run for our money."

The Talking Heads song ended, and the bar erupted in applause.

"We're on," Grace said, picking up her rope.

Susan cracked her bullwhip again.

Day straightened her hat.

In the next room the emcee, Bud from Wild Whitewater Expeditions, said, "And now, the Blue Cowgirls!"

WATCHING THE STAGE from just outside the broom closet—the men's dressing room—Nick willed his hard-on to go away. It would destroy the effect of his costume.

But he couldn't take his eyes off Day. Her attire was nothing unusual for the lip-sync. It shouldn't have bothered him or made him feel like dragging her off the stage and wrapping her in a sheet.

He wasn't crazy about the song she'd picked, either. "My Baby Thinks He's a Train"?

Beside him Zac said, "I don't know how Day will like England. We sure don't have anything like this."

Nick spun his head. Zac's eyelashes were blacked with mascara, his dark hair covered with a dishwater-blond wig. His stage experience had come in handy. With makeup and costuming, he had transformed them both. They'd put together their act in two days of practice upstairs at the River Inn, with Grace standing by as coach.

But this was the first Nick had heard about... "England?"

"Oh. It's nothing."

England?

On stage Grace swirled a lasso over her head. Nick's eyes flowed past her to the insides of Day's blue thighs, showing where her chaps were open. No. Day wouldn't go to England to see Pip. Trying to sound like it didn't matter, he asked Zac, "So, what? Is she going to visit your brother?"

The crowd howled as Grace lassoed sixty-year-old outfitter Carl Orson.

Zac smiled indulgently. "Visit? No. Come on, let's go get our props and the rest of our band. We're on."

The cheers for the Blue Cowgirls were deafening. Day doffed her hat, along with Grace and Susan, then exited the stage in single file with them, heading down into the crowd to watch the other acts.

Lew from Current Adventures wrapped his arm around her and held a beer in her face. "Congratulations, May-Day! To the lip-sync queen of Utah!"

Laughing, Day freed herself and helped herself to one of the beers that Jackie, a waitress friend of Susan's, had brought them.

Boatman Bud took his place at the mike in top hat and tails. "And now, as a special treat this evening, in honor of Dirty Bob, we bring you straight from Atlanta, Georgia, his favorite duo and their band—the Indigo Girls!"

Whistling and screams shook the floor, and Day watched two high-school teachers and a woman who worked at the state liquor store walk on stage and take their seats with a drum, a cello and an electric bass. They were all members of the community theater. Two very tall women in flannel shirts and jeans, carrying acoustic guitars, followed them.

Susan said, "I think we've been outclassed."

"They haven't done anything yet," Day grumbled. She hated to lose. Especially to Nick. "I can't stand it when he cross-dresses."

"I love it." Grace panted exaggeratedly at her husband.

A woman's sandpaper-rough Southern drawl came over the speaker, and Nick lip-synced perfectly with the words.

"We came here tonight for our friend Bob, and we want to play his favorite song for him, so he can watch it on video while he's mending."

Day's jaw dropped. "How did they do that? That really sounds like one of the Indigo Girls."

"Zac," said Grace. "That was his voice. Can you believe it? Isn't my husband the best actor in the world?"

As the high-school teacher at the drums began his perfect movements, in sync with the music, the voices of the Indigo Girls filled the bar, singing Bob's favorite song.

CHAPTER NINE

WHEN HE CAME OFF the stage, it was impossible to avoid meeting him. Saying hello. Breathlessness.

"That was really cheap," Day told him. "Whenever you dress like a girl, you win."

"Admit it. We were better." His eyes crept over her blue skin. "And with fewer assets." Losing the jesting spirit, he murmured, "Put on some clothes, will you?"

"Why? Bother you?"

Shelley Gonzalez was up next, performing "R-e-s-p-e-c-t," and Lew from Current Adventures said, "Hey, Day, dance with me."

She did.

Nick eased against the wall and tried to watch the lip-sync act, but his eyes drifted to Day, to the motion of her hips, to her naked back, painted blue, to her breasts in her bikini top. *Yeah. It bothers me a lot.*

What had Zac meant when he mentioned England? Was Day serious about Pip? Had something happened after he left town?

Another blue cowgirl appeared beside him. It was Grace, who asked, "Are you coming backpacking with us in March?"

"Yes." Spending time with Zac the past few days had been good. He wouldn't mind backpacking with him and Grace.

Lew stole Day's hat and put it on.

As Shelley's act ended, Nick and Grace applauded with the rest of the crowd, and Boatman Bud came on stage to say that the judges were tallying scores. "And in the meantime, let's dance."

Nirvana blared through the speakers, and Day continued dancing with Lew, laughing with him.

Nick gestured toward Day, addressing her sister as though he was just trying to catch up on news. "So, is she going to England?"

"What?"

Zachary appeared beside his wife and stepped on her foot. "All I said was we don't have this kind of thing in England. Day might miss it."

"Oh, yeah, that's true!" Grace agreed. "But Oakhurst is beautiful."

Oakhurst. Day *had* just responded to him like her old self. Maybe she was over him. Falling for Pip.

Boatman Bud announced the winners of the lip-sync contest, starting with third place. Second was the Blue Cowgirls. And first place was the Indigo Girls.

More music came on, a reggae beat, and the revelers in the bar whooped. Nick knew the song and liked it, and at first he didn't understand his sudden anxiety. The answer came with a loss of control—his body reacting on its own. Sweating. Accelerated heartbeat. Nausea. Dizziness. There were too many people in the bar. As he hunted for the nearest Exit sign, he was hot and scared, seeing the bumper stickers on the Subaru and the shattered glass in the road. Smelling blood. The red spurting everywhere and the fluid coming out of Bob's ear.

Between heads and shoulders around her, Day saw Nick's face. He was gray, visibly strained. As he pushed through the people, trying to get out of the bar, Bob Marley's voice filled the space.

Lively up yourself...

This was the song Nick had said was playing when he reached Bob's car.

Her instincts drove her toward him. Sweat glistened on his face as he smiled politely, blindly at a boatman in his path.

I have to get out. I have to get out, he thought. The other place had come. The dark and the smells and the fear. *I need to go out. Please let me out.*

He was afraid he might start screaming.

And then he felt her touch, her hand on his back, guiding him to the door.

IN THE CAB of his truck, with both windows rolled halfway down, he sank back against the seat, with Day's fingers woven in his. He didn't bother to say he was fine. ''This has never happened before.''

She was silent.

Nick was grateful. Day never said stupid things. Never said, *If you love something set it free...* When Day spoke, they were heart words. *I want to have your babies.* Yours, no one else's.

He whispered, ''You're the best.''

''You ought to know.''

Sassy tonight. It was that cowgirl costume. He moved to look into her eyes, to liberate a lock of blond hair caught in the blue paint on her cheek.

Day's fingers curled up, tensing, then relaxed. *Don't look at me that way, Nick. I don't know what it means.*

Nick couldn't stop looking. Tonight she'd seen him sweating, cramping, reduced by his humanity. It reminded him that he'd told her things after Sam died, that she knew other things. She loved him, who he really was. Only with Day was it okay to be filthy, gross inside.

He tried not to think about the pots.

Or about Kelly.

Edging back toward his door, Nick guided her down on the bench seat, and her chaps slipped away as she swung her legs over the stick shift and under the steering wheel. She grasped his shoulders, and he felt her trying to draw him with her, to lie on top of her. He did, gently.

"Day." He kissed her. Blue paint against his face. Their mouths opened together. Her arms strangled his neck, holding as tight as a woman's arms could, and Nick put his hand on her crotch.

"Nick..." She gave a small whimper.

He stroked her, his mind out of order. No thoughts. "Baby..." They were both so excited. Stifled words became a sound in his mouth. As his tongue felt hers, she strained under him, pressing up into his hand. If he slipped his fingers into her bikini bottoms, she'd be wet.

"Day..." He buried his face in her hair, squeezing his eyes shut, wanting to say the words that would make them both unravel.

I love you.

His hand felt like lead when he tried to move it to her thigh. His fingers dragged in paint.

"Don't stop," she whispered.

He tugged a string on her bikini bottoms and felt her unbuttoning his fly. Then touching him as he was her. Guiding his penis against her wetness. Almost silent, they teased each other, faces pressed close as they lay on the truck seat, knees bent to fit, chaps against blue jeans, breathing the shallow breaths of passion.

Love. Lying against her like that, it surrounded him. Day was the river spirit who'd come from the water before he was a man. She'd helped teach him to read. Touching her body that was too pretty for him, he had learned tenderness.

He pressed his mouth to hers again, caressing her tongue, giving her his love, giving her the most he had, more than he ever gave anyone.

Day felt it all, felt his soul coming into hers, surrounding hers. The darkness and intensity and love that was like nothing else in the world except the earth. The grit and beauty of the desert. The scents of caves where bats hung. Nights with flames leaping toward the sky. This primal enchantment was the truest thing in her life.

Nick took his left hand from her to open the glove box and get a condom. As he knelt over her, Day watched him put it on, then looked up at his mascara-rimmed eyes.

He met hers, and they were suspended in knowledge.

That their love might be strong enough this time.

Silently he brought his body to hers, opening her, soothing her as he entered her, as he saw her eyes watering. "Okay?"

"Yes."

His hands cradled her blue-painted face, now smeared from his excitement, from their closeness. Day's eyes were the real blue, the true ice blue, like the wildflowers called pale trumpets. "You're so pretty."

Her lids were dropping shut, her face caught in feeling. Their bodies were together, joined, and Nick knew what it did to her. He tried to keep his head clear, for her. "Sure you're okay?"

Her answer was an incomplete sound. He cradled her closer, and as he felt her fingers in his hair, felt her clench around him, he whispered to her softly. No lies. Just words no one else could hear, even if they'd stood just two feet away. "I won't ever hurt you again. I belong to you. You know that? Even if we're apart, I'll be yours. My heart and my body."

There were tears on her face, and he knew she didn't believe him, so he stopped and tried to tell her without words.

THEY HUGGED for a long time afterward, then rolled up the windows to shut out the cold and hugged again. Nick kissed her hair and her face, the flavor of blue body paint in his mouth. "That stuff doesn't taste too bad. Kind of like sourdough that's got something wrong with it."

Day pulled herself from her thoughts, took his cue to keep it light. "Grace thinks it smells like Play-Doh."

"What's that?"

"Play-Doh?" Why should it surprise her? Nick never knew these things. "It's kind of like modeling clay for little kids, but it has the texture of cookie dough. It comes in a bunch of different colors in a yellow can."

"I know what you mean."

Day doubted he'd ever smelled or touched Play-Doh. Definitely not as a child. She drew back to see his face. With a small laugh, she reached for the glove box and opened it and found some tissues. "I wore off on you." She wiped his cheeks, trying not to think. Thinking could destroy this moment of happiness. He'd made her learn to live in the present.

She found her bikini bottoms. As he tied the strings for her, she said, "I can't believe I had sex in the parking lot at the Dry Gulch Saloon."

"Mm." Nick finished buttoning his fly and sat back in the seat, then turned the rearview mirror toward him. "My mascara's running." A glance at her. "You're all smeared."

She examined the state of her body paint.

"I'll drive you home," he said. He couldn't plan further than that.

"Thanks. Will you get my stuff, too? It's in the back room. I just have a straw tote bag."

"Sure." Nick took the tissues from her and wiped traces of blue from his face and neck, then got out of the truck and walked back to the bar. Grace and Zac were sitting on the edge of the stage outside the dressing room, and when they saw him, both leaned forward, like nearsighted people trying to recognize an approaching figure. Then, suddenly, they burst out laughing.

"Hello." Uneasy, wondering what joke was at his expense, Nick slipped into the back room and grabbed Day's bag. Then he saw.

His hand was blue. And that was just the start.

"YOU STILL OKAY?" He shut the driver door.

"Sure."

Her face was a mask. He needed to say something, but everything that came to mind seemed empty. Even *I love you.*

Take her home. Make sure she's okay. Leave.

His hand hovered over the ignition key. He sat back.

Day was afraid of what he might say, so she spoke first, treading far from what had just happened. "I don't know what you're planning to do about Rapid Riggers. But could you please row our first Cataract trip? It leaves April twenty-seventh. Private trip, one passenger. A tour operator set it up, and he wants VIP treatment for the passenger." In other words, the best guide they had. "The guy is Japanese and doesn't speak a word of English. Zac's going as translator."

"Zac knows Japanese?"

"Two years at Eton. He can't remember much, but he's brushing up. The guy's going to stay at the River Inn. He's going to take some four-wheel-drive tours, too. Anyhow, Zac can go with you on the river, help you communicate."

Nick started the engine. The last time Zachary had gone down Cataract, it had become a medical emergency. "Just make sure he brings his meds."

"I don't think he needs them. That was kind of a rare thing. I think he was dealing with some issues from his childhood."

"Mm." Draping his arm over the back of the seat, Nick maneuvered out of the parking space. He liked Zac, but he didn't want to run Cataract with a psychotic person and a passenger who couldn't speak English. *Rub-a-dub-dub, three men in a tub.* He drove over the gravel and turned out of the lot, heading toward Main Street.

Day closed her eyes, taking some slow deep breaths. Still shaky and feverish-hot. When she opened her eyes again, the truck was on Uranium Street, and she reached for her straw bag so that she could get out fast. Not ask him in. She needed to think about this.

The blocks passed. When the Chevy stopped, she faced him and noticed the blue patches on the tan bench seat. "You've got a blue interior now. I'm sorry, Nick."

"I'm not."

She smiled. "Wait here a minute, okay? I have something for you."

"Okay."

Day hurried inside. She returned to him covered with goose bumps and shoved a gift-wrapped package across the seat. It had Christmas paper on it. "You can tell your girlfriends that your auntie made it. Good night."

As they leaned toward each other in the cab, kissed in friendship and love, Nick recalled the charm he'd thrown in the river. The package on the seat was the other half, the gift he could never match. "Thank you." He held her wrist, keeping her so that he could kiss her again. "Thank you," he repeated, *for your love.*

Shivering, she asked, "Are you coming into the office tomorrow?"

"I have to work tomorrow night. On the ambulance."

In Salt Lake. Day knew it was an excuse. He was running again. Probably from what he'd said to her. "Drive safely." She shut the door and ran back up to her house, rushing from the cold.

Nick unwrapped the present. Inside the box, laid in tissue paper, was a cream-colored handmade chamois shirt. He rested his arms on the steering wheel, pushed his hair back from his face.

Day never had to know that he'd stolen a few pots. He could hide it from her forever, and they could be happy together.

Really, Nick?

He started the truck.

Day wasn't just a good storyteller, she was a good listener. When they spent night after night together as lovers, things came out. In the past, it had been good, like entrusting pieces of himself to her safekeeping. She knew him better than anyone else did. There wasn't much left for him to give.

He didn't want her to see the parts he still held.

And he didn't want to live with her in a world of lies.

GRACE STOPPED at the Rapid Riggers office the next morning and found Day fiddling with a buckle on one of her high-heeled platform sandals, accessories for her ivory suede pants and cotton-Lycra blouse.

"You know, I used to think you dressed like this to avoid carrying out the trash." With a knowing expression, Grace readjusted the Ensulite pads on the couch and took a seat. Thoughtfully she surveyed Day. "You look better. Was that your blue paint all over Nick?"

Day *felt* better. Alive. Nourished. No regrets. And she didn't have to look at that present in her guest room anymore. "What a pointed question." She stood up. "Want some coffee?"

Grace jumped up to follow her sister into the kitchen. There, she wrinkled her nose at the pot. "How old is it?"

"Just a couple of weeks. All you have to do is scoop the scum off the top with a spoon."

Grinning, Grace helped herself to a coffee mug. "I came by to ask you something. Since you've been cycling and you did that rappelling stunt with Nick, I wondered if you'd like to go backpacking."

"You're hilarious." Day hadn't been backpacking since high school, with her father and Grace and Nick. "Who with?"

"Me and Zac, maybe someone else. Susan said she'd take care of the dogs. She wants to take them to visit Bob."

Soberly Day remembered Nick in her arms the night before. It had started with Bob. "Where are you going?"

"The Maze."

"*The Maze?*" The Maze was perhaps the most rugged and remote section of Canyonlands National Park. "Do you think I can do it? How long are you going for?"

"Five days. We'll get home the night before your birthday. You'll maybe want to work out a little harder. I'll ride my bike with you."

When Grace rode her bike, she took it off-road, onto trails Day had traversed only in Suburbans. Poison Spider Mesa, the Amasa Back, the Moab Rim Trail. Though Day had bought a Rockhopper years before with the intention of taking the bicycle off-road, trying Moab's world-famous mountain-bike trails, she had attempted it only once, with Susan and Dirty Bob on the Slickrock Trail. Petrified by the steep slopes of uncompromising rock—no forgiveness in a fall—she had returned to the parking lot and pedaled a half mile up the gravel of Sand Flats Road.

Such was her all-terrain bicycling experience.

Backpacking, though...

Would it make a difference to Nick if she could say she'd spent five days backpacking in the Maze?

"No Slickrock Trail," she said.

Grace laughed. "Does that mean you'll come?"

"Okay."

The doorbell rang as someone entered the reception area. Stepping through the swinging doors, Day met a small long-haired brunette in a short cotton skirt, a Slickrock Café T-shirt and hiking boots. The most noticeable thing about her was her dynamic athletic energy. Her legs were brown and hard as tree limbs and bare, though it was February.

Day felt ill when she saw her.

She had river guide written all over her.

And she definitely looked like Nick's kind of woman.

"Can I help you?"

"I'm Leah Fox. I've been a Grand Canyon guide for the last few years for Western River Ways, but a friend lent me a house in Moab for the summer. Do you have any openings? I'm interested in rowing Cataract."

Cataract boatmen were hard to come by, and Rapid Riggers was missing Bob. If Leah Fox had rowed the Grand Canyon for "the last few years" . . . *I'll never be able to explain it to Nick if I turn her away.*

On the other hand, Nick never had to know.

But she couldn't run an all-male river outfit. She couldn't discriminate against pretty women.

And the night before, when they were making love, Nick had promised her things she *wanted* to believe. Because the thought of him with a new girlfriend was more than she could stand.

"Let's see what we can work out, Leah."

DAY WAS TO MEET Grace and Zac at the River Inn on the second Friday afternoon in March to finalize plans for the Maze trip. They would leave early Sunday.

It was a sunny afternoon, the river showing the reflection of the blue sky, of the towering sandstone walls on either side of the corridor, of the green tamarisk dipping over the water. Day rode her bicycle alongside it, from Rapid Riggers to the inn. Ten miles. She was dusty and sweaty when she steered down the narrow drive where Zac had laid gravel for the guests who would be arriving next month. Hearing a vehicle, she glanced back and almost fell off her bike.

Nick drove up beside her. His windows were down, and in the shadows of the cab, he was half-naked, all brown arms and ribs and chest, muscular legs showing under the hems of his climbing shorts. Climbing gear obscured the floor of the cab—ropes in nylon sacks, a rack of carabiners, his shoes. He was barefoot.

Instant spring fever. Day stared for only a moment at the cotton keeper strap—that same brand—holding the sunglasses around his neck. For only a moment did she go away.

Then there was Nick, smiling, melting her. "What are you doing?"

"Oh, I . . ." Day was embarrassed to tell him. "I'm going on this Maze trip with Zac and Grace." She swiped at a mosquito on her arm. "We're having a planning meeting."

"Oh."

"I didn't know you were in town. Is everything okay at school?" She unfastened her bicycle helmet, hung it on her handlebars, ran her fingers through her damp hair, caught another mosquito. Resisted checking her reflection in his side mirror.

"Everything's great." He seemed preoccupied until he said, "Did you know I'm coming?"

"What?" Day held the passenger door, trying to keep her bicycle from banging the side of his truck. There were still traces of blue on his seat. "To the Maze?"

He nodded.

Grace. Day edged away from the truck. "I didn't know."

Nick set the brake and opened his door. He walked around to her side, and she caught his scent as he grabbed the right hand grip on her bicycle. "Get in. I'll throw your bike in the back."

She swung her leg clumsily over the seat and rear wheel of the bicycle, unsteady because he was so close. While he lifted her bike into the truck bed, she made herself comfortable in the cab. Remembering.

As he arranged her bike, Nick noticed the dirt dried on the frame. Had she been riding off-road? The signs that she had seemed like an omen. He'd planned to see her, anyhow, while he was in town. They had a lot to talk about. Their relationship. Rapid Riggers. And Bob.

Now Day was going to the Maze—though she hadn't known *he* was going. It must be something she was doing for herself. Nick remembered long-ago Sutter family backpacking trips, river trips. Day had groused, but she had gone.

It was after Jim Antonio's accident that she'd begun to change. She'd left for Salt Lake to study fashion design, and when she came back... His sweetheart, his lover, was different. Hiding fear under a Sutter's bravado. Under costumes he stripped off her once a year.

Was she changing again? Coming home to herself?

Nick like the idea very much.

THEY ATE DINNER, Grace's homemade pizza, on the screened porch of the River Inn. When they finished eating, the sun had disappeared behind the walls of the river. Not much time left for bike riding.

Day said, "I better get home."

Nick drew his feet off a porch railing. "I'll take you."

Grace and Zac exchanged looks.

Noticing, Nick said, "Thanks for dinner, Grace. I'll see you Sunday. Let's try not to have any more surprises on this trip, eh?"

Zac cleared his throat, jumped up and began collecting plates from the table. *Two matchmakers,* Nick decided.

"Surprises?" Grace asked.

Nick cuffed her lightly behind the ear and addressed Day. "Ready?"

On the way home he said, "Your bike looks used. There's dirt on it."

"Whenever it rains, I paint it with mud."

"Mm. Want to go for a bike ride tomorrow after work?"

This was her chance. Even before the backpacking trip, she could start proving she was Nick's kind of woman.

What if she failed? What if he figured out the truth, that she didn't have it in her to do thirteen fingertip pull-ups on a door frame?

And what would happen when Nick got a look at Leah?

Day was pressing her arm across her stomach.

She wasn't answering.

"Day?"

Prove it, Day. Show him what you can do. "Sure."

At her house he took her bike out of the truck. "Thanks for the shirt," he said; he'd been planning to tell her. "I wear it a lot. Haven't even gotten any blood on it."

"I don't mind that. Just as long as it's not yours."

They both recalled another person's blood. Nick tilted his head toward her porch steps. "Let's sit down." When she'd settled beside him, he said, "I saw Bob this morning. He's doing a lot better, and I asked the people who're taking care of him if he could leave that place and come home. It happens in stages, I guess, and won't happen real soon. But they let me take him for a drive up to Colorado National Monument. We didn't get out of the car. You know he can hardly walk. But eventually they'll let him out for a whole day, then a weekend, under supervision. If everything goes okay, he can come home. But he still shouldn't be alone. I had an idea I wanted to run by you."

"Run it."

"There's that sink upstairs at the office and the old stove. Remember I lived up there one summer?"

"I follow you. But who's going to be with him at night?"

"I'll stay with him for a while. We'll have a good time. But his living there... We couldn't kick him out later. Whatever happens..."

Between us, finished Day. Nick's suggestion was what her father would have done. She couldn't walk in Sam Sutter's footsteps as a river runner, but she was still his daughter, still committed to doing certain things his way. Taking care of her "family" was part of it. "His living upstairs isn't a problem. But what about that Cataract trip in April? You'll be gone for several nights. And now you're still in school."

"As I said, this can't happen right away. I was thinking after Cataract. But you're right, Day. It'll be a major commitment—from all of us."

"I want to help, Nick."

He saw her resolution. The Sutters had been pioneers, and she possessed her father's pride and commitment to caring for her own. Bob had worked for them eight years, almost as long as Nick.

Nick whispered, "You're a good woman, Day."

"I haven't done anything yet. I might have him carted off by fall."

"No, you won't." It was hard to take his eyes off her. Nick had spent the weeks since the lip-sync thinking about her. Wondering if they could have what they both wanted.

Without her discovering exactly what it was she loved. Who he really was.

He wouldn't think about it now. "So, tomorrow," he said, "bring what you need for the bike ride to work. We'll probably be out till the sun goes down." A teasing remark stuck on his tongue—a joke about bringing a traction splint, just in case. He didn't say it. He wanted her to be able to do this. The bike ride. Then the Maze. He wanted her to enjoy herself, to discover her own strength. To feel the pride he'd seen in her eyes after she rappelled into the Marble Quarry.

So he just smiled and stood up. "See you tomorrow, Princess Day."

SUSAN AND LEAH were rigging for a four-wheel-drive trip and Day was helping when Nick banged through the kitchen door of the river office the next morning.

"Howdy, stranger," said Susan, giving him a quick hug. "Day told me the plan for Bob, and guess what?"

"What?"

"You don't have to stay here nights with him at all. I will. I hate making that drive out to Castle Valley in the summer. Too many tourists on the road."

"Let's see if they'll let us bring him home first," said Nick. "But I appreciate the offer. Maybe we can spell each other." He eyed the unfamiliar person by the refrigerator. A guide obviously. He held out his hand. "I'm Nick."

"Leah."

Folding an oilskin tablecloth, Day felt as though someone was strangling her. *I can't go through this again.* Almost dizzy, she listened to Nick ask Leah where she was from.

"Tahoe, but I've been rowing the Grand for three years. I'd like to train for Cataract."

"We can do that."

Day made it past them into the reception area and out onto the front porch. She was still watching the parade of eighteen-wheelers and RVs on the highway when Nick came outside with a cup of coffee. "Ready for our bike ride?"

"Sure." She hoped her smile look genuine. Until minutes ago she *had* been looking forward to the ride. But seeing him with Leah had changed everything. What if she couldn't keep up?

There were plenty of women who could.

AT FIVE they gave last-minute instructions to Fast Susan for the week they'd be out of the office. Then Day slipped into the bathroom, changed out of her dress, coated herself with sunscreen and donned baby blue bicycling shorts and a matching crop-top.

She joined Nick in the sun outside the back porch of the office to find him and Leah comparing bicycles. But when Leah saw Day, she climbed on her own, saying to Nick, "Well, I'll see you later."

It looked for all the world like they'd made a date.

Leah pedaled off fast and hard, muscle in motion, waving and whistling to another cyclist on the highway, a friend with whom she quickly caught up.

A hard act to follow.

Nick reached for the guide shell and rolled-up T-shirt Day held—extra clothing. "Want me to put those in my panniers?" His bicycle had a rack and two canvas bags.

"Please."

As they strapped on their helmets, Day asked, "Where are we going?"

"The Moab Rim Trail? Leah just told me a way we can meet up with Behind the Rocks and come down Pritchett Canyon."

Before dark? Day contained her feelings. So what if the Moab Rim Trail was vertical slickrock, an ought-to-be-condemned four-wheel-drive road? So what if Pritchett Canyon was a million miles downriver from there. Nick's kind of woman wouldn't be afraid. And Nick's kind of woman definitely wouldn't bellyache about the fact that the trail began six miles away. Only wimps drove to the trailhead.

As they pedaled out of the lot and over the Moab Bridge, Day was thankful that it wasn't July with 106-degree temperatures. Nick rode fast, but she sensed that he was actually slowing down for her, so she tried her best to keep up.

When they got to the trailhead, she stopped and gulped water from one of her water bottles. "This seems like an ambitious ride to make before dark."

He squirted some water into his mouth. "Nah."

Day scooted her bike to face the trail, a rock grade breaking through the foot of the towering magenta cliff. She climbed back on. "Okay." She pedaled in a circle on the gravel turnout, glancing across the road at the river, and shifted her bike into the lowest gear.

Nick was waiting.

Day started up the rock trail, pedaling as hard as her legs would work. The grade was steep, and she rode for only a few yards before the wheels would turn no more. She stopped, and Nick passed her. Lifting the front wheel of his bike, he powered up a vertical ledge.

Leah had told him about this route. And Leah would have been able to keep pace with him. Stifling desperation, Day climbed off her optimistically named Rockhopper to walk.

Almost an hour later they reached the top, and Nick didn't have to say a word for her to know he was disappointed. She hadn't fallen; the trail wasn't technically difficult so much as steep. But she'd pushed her bicycle most of the way to the top, riding only on the flatter stretches.

From the Moab Rim, they drank water and admired the 360-degree panorama. To the east lay the river portal. To the south lay Moab. They could identify the Rapid Riggers building, a distant spot near the bridge. The view was exquisite, the heat of the sun perfect.

As they stood side by side with their bikes, Day said, "I'm sorry I had to walk so much. It's gorgeous up here."

"It is. Thanks for coming." Nick didn't know what to say about her pushing her bike. Some women had natural athletic ability; Day's needed development.

So what, Nick? Slow down. Enjoy her company. Unfortunately now they'd have to make up lost time in order to be home by dark.

"The trail's pretty flat up here," he said. "Ready to go?"

"Sure." They struck out on the sandy trail, which wound past tall sandstone formations. The river and the town were behind them. Ahead golden sunlight shimmered on the red rocks and yellow-green grasses and sagebrush, on gnarled junipers. Day began to enjoy riding. In some places the sand was deep, but nowhere did it stop her. It was worth the dust and sweat to follow Nick's back, to see the ribbons of muscle in his brown shoulders. Just to be with him, because she loved him.

The rocky dirt road turned west, and soon there was nothing to see but sandstone and grass for miles. In the distance, the fins of Behind the Rocks jutted against the sky. When the Moab Rim Trail forked with a rutted double track, Nick took the less-traveled way, Day a few yards behind him. Her front wheel tried to mire in a hole full of sand; through sheer determination she kept pedaling, jouncing over the gouged-out holes in the road, looking toward the sun.

The new road twisted again, heading west, away from the river, and she asked Nick, "Do you know where you're going?"

"I think so."

It wasn't the assurance she'd been looking for.

"It's kind of late, Nick."

"You can't get lost up here."

"*I* could."

"Yes, but you're with Nick the Pathfinder, so relax."

She did. Now that they were on top, this wasn't bad at all. Following his purple-and-blue mountain bike, custom-made by a Park City frame-builder, Day asked, "Am I riding fast enough?"

He'd been wondering if anyone could ride more slowly. "If you could push a little harder, it would help."

She picked up her pace, and he watched the sky, tried to keep his bearings. They should have hit another trail by now, but he knew he hadn't missed it. They rode on, and eventually he saw the turnoff and took it, with Day lagging after. *Just a little farther,* he thought, *and we'll stop for a snack.*

The sun was going down.

The track led onto slickrock, and Nick followed what appeared to be tire marks from a vehicle. Beyond the sandstone, he thought he could see the trail, but when they reached it, it only led to another slickrock section. He relied on landmarks. If they headed just to the right of Behind the Rocks, they'd eventually hit a four-wheel-drive road that would lead down into Pritchett Canyon.

The sun was dipping against the distant fins when they met an impassable section of rock rising from the landscape in curves and waves and bowls. Her legs almost numb from pedaling—they must have ridden twelve miles from Rapid Riggers, half of it off-road—Day stopped her bike to rest and drink.

Nick circled back and stopped his own bike. "Want something to eat?"

"Sure. Where's the trail, Nick? I don't see it."

He handed her a bag of sunflower seeds. Leaving his helmet and his bike lying in the sand, he said, "I'm going to climb up there and see where we are."

As he hiked up onto the hump, Day scanned the area from which they'd come. They'd crossed several long sections of slickrock, riding around potholes full of water. Now the wind was kicking up, the cool wind of spring. She opened Nick's pannier, removed her guide shell and put it on.

When he came down from the rocks, he admitted, "I'm not sure where we're going. I think we'd better head back the way we came."

"That's too bad," Day said gently.

"No point in getting lost. We still have to pack tonight."

For the Maze. Day had almost forgotten. She wished she was already home preparing for the trip; she'd be exhausted in the morning. The sun was down now, leaving only its rosy signature in the sky.

They set out again, riding onto the slickrock. Another high outcropping grew up before them, and they pedaled around it, then had to carry their bikes over a vast cactus patch.

"Nick, obviously we didn't come this way before."

"That's true. I'm kind of heading toward the river."

"Are you sure? I mean, sure that's the way we're going? The river turns."

"Yeah, I know." He didn't sound impatient, just apologetic.

Day asked, "Are we lost?"

"A little. Don't worry. I'll get us home tonight."

Day hoped so. She wasn't an EMT like Nick, but she'd taken enough first-aid classes to know how most people died in the wilderness. And that a person didn't have to get very cold to die of exposure.

CHAPTER TEN

"WELL, IT'S A GOOD EXCUSE to hold each other all night."

They'd found shelter, an alcove, not quite a cave, in one of the monoliths, and Day sat between his legs, with Nick wrapped around her. Still she shivered. Fatigue had made her defenseless against the elements.

"When the wind dies a little more, I'll build a fire. I've got lots of matches." He rubbed Day's arms through her mango-colored guide shell. "Nice jacket."

"I bought it for the Maze."

Her words were slurring. He should try to build that fire now.

Nick squeezed her shoulders. "Let me see what I can get going. Help me gather some kindling. Moving will keep you warm."

There was no moon, and Day was afraid of picking up a scorpion or a spider. But in the starlight, she collected twigs around the trees while Nick found larger pieces of driftwood.

With rocks, he constructed a fire pit close to the alcove, where a stand of junipers helped block the wind. He used five matches before the kindling caught fire, and then he added larger pieces slowly, while Day watched.

When the blaze was burning well, they huddled side by side on the slickrock.

"Better?"

"Thanks." The fire warmed her skin. Nick made her feel safe. It would be a long night, probably without sleep, but in the morning they could refill their water bottles from the potholes. And then Nick would get them home.... "Grace and Zac will be worried when we don't show up tomorrow." They were supposed to meet at the River Inn at 6:00 a.m. to leave for the Maze.

"I know." Nick had never been in a situation like this, though he'd participated in plenty of searches for others. If he'd been alone or with a different woman, he would have risked trying to find his way in the dark. Not with Day.

"What are you thinking?" she asked.

"I'm having an experience in humility."

She didn't laugh. Nick was a professional guide; she doubted he'd ever been lost before. Why did it have to happen with her? No one would let him forget the incident, and Nick would always associate the humiliation with her.

"Nick, I don't mind walking. Trying to make it home tonight. I don't want Zac and Grace to worry."

Nick wished they could be back in Moab before anyone discovered them missing. But trying wouldn't be wise. "When people are missing, Day, nothing matters but the outcome. We'll do Zac and Grace a favor and sit tight till morning, okay?" He changed the subject. "Want to tell stories?"

"Oh, God, there's a centipede." Repulsed, Day leapt up and darted away from the inch-long insect.

Another raced over a boulder nearby. Bugs. Nick hated centipedes, too, but he'd become inured to them long ago. And he and Day would see more of them that night. "Ignore them."

His voice was resigned but also stern. Day knew why. *Nick, you're used to things like this. I've always lived in houses, slept in a clean bed.*

She sat down on his other side, away from where she'd seen the centipede, his arm snug around her. "It's all right, Day. Let me tell you a story. In the Behind the Rocks, there lived a chipmunk named Weather...." It was a story he'd told before. He'd changed the kind of rodent, changed its name, changed its home. But he'd told the same tale to a little girl he'd loved who was afraid of centipedes, who grew frantic whenever one crawled on her. "Weather gathered the food for the other chipmunks in his colony. He was the leader, and his enemy was the wildcat Dark Face...."

Her head against his shoulder, Day relaxed, listening to the adventures of Weather, until she felt a bug on her and jumped, frantically brushing it away. The centipede squirmed on the ground in an S shape.

Day crushed it with her hiking boot. Her whole body shook, and Nick pulled her closer.

He said, "My sister hated them, too."

The fire crackled. Sparks shot toward the stars.

Day hardly breathed.

Nick never talked about Kelly. Not since after her own father's death, when he'd told her about his childhood. His sister was younger. When they were taken from Nick's father, she'd been sent to a different foster home. Nick had never tried to find her.

Day still wondered why.

Had he comforted Kelly this way? Had he told stories to calm her?

They both must have needed the calming. They both must have had centipedes crawl on them—only maybe they hadn't known what was touching them in the dark.

Nick wished he hadn't spoken. That he had was a dangerous sign, a portent of things to come. He badly wanted to tell her about Kelly. To tell her the *truth* about Kelly. The need had been building for weeks. Months, even. Since Bob's accident. Since things had begun to change.

But what would Day think of his turning his back on a seven-year-old girl? He could have protected her.

Not a chance, Nick. You tried. You were a skinny little twelve-year-old. He broke your arm like a twig.

How much did Day love him? Would she love him if he told her the truth? She'd never turned *her* back on him. His monsters hadn't chased her off yet.

"Do you think Leah's pretty?"

He spun his head, startled. "Leah?"

In the firelight Day gazed down at her hiking boots. "Our new guide."

Get a clue, Nick, he thought. Hurting inside for the times he'd hurt her, he twisted his torso and put his right hand on the side of her face, touching her smooth skin, stroking the delicate bone beneath. "Nobody else is pretty, Day."

Something ran up her thigh, and Day jerked away, brushing it off. When it raced inside the sleeve of her jacket, she leapt up and yanked off the shell. Nick, on his feet instantly, snatched the jacket before it could go in the fire. He grabbed her.

"Stop it! You're all right."

Half-hysterical, she tried to take the shell from him.

Nick held it away from her and shook it once, hard. A centipede dropped to the ground. His eyes met Day's.

This is what it was like for you, she thought. *Every single day.*

She understood him more.

After a bit she put the jacket back on and they sat down again. Day folded her knees against her chest. "You were saying?"

His hands were templed against his face, casting shadows, a pattern of gold and black in the firelight. To Day, he was a big man who had been hardened by life since he was a child, yet had managed to learn gentleness. She found him brave and somehow larger than life.

For fourteen years, she'd been looking for a man who compared.

The problem was, she was an ordinary woman. She had never climbed a mountain. She could not kayak. She did not do the things he valued.

"Day, I think since the solstice, we've both been changing a lot."

His voice came out of nowhere. He spoke slowly, as though weighing every word.

"I have . . . problems . . . that you don't know about. I'm trying to be a good man."

Day's heart pushed her chest hard, in and out, in long-spaced beats. She never moved her eyes from his face, with his dark hair hanging uncombed around it. The cave boy who'd grown into a man. And who was telling her he had problems she didn't know about.

She knew plenty. She knew about his alcoholic parents, his mother who was gone weeks at a time, working. His father, who had beaten him, who had made the scar that stretched across his lower back and joined another below the waistband of his shorts. Scars so wide and puckered that it was hard to believe they'd been made when he was small. Nick had said they'd gotten infected.

She knew about the shack at the end of a ranch road, a road to nowhere in southern Utah, one of those pockets of wilderness where you could hide a house in the landscape because the desert went on so far. His father had locked him in the dirt space beneath the house and left him, going away for days at a time.

Nick and his sister had eaten bugs.

And when the man upstairs came home, things were worse.

Day believed him that he had problems she didn't know about. Nick Colter should have problems coming out of his eyeballs.

"You've changed, too," he was saying. "You've stopped smoking. You're trying this kind of thing."

Mountain biking. Getting lost, Day thought.

"When Bob had that accident, I thought it could have been me. And . . . I haven't been . . . good. Everything I've done has been for me. I don't want to be that way.

And...us. I've never used you, Day. I've always loved you." His face was close to hers. Their cheeks touched as he said, "I love you, Day. I can't turn away from it anymore."

"Why have you ever?" She didn't intend the words to come out, not in that higher-than-usual voice that was really saying, *Why are you crazy? Why have you always hurt us both?*

The heat of the blaze pinpointed on Nick's cheeks, warming them, heating his eyes, burning at truths that couldn't be told. But this talking had to happen. There were truths he could say. Things that could be better.

"You give yourself up for me, Day. It's not right."

"It's *love*."

"No. You pretend things don't bother you when they really do. You pretend to like things you don't." He stopped himself before he could name his doubts. This bike ride. The trip to the Maze. She wasn't doing *those* things for him. But the knowledge of what she would sacrifice, of all she *had* sacrificed, weighed down his heart. "You lose your*self*."

"If I don't, you'll find someone else. It's not a lot of fun to get a card from Nepal on my birthday from *Nick and Bonnie*."

"I was trying to make a point."

"You made it. Don't say this to me. Don't say I give you too much. I give you the very minimum that you take. And that's everything. You think I'd let Pip or some other guy screw Elizabeth Shephard one month and me the next? You know why I've done all this for you? Because I love you. Don't try and judge that."

"Why don't you stand up to me? You think Shep or Bonnie would let me—"

"Shep and Bonnie don't know shit about you, and obviously neither of them is around. I am. I'm not going to make a career of keeping you out of the beds of twenty-two-year-old boatinas. Why don't you grow up?''

There was enough truth in that to sting. "You *have* made a career out of it. Out of me. That's the problem. You love me too much."

Day was angry. Angry enough to stand up and move away from him and step on a few more centipedes. "At least the feeling's mutual. Unless you've started breaking one of our rules." No lies. She was sure he knew what she meant—the night of the lip-sync. Whispered promises. "Did you mean what you said? Or were you just... excited?"

The last word was barely distinguishable. He got up and reached for her, and after a sulky moment, a mad moment, she let him pull her against him.

Day felt the familiar shape of his body. Its strength. Warmth. His muscles and the male flesh nestled against her pubic bone. His smell and his smooth skin were so familiar to her.

It was good to be held.

"I meant it," he said. "And maybe we need some new rules."

"What—you've found a new way to say 'no strings'?"

She *had* changed, was changing. He didn't regret what he'd said. Hearing her answer had altered his perception. She'd let him have his way out of love, not weakness. And because she'd understood him.

She knew he needed her. Had needed her all the years she'd been there. She'd never turned her back.

"'No strings' was the old rule," he said. "Let's try 'no others.'"

Day was tired. Exhaustion brought her emotions to the surface, made her incautious. Now, anger had a hold on her and wouldn't leave. "So I get to be the flavor of the month?"

His breath escaped like the air from a fatally punctured tire. A spark from the fire rocketed into the desert, away from them. A bug crawled on him, and he knocked it off and killed it. Sometimes truths came easy, and he knew wisdom when he spoke it. "If you treat me like I deserve, we're not going to have much of a chance, Day."

Her body eased. She melted into him, and her fingers found a way through the fabric of his jacket, to hold his muscles.

She knew that, for the first time in their lives, he was really hers.

And that he could be forever.

THEY SPENT TIME in tenderness, holding each other, kissing. Forging a new bond that felt stronger than any Day had known with him before. Neither of them slept, though Day knew Nick could have. He stayed awake for her, held her between his legs by the fire while she told him a fairy tale, "Iron Hans," about a boy who released a large wild man—a man covered head-to-toe with rust-colored hair—from a cage and thereafter received his help. Nick told her about his classes in Salt Lake City and about working on the ambulance.

Inevitably the conversation came around to Bob.

"I like your idea," Day said, "of having him live over the office. And I'm sure my dad would have liked it."

The mention of Sam made Nick queasy. Sam had cared for him, too. So much that Nick had been fooled into thinking it meant more than it had.

Not fair, Nick. It's not fair to him to think that way.

They'd gone through periods where they fought often. But in the last few years before Sam's death, the outfitter had retreated into silence. The silence of resignation—and reproach.

The will should have been no surprise.

Nick said, "I'm glad you agree about Bob." The two of them had enough differences to resolve. Her coming to the Maze, spending more time in the outdoors, would help. For his part...

I'll have to slow down.

As soon as the sky began to lighten, Nick put out the fire. Day saw him studying the horizon where the sky was brightest.

"What time do you think it is?" she asked.

"Five."

Day longed to go home and curl up in her bed, to celebrate her new relationship with Nick in the familiar safety of civilization. Instead, if they made it home soon, they would leave for the Maze with Zachary and Grace. Their commitment would be tested in an environment comfortable to him—and harsh to her.

When the fire was out, they geared up and began to ride, heading in the direction Nick was sure would land them either on the Moab Rim, looking over town, or above the river. Either way, they could find their way down.

In twenty minutes, they came upon the road and their own tracks, and in two hours, they were at Day's house.

In the kitchen, putting on coffee for both of them, she listened to Nick speak with Grace on the telephone. "We were biking, and it got too dark to ride. We had to stop for the night. I really apologize. I haven't even had a chance to do the shopping.... No, we still want to go. I'll help Day get her stuff together, and then we'll go out to my place and get mine. We'll be over in ... two hours. Thanks. That's probably a good idea. Okay. See you soon."

He hung up. "They're going to do the shopping."

"Mm."

"What are you smiling about?"

"I notice you didn't mention the L-word, Pathfinder."

Their time constraints didn't stop him from pouncing on her and tickling her till she begged for mercy.

DAY WAS EMBARRASSED to tell Grace about her new commitment to Nick—and his to her. He'd had so many girlfriends, Grace might respond; who was to say she wasn't just one more? Anyhow, her sister would figure it out on her own that night when Day slept in his tent. Keeping the news to herself seemed a fair exchange for Grace's mischievous plans for the Maze trip.

The four of them took Grace's Toyota 4Runner to the Maze. Nick and Day slept in the back seat on the way. It was hours to the ranger station to pick up their permit, hours further, bouncing and jolting off-road, to the place from which they would descend into the Maze. Day awoke only when Zachary slowed the car to park, and she found that Nick had been holding her while she slept. His hand slid down her arm as she sat up, with a tender lover's touch.

In the front seat Grace smiled as though this was all her doing.

The rim of the Maze was white sandstone, with the colors of geologic time stacked beneath like cake layers, falling vertically into a wild twisting canyon with a rust-brown sandy floor. The area had been well-named, for the canyons formed a labyrinth on a scale that could be seen only in the American West. This was wilderness, not a building in sight, just sandstone spires and buttes and the white rim stretching as far as the eye could see. But there was more than rock; even along the stark white rim were piñon trees and junipers with light blue berries. As Zac parked the 4Runner, a chipmunk sped over the slickrock, disappearing into a crevice.

It took time to get organized, to double-check that they had everything. Though it was years since she'd been backpacking, Day remembered some tricks. She hefted her pack up onto a boulder and sat down to slide her arms through the shoulder straps and fasten the sternum and hip buckles. Rising, she staggered under the weight. She had a frenzied recollection of the person she'd been months before, a woman with a very sane attachment to her espresso maker, hot baths and a bed with sheets. *What am I doing here?*

Nick appeared beside her, wearing his pack. "You need some adjustments." Expertly he tightened some of the straps. "How's that?"

Something stopped her from saying, *Can I wait in the car?*

He thinks I'm going to love this the way he loves it. I have to try to be like Shep and Leah. I have to have a good attitude.

Nick's adjusting the straps *had* helped her pack fit. "Thanks."

Zachary locked the 4Runner, and they set out hiking under a cloudless morning sky to the rim over the Maze. When they reached the edge, Nick dropped his pack and scouted the rim, covering what seemed to Day a huge distance in minutes. Returning, he said, "Okay. I see where we go down."

He slipped into his pack, and the others followed him on a winding path over the slickrock to the rappel site he'd chosen. As Nick and Zachary dug out the climbing gear, Day neared the edge and looked over. It was a straight drop for seventy-five feet or so to a slickrock shelf that thrust out over the twisting canyon.

Nick set up a belay for the rappel, using a rock not far from the rim. He told Day, "I brought my lucky rope."

The turquoise rope they'd bought to go into the Marble Quarry.

"How about your compass?"

"Shh!" he whispered, putting his finger to his lips. Eyes smiling at hers.

As Day rubbed on sunscreen and took her black Rapid Riggers baseball cap from her pack, Nick brought her the same harness he'd tied for her in Marble. "Remember this?

I'm going to have you go first, and when you get to the bottom, send the harness back up, so Grace can use it."

"Okay." But when it came time to rappel, Day was confounded. "So... what wall do I put my feet on?"

"You don't. This is a free rappel."

"Oh." Hanging in midair with no wall to touch couldn't be any more dangerous than rappelling into the Marble Quarry.

Grace asked, "Want me to go first?"

"Oh, no." Rappelling was fun. Her enthusiasm could be genuine here.

"Day," Nick said when she was ready, "I think the best way to start here might be with that upside-down trick."

He was serious.

"Okay. On rappel." She let herself fall all the way back, upside down, so that she wouldn't run into the overhanging ledge. When she was beneath it, she pulled herself upright and lowered herself into space. *If I'm not Nick's kind of woman now, I don't know what I am.*

But she remembered another woman, a woman whose interests were the local theater and... well, whatever. This year's spring musical was *Camelot,* but she'd skipped the auditions. Nick's being in Salt Lake required more time from her at the river office. Zac wasn't participating in the play, either, because of the grand opening of the River Inn next month.

But last night, she and Nick had taken an evening mountain-bike ride. And here she was, taking a week off for a backpacking trip. Here she was, rappelling into the Maze.

Pride in her accomplishments was touched by loss. *Why can't I just be me, Nick? Why can't you love me for me?*

WHEN THE OTHERS AGREED to stop and camp for the night, Day's legs were burning, her hips raw and bruised from the weight of her pack.

Their campsite was above a wash on the floor of the Maze. As Grace brought out pots and the camp stove from her pack, Zac asked, "Where should the tents go, do you think?"

Grace pointed out two flat sandy locations, each with twisted juniper trees growing nearby. "How about there— and there? And..." She scouted for a third site.

Nick cleared his throat. "That'll work, Grace."

She gulped. "Oh." Then, coloring and smiling and glancing over her shoulder at her sister, she hurried away to set up the kitchen.

Day knew how to pitch a tent. Checking the tents at Rapid Riggers when they returned from trips was part of her job. Together, she and Nick laid out his ground cloth, securing the corners with rocks, then assembled the tent. When they were done, Nick climbed inside, rolled out their Therm-a-Rest mattresses and their sleeping bags. Day came in, too, to change into her blue jeans.

As she pulled off her canvas hiking shorts and tugged on a pair of Ben Rogan designer jeans, he watched her and saw the bruises and red skin where the weight of her pack had been. The sight upset him. "Sore?"

"A little." She wouldn't make a deal of it. Shep and Leah wouldn't.

But it hurt to button her jeans, and when Nick touched her hip, she flinched from the bruises where her pack had rested.

"Okay, so I'm having a great fantasy about Club Med."

"I'll make you a deal," he said.

"If it includes room service, you're on."

"It can include room service. If you tell me a really good story," he proposed, "I'll take you to Club Maze. Or bring it to you."

"Club Maze?"

"Yes, Your Royal Highness."

"What kind of story?"

"Something with knights."

Day could grow old telling him stories—and making him clothes and holding him when he needed to be held. He'd spent the years of his life when someone should have done those things with no one to do them for him.

"I know a knight story, but it would take hours to tell."

"I'll have it in instalments. Club Maze is expensive."

"I see. Shall we start now?"

"Let's check and see if they need help with dinner first."

Zac was helping Grace with dinner, talking with her, so Nick and Day found a rocky overlook, from where they could watch the sunlight disappear down the canyon. Day leaned back against a boulder, and he reclined on the shelf with his arms behind his head.

She began telling "The Knight of the Cart."

"On the Feast of the Ascension, King Arthur held court at Camelot, and after the meal he did not stir from among his companions." Day explained how the queen came to be abducted by the bad prince Meleagant and how an anonymous knight was so determined to save her that, after two steps' hesitation, he suffered the indignity of riding in a medieval cart used for carrying criminals because he was told it would bring him to Guinevere.

"It's Lancelot, right?"

Day merely smiled. She had just reached the part where the Knight of the Cart had defeated another knight in battle and was about to grant him mercy, but was interrupted by a woman who demanded the knight's head, when Zac yelled, "Dinner!"

Nick sat up. "Wait. Is he going to cut off the guy's head just because she wants it?"

Day stood to walk back to the campsite. "Well, he's very Generous, so he might, but he's also Compassionate, so of course he has a dilemma. Anyhow, you've had your instalment for today. Now you owe me."

He caught her, turned her toward him. "Day."

His face had that peaceful relaxed look, the look she'd seen when they snowshoed up to the Marble Quarry. "Thanks for being here with me."

She wanted to remind him that she'd agreed to come to the Maze before she knew he'd be there. She wanted to say, *I'm doing this for me.* But it wasn't true.

And never had been.

"THAT MUST HAVE BEEN some mountain-bike ride," Grace remarked to her sister as they went off into the darkness to brush their teeth.

"Mm," Day answered.

"I'm going to take credit," said Grace. "You wouldn't have seen each other Friday night and decided to go mountain biking the next day if it wasn't for this trip. Are you having fun?"

She could barely walk, and she was craving a jelly doughnut. But being with Nick, being the woman he loved, made up for it. "I'm having a great time."

When they returned to camp, Nick had disappeared, and Zac was waiting for Grace to turn in. Day said good-night to them and went into Nick's tent. He wasn't there. She groped for her headlamp and shone it on her sleeping bag, which was zipped to his.

On the place where her head should go lay a Godiva chocolate and a note in Nick's messy writing. "Enjoy your stay at Club Maze. The Management."

She was devouring the chocolate when he came in carrying his toothbrush. "How did you happen to have a Godiva chocolate along?"

"They sold them in the gift shop at the truck stop in Green River." He lay down beside her, on top of his sleeping bag. "I thought of my lady, the Queen of the Dry Gulch Parking Lot."

"*You* were the Queen of the Dry Gulch, Nicholas."

"You're just jealous because we won." He slipped his hand under her T-shirt. "Though when Bob saw the video, he said you should have."

"Ah, he *is* getting better."

"Actually I thought it was a sign of impaired judgment." He could feel Day's breaths growing shallow from his touch. Aroused, he kissed her, and they slid into their sleeping bags and cuddled closer.

She unbuttoned his jeans, as he did hers, while his mouth found her breast, her nipple. Wanting him desperately, Day nonetheless remembered how many women had shared this tent with Nick. *He wasn't like this with them,* Day told herself as he kissed her, as their tongues began sharing an intimate tenderness. *He was never in love like this.*

But tonight, in an environment that must have become familiar to Shep and many others, it was hard to believe the thought.

New Mexico

RORY LEFT HER TENT in the dark. John Frazier, the expedition director, stood outside his tent with the artist, an undergraduate named Theresa, and Rory made her way over to them. They were examining the contents of a box.

More bones, like those found at the other Chaco sites. Bones that had been bleached white in cook pots. John, and others, were sure they indicated that the Anasazi had practiced cannibalism. But the descendants of the Ancient Ones, the modern-day Pueblo peoples, were offended by the idea.

Archaeologists opposed to the cannibalism theory said that they would only accept it when human remains were found in prehistoric excrement. Unfortunately the place where they'd found some preserved human feces was the same area that had been ravaged by a pot hunter some time before.

"I'd love to get my hands on that guy," John said.

Rory was quiet. She'd never met an archaeologist who liked pot hunters, but she knew many who understood them better than John. If Rory had gained anything from her earliest memories, from recollections of ghastliness, it was compassion for the human condition and pity for weakness.

She had been where weakness was born.

Rory could imagine the sort of person who would destroy history for greed or simply for the love of digging. She could imagine the vacuum in his soul that craved satisfaction and hunted it in ruins. She knew the kinds of pain that could cause such a void.

Rory walked away from John Frazier before she could reply. The expedition leader would never understand if he heard her defend the pot hunter.

Her colleagues worked in dirt every day—but Rory had lived in it.

CHAPTER ELEVEN

"WE CAN'T GO AROUND?" Day asked the next morning. They'd been hiking for three hours. Despite being fortified with cowboy coffee in bed—compliments of Club Maze— and despite Nick's pile sweater padding her hips under her pack, Day was unprepared to scale the sandstone wall before them.

"It's twenty miles around the hairpin," Nick said. During the planning meeting, he and Grace and Zac had agreed that they would cross up and over the tongue of land. Now he realized Day hadn't been paying attention. "Anyhow, you're going to have to climb to get out of the Maze, Day. But this is just a walk up. We almost don't need a rope."

Day scanned the wall. He was right. If she weren't wearing a pack, it would be easy. But her pack weighed half her own weight.

"I'll lead," said Nick, "and set up a belay."

As he started sorting out the ropes, preparing for the ascent, Day zipped up her jacket. She listened to him consult with Zac, who was to belay him from the bottom once Nick placed protection. Then he turned to her. Including the others, he said, "Let's clarify communication."

There were new phrases to learn. "On belay," "Climbing," *"Rock,"* "Up rope," "Slack," "Falling!" Day thought she could remember the last one. Nick showed her how to tie into her harness. "Three components of your safety system can't be backed up. Harness, rope and tie-in knot." He showed her how to tie the rope through all the layers of webbing on her harness with a figure-eight fol-low-through knot. Grace and Zachary, who both had experience climbing, watched anyhow as Nick made her practice the knot three times, testing her as he had in Marble. "And when you're off the rope, you say...?"

"Belay off."

He checked the sky for clouds. In the southwest, weather came in fast. But from where they stood, he couldn't see beyond the high canyon walls.

"Okay, I'm going up."

When he was at the top, had set up an anchor and thrown down the rope, Grace suggested, "Day, why don't you go next?"

Day put on the climbing harness, tied in as Nick had shown her, approached the wall and tugged on the rope.

He called, "On belay!"

The rope was slack, so she yelled, "Up rope!" and Nick pulled it up.

"Climbing!"

"Climb."

She started up. It was *not* almost a walk up, as he had said, but there were plenty of ledges and handholds. Nick kept perfect tension on the rope from the top. When Day was two-thirds of the way up, it became trickier. A sheer stretch of rock ten feet high lay in front of her. From the bottom, Zac coached, "Go to your left."

Fatigued, unused to climbing, let alone with a pack, Day scanned the face until she saw where he meant. There was a foothold, but above it, nothing. She moved over to the right and placed the sole of her boot onto a tiny shelf, but when she put her weight on it, her toe slipped out.

She heard Nick above her. "What's up?"

"She's at the crux," said Zac. "Try the left, Day. What you're doing is harder."

Stay calm, Day. Don't feel pressured. You can do this. "But there's nothing above there."

"There's a handhold on your right."

Day put the toe of her boot in the foothold and pulled herself up, wobbling under the burden of her pack. Nick drew up the slack.

"Reach up with your right hand," called Grace.

Shaking, she put her bare fingertips up to the right.

"You're almost there," Zac said. "It's a ledge."

She found the ledge. *I can't do this. I'm not strong enough.*

"There's a little crack on the right, under your handhold," encouraged Zachary. "Put the toe of your boot in there."

She did as he said, but it wouldn't hold. Her leg muscles vibrated madly, and her left boot began slipping from its purchase. "Falling!"

The rope caught her, and she landed clumsily on the ledge where she had stood before.

Try again. Don't panic. She wondered what Nick was thinking. Was he wishing he was with Shep, who had climbed El Capitan? *Don't think about it. You're not Shep.* She tried the same foothold, the same handhold.

"Falling!" Her knee scraped the rock.

Up top, Nick spotted storm clouds approaching from the southwest. It was noon, late to be doing something like this. On this spit of land, they would be magnets for lightning. But going around would cost them a day, leave them short on food and water. "Zac. Tell her to untie and wait on that ledge. You and Grace come up, and I'll go down and help her."

Grace, then Zachary, climbed up, and both easily passed the crux while Day watched, feeling hopeless. Within ten minutes Nick stood beside Day on the ledge. "Take off your pack. I'll carry it up for you."

Day acceded with regret. She wasn't doing it all herself if she couldn't carry her own pack. Grace had made it up that stupid crux. But she leaned against the wall, bracing herself, unfastened her hip and sternum straps, and removed her pack.

Nick retied the rope to her harness. The shadows of the afternoon had faded to light gray. "Feeling a little shaky?"

"Yes."

"You can do this, Day."

He had hoped that Grace would find a route Day could use, too. Sometimes women were subject to different limitations than men. But Grace had gone the same way he had.

Day lacked the upper-body strength and the climbing experience.

Nick considered the wall, looking for possibilities. "Come over here. Left foot here."

"It won't hold."

"Don't say that till you try it."

She already had. But she tried—and fell on the tense rope.

"Try again, and use this handhold." Nick supported her as she started to climb.

"Up rope!"

The rope went up.

"Day, reach over to your right. It's a long stretch with your right leg."

She tried it and felt herself slipping. As she attempted to pull her leg back, she suddenly flipped around so that her back was against the wall. "Falling!" Her elbows scraped the sandstone.

Nick saw the blood.

"Day, look at me."

She did, her chin trembling.

"Day, this is a hard backpacking trip, and you're doing great. You can go up this wall. You can go the way you just started to go. Just trust yourself."

"I'm not strong enough. My arms won't pull me up."

"I know. But it'll work. You can make it work. It's just this little wall, and then it's a walk to the top. You can see it from here. You can see the way to go." If she didn't make it this time, they'd pull her up. The storm was coming.

Day glanced at the sky nervously, and he knew she was thinking about the weather, too. She knew the dangers. Sandstone that became slickrock when wet. Lightning.

She faced the wall again. *I have to go up.*

She tried the foothold he had suggested, then the handhold. Then that second elusive foothold. His hands spotted her, but it was the memory of his words that emboldened her. For just a moment she knew that her three holds were in perfect balance.

"You've got to trust your right foothold. See that big stair-step?"

She understood. She forced herself to trust her weight to the ledge, then lifted her left foot. When her right boot started to slip, she held the wall with her knee while she dragged her left foot to its new purchase. Then she fell. "Falling!" she cried, twisting and banging along the wall.

Nick steadied her as she landed on the ledge. "Don't use your knees."

She gasped for breath, quaking from tension.

"Okay? Look, we've got to outrun this storm, so—"

What he was going to suggest was something she couldn't face. Failure. A weakling. "I'm going up. I'll get it this time." She turned to the wall again, and as her right foot reached for the skinny toehold, she felt herself starting to cry. *Dammit, you stupid rock. I'm going up.*

Watching, Nick bit his lip hard. He'd never seen anyone so determined.

She held on tenaciously with her right hand and put her left boot in the new foothold. As she hauled herself up, she almost fell again, but she regained her balance, grabbing clumsily at the wall. Then the hard part was over, and as Nick had said, it was a walk to the top.

Nick came up two minutes later, carrying her pack. The memory of her tears burned in his mind, disquieting him.

Months ago she'd asked him if it would make a difference if she could follow him the places he wanted to go. *Say that effort wasn't for me, Day, but for you.*

He wondered if it might be for both of them, if Day had needed to come for her own reasons—and needed something stronger than personal challenge to bring her here.

She had already taken off her harness, and the four of them worked together, coiling the rope and stowing the gear, then putting on their packs as the first raindrops fell. Far across the white rim thunder rumbled, and jagged lines of white split the dark sky.

Time to move. "Let's go." Nick had taken this route through the Maze before, and he remembered the trail down. It was a scramble, but Zac and Grace would have no problem. As he took the lead, avoiding the slickrock that was already becoming dangerously slippery with rain, he planned their route.

At the top of the trail he told Zac, "Go ahead."

Grace followed, then Day.

A less-experienced hiker, she descended more slowly than the others. Zachary and Grace were cross-country runners, and Nick saw them waiting for him and Day. "Go on to the bottom." He'd hang behind with Day.

The trail was loose sandy soil, crusty dried mud, and rocks. As she rushed in the rain, Day's feet slid out from under her. She slammed backward on her pack.

"Okay?"

"Yes."

From behind, Nick lifted her pack so that she could stand.

"Thanks."

The trail grew steeper, then edged along wet sandstone, a long stretch of slickrock leading past an alcove containing an Anasazi grainery. Zac and Grace had only glanced at the ruin before going past. The floor of the canyon was a better place than an alcove to wait out an electrical storm.

Day stepped tentatively on the slickrock. How could she cross it? It was more slippery than algae on a stream boulder. The air smelled like ozone. She put her weight on her boot, and Nick grabbed her hand.

"There's sand in that trough there. Walk on it."

She did, and it was easier, but through the wet hair plastered to her face she discerned that beyond the alcove was only more slickrock, with a fifty-foot drop below. She edged toward the overhang, balancing in the crease between two swellings of Entrada sandstone.

Through the rain came a bright flash of light, then almost immediately a shattering bang of thunder. Water coursed down the slickrock.

"Come on, babe. Keep going. We're almost there. We'll wait it out at the grainery." And pray the lightning didn't decide to take a shortcut through their bodies to the ground.

The sandstone glowed blue with St. Elmo's fire. The tiptoe patter of desert rain punctuated the silence before the next searing light, before the boom that made Day jump. But she had reached the alcove, and she ran inside.

"Back, to the wall," said Nick. "Take off your pack and sit on it, and keep your hands and feet off the ground." The alcove was about ten feet deep and twenty feet wide. At the farthest side was the ruin of a round grainery of mud-and-dab construction. The door was oval. Water poured from overhangs across the canyon, and Nick heard the water all around before the light blazed again outside. He relaxed. The Anasazi were good at building where they wouldn't be hit by lightning.

Anasazi... Pots.

Feeling like the thief he was, he removed his own pack and sat on it a few feet from Day. She was staring out at the canyon and the storm, her face white. He knew she felt she was slowing everyone down, holding them back. He'd seen her tears and her courage, and they had brought his own feelings to the surface, as though the thin shell over them could be scraped off if he even bumped into someone else. She'd been so brave.

The secrets he was keeping from her felt like cowardice.

She would hate him if she knew.

He hated himself.

Tell her. Be as brave as she is.

No!

He jumped at the next flash, the next sound.

Day asked, "Do you think Zac and Grace made it down?"

She was worrying that she'd put them all in danger, Nick reflected. "I'm sure they did." The thunder and lightning were still close, and they should wait for the rock to dry before walking. "Let's hear some more of that story."

"All right." Day remembered where she'd left the Knight of the Cart. "Well, the knight had a dilemma. The knight whom he'd defeated had asked for mercy, yet the damsel who had just arrived urgently beseeched the victor to grant her his head."

Nick winced when the Knight of the Cart did cut off his opponent's head and gave it to the damsel. But the story soon took a turn. In a joust, the hero won the freedom of the queen. The Knight of the Cart was revealed to be Lancelot, but when he was granted an audience with Guinevere, the queen would not speak to him.

"Why not?"

"She didn't say, and Lancelot could do nothing but grant his lady her wish and withdraw. Very depressed, he went off to find his companion Gawain, from whom he had been separated."

The storm had stopped and a filtered sun was warming the rocks.

Finished with her installment of the story, Day stood up to inspect the grainery. She gave a small cry. Barely visible from beneath the sand in the ruin was the rippled gray side of an Anasazi pot. Just as someone had left it centuries before. "Nick! There's a pot here. Come look. I've never seen a pot anywhere but in a museum."

He went to the grainery to see the piece. Dolores corrugated style. Day would have been interested to know. He didn't tell her. Crouching beside her, he eyed the section exposed in the sand and didn't suggest uncovering it. The right thing was to leave everything untouched.

Nick had never done that in his life.

He felt vulnerable and longed to throw himself at Day's feet and confess. But he could only crouch beside her, feeling her goodness, knowing that any decency growing inside him was because of her. Wanting to be as fine as he could be for love of her.

THEY CAMPED in the canyon below the alcove, about two hundred yards from a pour-off that had worn a pool in the curving sandstone. As soon as he'd helped Day pitch the tent, Nick disappeared, and he was gone so long that at last she searched for him.

Weaving through the cottonwoods on the canyon floor, she found him working in the sand beside the pool with Zachary. It looked like they were building something, but they were also skipping stones in the pool, doing pull-ups on the overhanging rock ledges, having fun.

She left without disturbing them.

When she and Grace had made dinner, cheese biscuits and curried rice with nuts and dried fruit, she went to get the men. They were just wading out of the brush near the pool.

Zachary said, "We built a sauna."

Slapping at mosquitoes as she peered through the brush, Day spied a black tarp spread over some kind of dome.

Nick rubbed his hands in anticipation and winked at her. "Club Maze." As Zac returned to camp ahead of them, Nick explained, "The sauna's kind of small. We made a frame out of branches. I thought you and I could let Zac and Grace use it first.''

A backpacking sauna. A vision of warm transparent water, a white beach and a clean hotel room with a wet bar filled Day's mind—Club Med, not Club Maze. But she appreciated what Nick had done. ''Thanks.''

Day's conflicting emotions confused her. Her father used to build saunas by the river for her and Grace. Day remembered playing with her sister in the silt at the shore of the Colorado, swimming in her life vest while he kept a careful eye on them. The memory was earthy and distant.

What had happened to that part of her?

In her mind she saw a man emerging from white foam, screaming, then pushed under by the force of the torrent. His glasses were twisted sideways on his head, dislodged but not coming off because of the cotton keeper strap. It was stretched tight, making a diagonal line across his cheek. Jim Antonio.

His death in Cataract Canyon had taught her that the wilderness *was* an abyss. It terrified her, and yet something in her craved it, made her long to be like Shep and Leah—and her own sister. And her whole being had always, since the first day she'd seen him, longed desperately and incurably for the person who was, to her, the earth and the wild.

Nick's arm was around her, guiding her through the trees. He smelled like earth, like the piece of herself she'd lost. Maybe she was finding it again now.

Not in him—but in herself.

WHILE ZAC AND GRACE enjoyed the sauna and the natural pool, Nick and Day lay on Therm-a-Rest pads by the fire, two dozen feet away, and she continued ''The Knight of the Cart.''

''Now, while Lancelot was searching for Sir Gawain, he was captured by men in league with the prince Meleagant,

who had carried off Guinevere. The cruel captors sent word
to the queen that Lancelot was dead. Hearing that news,
Guinevere almost died herself, because she could not eat.
And some people rejoice in bad news, and so the captors
felt compelled to tell the captive Lancelot that the queen
was dead. When his captors were distracted, Lancelot made
a loop of his belt and put it around his neck and hanged
himself from his saddle horn.''

Nick laughed at the melodrama.

''His captors thought he'd fallen from his horse, but then
they saw the belt, and they cut him down. He had nearly
severed the veins in his neck, and he couldn't talk for some
time. . . .''

But soon after, Lancelot was taken to the castle where the
queen was being held, where Meleagant's kind father ordered his release. ''Lancelot and the queen were overjoyed
to see each other alive. In her good graces again, Lancelot
asked why she had shunned him after he'd first defeated
Meleagant in a joust.

'''Because,' she said, 'you hesitated two steps before you
got into the cart.' ''

Nick groaned.

''Lancelot knew she was right, that he should have
obeyed love when love ordered him to mount the cart and
that he should never have been afraid of what love demanded. He apologized to the queen, for she was right.
Delighted with his company, the queen suggested they meet
that night to enjoy each other's love, and Lancelot readily
agreed.''

Day stopped speaking, and Nick realized she was finished with the tale for the time being. He sat up on his
mattress. Resting on one hand, he studied her face in the
firelight. ''Do you believe that? About love?''

''Yes. I think it's *right* to trust in love. But we're human. Sometimes it's frightening.''

Nick already knew that. *Do what love demands*. Was he that brave?

Grace and Zac came out of the pool, shivering, and made a beeline for their tent. "It's all yours," Zac called over his shoulder, waiting for his wife to enter first.

Nick used a broken tree limb to roll rocks out of the fire onto a sled of branches that Zac had constructed. He dragged the sled with the rocks over to the sauna and shoved the hot stones inside, into the pit he and Zac had dug. While he collected water from the pool in the coffee-pot, Day removed her boots and socks outside the sauna. Nervously she waited for Nick.

He set the coffeepot just inside the door of the sauna, and they stripped together. It made Day feel young as a child, and the hut of branches seemed like a child's fort, too, when they ducked inside and she pulled the plastic tarp closed behind them.

"Watch out for the rocks." His hand touched her leg, and she grabbed his wrist, blind in the darkness. "Come over here."

Nick. She could smell him, the earth smell that made her whole. The skin and hair on his nearest thigh brushed hers as he poured water over the rocks, and the sudden spraying sound made her huddle closer to him. His arm went around her.

"Nicholas."

"I love you." Wet heat filled the small cramped space. Under its cloak Nick kissed her cheek, then her nose, then her lips. Their mouths opened, tongues sliding together in a kiss of mutual adoration. Her hand touched his stomach and slid down to hold his erection. "Day..." His voice shook.

You hesitated two steps...

The story spoke personally to Nick. He would never forget it. Lancelot had not been a criminal. Yet Nick was, and he deserved to ride in the cart. Love told him it would bring him to his queen and make their love whole as it never could be with secrets between them. Yet she would hate him! They wouldn't end up in each other's arms.

Tell her about Kelly, Nick. Start there.

He poured more water on the rocks, reminding himself how it was after Sam died, what he'd told her. *It wasn't even a house, Day, where we lived. He locked us in the dirt space underneath, and sometimes we were there for days, like animals, like rodents.* She'd listened. She'd held him, never let him go. When he was done, she had made love to him.

The heat in the sauna built, like the heat underground in August.

"You tell a story," she said.

He swallowed. His lady had asked. "Once... Once there was a..." A boy. He couldn't. "Once there was..." *It's Day. It's okay.* "When Weather the chipmunk was small, he was trapped in a shoe box with his sister... his sister, Squeak."

Day felt keenly alert, as though the sauna was washing a fog from her mind. Weather the chipmunk had a sister.

"The wild cat, Dark Face, who was their father, liked to leave them in the shoe box while he went out carousing far away, and sometimes he forgot them. They were hungry, and it grew foul in the shoe box. So when they were let out, they ran into the desert and hid. They didn't want to be locked up again. One day, when Rousel's— When Weather's father..."

Rousel? Where did that come from? Day wondered.

"When Dark Face found him hiding, he broke his arm. A chipmunk can't live with a broken arm, and his father knew that, but he had to wait to take him to the doctor until the other things he'd done to Weather had healed up."

Day was glad he couldn't see her face. *Oh, God, what's wrong, Nick? What are you trying to tell me that you can't say without a story?* The heat made her dizzy, but she listened so as not to miss a word.

"Two weeks later Dark Face took Weather to the doctor, and he took Kelly— he took Squeak, too." Nick poured more water on the flames, wanting more heat to sweat it out of him, to make the story leave him, to make it gone and make him clean. "Squeak had something wrong with her. She had a condition on her chipmunk face that was a birth defect from her mother liking to carouse like Dark Face. To drink. She had... a cleft lip and palate. And the chipmunk doctor told Dark Face that it could be fixed, and Weather heard.

"One day when his father was sleeping off a drunk, he took Squeak and hitchhiked into town to the doctor's office. The doctor remembered him and Squeak, and when Weather said that he wanted his sister's face fixed, the doctor told him that if... that if Squeak went to live with a chipmunk couple he knew, they would pay to have Squeak's face fixed."

Nick poured on more water. The sweat drove down his face. It was too late to turn back now. Too late to leave the tale untold. Day knew. She wasn't speaking. Just breathing. Waiting.

"Weather..." His voice was hoarse. "Weather loved Kel— Squeak, and he didn't want her to go live with anyone else, so he took her home. And when many days and nights had passed, his father took his sister upstairs and locked him below. Locked him in the shoe box. And he heard his father... trying to... have sex with his little sister, Squeak."

The sweat was coming out of his eyes. Why was he choking this way? His body felt so awful. He was dirty, like that place.

"I— Weather— He took her back to the doctor, and the doctor took her and told him to go away. And that was the last Weather heard of his sister."

Day grabbed his body, slick with sweat, clinging to the muscles in the heat. Her fingers and limbs slipped on his skin, and she held tighter. "What did Weather do then? Tell me." Running her fingers over his back. Feeling the hideous grooves at the bottom.

"Weather was afraid of his dad, because of... because he hit. But he was afraid of going to jail, too. The doctor said Weather shouldn't tell anyone, or he and his father would go to jail. So he hid in the desert. He knew where the spring was, where his family got water. But he had to steal food from the supermarket and he got caught. Someone knew where he lived, and the police took him home, but when they saw the shoe box they took him away again, to live with... other people."

And when he was twenty, Day continued to herself, he returned to southern Utah to find out what had happened to his father. He'd learned he was dead, that he'd passed out drunk in the road and been run over by a truck.

"Didn't anyone ask what happened to Kel— to..."

"I said I didn't know. I said we'd gone to town and I'd lost her."

Nick poured the rest of the water on the rocks.

The hissing was explosive, the heat instantaneous and intense. Day had to lower her head against his back to breathe without the steam singeing the insides of her nostrils. Her sweat stung the scabs on her knees and elbows from her climbing falls that morning, but she didn't notice. She noticed nothing but his heartbeat.

"I love you. I love you, Nick."

"I hate me. I think she's dead or something worse. I think I gave her to someone evil. Nobody good would want a seven-year-old with a harelip."

Day clutched him more tightly. *I can't handle this. I've never been exposed to anything this bad. I don't know how to help him.*

"There's no more water."

They left the sauna. The night was cool, the water in the pool like ice. Day plunged in, her feet sinking into the slimy silt on the bottom. Nick did not come in. Abruptly he pushed into the brush, naked, and disappeared.

She stepped out of the frigid water, dripping. "Nick?"

"Don't come!"

The words drifted back to her. She heard him running, breaking branches, and the sounds became smaller and more distant in the forest.

He could step on a scorpion, get cactus spines in his feet. He could get lost. They were in the Maze, for God's sake.

Day dried herself with her clothes and put them on, knowing she wouldn't follow him, wouldn't be able to find him. *She* would be likely to take a wrong turn, to disappear forever.

But Nick was made of harder stuff. Desert-rodent stuff.

She was the one who'd told him about Iron Hans. Maybe now he was running to a place where he could call for the help of some wild hairy friend of his own—a giant to give him a strong war-horse and a band of warriors to fight the monsters in his head.

But if Nick had ever had such a helper, someone who gave him armor in which to face the world, it had been Sam Sutter.

And he was dead.

CHAPTER TWELVE

HE HAD TOLD HER.

She'd held him, with her hands and arms and breasts against the sweat on his back. She still loved him. But Day's father had been good, and she could not understand how Nick felt now. She couldn't possibly know incest. Nick ran along the floor of the canyon, the sand and prickly plants under his feet, branches scratching his arms and legs and the sides of his chest like memories.

This wild place where there were no others, this lightless Maze of rock, was the place where it didn't matter that he came from badness. He breathed hard, and in sweat remembered who he was. Digger, EMT-I, outfitter, guide, lover of women. Day was distant from him, something he wanted but couldn't quite touch.

Why did she love him?

The thoughts hurt, and he ran faster and harder and didn't think at all. He ran until he fell, tripping in the sand of a dry wash. He rolled in the sand, covered himself with the dust that had come off the canyon walls.

I want to be good.

The need hurt so much he didn't know what he would do. If only he could start over, and all the pots were still lying in the sand; he would leave them alone. If only he could have taken Kelly to the police, to someone who would have helped, instead of giving her away. He'd been so stupid. Why was he stupid?

Well, I think you're smarter than that, Nick.

One of those things Sam had said. Before Sam had stopped talking to him. Before Nick had felt the silence that meant, *You're an adult, and there's nothing to be done with you anymore. Pity you didn't turn out any better.*

"Sam," Nick whispered into the dirt.

How could he go back to Day? How could he take her, have her, when he didn't deserve her? From Salt Lake City, it had seemed possible. There, he lived clean and worked hard and tried to save people, tried to resurrect corpses that vomited on him, tried to stop blood from running out of bodies. With distance, it had seemed possible that if he tried to fit in with civilized people, he could be enough like her that they could be together.

But seeing her and Grace and cultured Zachary, remembering Sam, reminded him how far from them he really was. Saying the words to her, saying that he'd heard his father trying to have sex with his sister, he had seen how different he was.

He was a dirt creature, the sandman. He was Weather. He was Rousel.

He dug deeper in the sand.

DAY WAITED by the fire, feeding wood to the blaze. She finally went to the tent to get her sleeping bag. She brought it out and lay by the fire to wait for her lover.

He didn't come back, and she fell asleep and dreamed about chipmunks and awoke with something dripping on her.

"Nick."

The fire was out. He was zipping his sleeping bag to hers. He smelled like smoke and was naked and damp from the pool.

"Are you okay?" she asked.

"Sure."

In the starlight, they pulled the joined sleeping bags more tightly around each other and searched out each other's mouths, with only her clothes between their bodies.

"I love you," Day said. "What you did wasn't wrong, Nick. You were just a little boy."

"I was twelve."

"Like I said."

"Let's not talk about it anymore." *Let's pretend I'm like you, that I'm one of you.*

Day wanted to talk about it—wanted *him* to talk about it. "Have you tried to find her, Nick?"

"I hired a private detective. Thirty thousand dollars."

"Oh, Nick." Each of her fingers clung to him, trying to tell him how she loved him. "You shouldn't keep it bottled up."

"I told you."

"You should talk to other people. Susan gave up a baby for adoption. You've seen Zac psychotic and Bob in a coma. We're all human. That's what your friends are for."

She was the only friend he needed. Nick changed the subject. "Tell me some more of the story." The lowly knight and his queen. But even Lancelot was a nobleman, the son of a king. Like Zachary or Pip. Nick was not. But in stories he could become Na-chu-rú-chu the weaver, or Tiyo who went down the Far Far Below River in a hollowed-out log... or Lancelot. *Will our love always be forbidden, Day?* Yes. It would be forbidden while he avoided the cart, avoided the disgrace of exposing his crime.

Day allowed the change of subject, and she drew his head to her breast. "Let me see. Where were we? Oh, yes. The tryst. Lancelot came to her window that night, and they held hands through the iron bars but were frustrated to be otherwise kept apart. Lancelot boasted that if the queen wanted him inside, no iron bars would keep him out. She *did* want him, and Lancelot pried the... bars... and he... Oh, Nick. Oh, God."

"Shh. I love you." He was unfastening her jeans, and she felt close to crying as she felt his hand between her legs, making love to her. "Let me tell the story now," he said softly. "I think I know how it was between them."

Over her, bare-shouldered and strong, he took her face in his hands and said, "He came to her bed, and when he was in bed with her, he said, 'My lady, thank you for letting me be with you this way tonight. This is the greatest joy I know, for there is no woman in the world as beautiful as you, or as good. All good I do is for love of you.' And he..." As he told about the tryst, about how Lancelot loved his lady, Nick caressed Day, imagining he was a king's son, like Lancelot, and half-worthy to touch this woman he loved.

Hearing him, seeing the look in his eyes, Day understood. He thought he was bad, and he wanted to be her knight. *You are.* While he was inside her, Day took his face in her hands and said, "I love you more than anyone. You're like all the stars in the sky to me."

Nick's arms squeezed the breath from her.

God, he couldn't lose her. She'd accepted the mistake he'd made as a child. But she'd never forgive what he'd done as a man. If she ever discovered it, she would leave him.

The thought of Lancelot du Lac hanging himself from his saddle horn no longer made Nick laugh.

THEY RETURNED to the River Inn late Saturday night, and Nick and Day drove to her house and showered together and made love. Day was blissful. The next day was her birthday. No card from "Nick and Bonnie" this time. Nick wanted to take her to Grand Junction. They would visit Bob and have dinner.

But after they'd made love, Nick seemed restless in her bed. At last he asked, "Would you care if I went home and came by to get you in the morning? I want to check my answering machine.''

Who are you expecting to call?

It was happening again. This was the first subtle sign that she mustn't hold too tight. Day didn't know what to do. Except say, ''That's all right.''

Her voice was relaxed.

Nick knew everything she was thinking.

And she was completely wrong.

AT HIS TRAILER an hour later, Nick unlocked the cable that held the door shut. He carried his pack and some mail he'd picked up at the post office and left them by the door while he showered and found clean clothes.

When he was dressed, he opened a cabinet beneath the sleeping loft and dragged out the cardboard box he used to store his collection of artifacts. Besides the coyote effigy, there were three: a black-on-white Pueblo III double mug, two mugs joined together; a black-on-white Mesa Verde bowl, flawless and uncracked; and a basket. They were perfect and intrinsically beyond price. If sold, the three items together would bring seventy-five thousand dollars or more.

They, not his answering machine, were why Nick had wanted to come back to the trailer. Sitting on the floor in the cold, just outside the glow of the single bulb over the sink, he lifted each object from the box. Nick had never felt a need to display his finds. He had coveted them to enjoy himself, to handle and admire in solitude.

Now, however, they threatened him with the same intensity as the childhood threat of the trapdoor lifting on the roof of his prison, or of his father's voice calling him when he ran away into the desert.

He had to get rid of them—and the coyote effigy.

Panic made him want to throw them in the river, where no one would ever discover them.

That would ease his fears—but not his conscience.

Perhaps he should donate them anonymously to the museum. He could provide information about where they'd been found.

That solution didn't sit well. Day would learn of the donation, see the pieces. The artifacts would continue to haunt him. The only way to be free of them was to return them to where he'd found them; he remembered each place.

Nick couldn't accomplish that tonight, and tomorrow was Day's birthday—and they needed to see Bob and talk to his caretakers. So Nick boxed the treasures again and put them away, feeling as though he was hoarding dynamite that might someday explode. He had to get rid of them *soon*.

As he moved to prop open the door of the trailer, preparing to go to sleep, the mail he'd laid on the kitchenette table caught his eye. He glanced through it, stopping when he found an envelope from the West Fork River District in Idaho.

Nick didn't have to open it to know what it contained.

The Selway.

Only one private trip launched each day during the Selway River's brief season. Permits were hard to come by; this year, with Shep, was the sixth Nick had tried.

And this was the year it had worked.

He was joyful as he got ready for bed, and it was only when he slid between the sheets alone that he remembered Day. And felt disappointment that she couldn't care about the Selway permit as he did.

Running that river was an experience she could not share.

THE NEXT MORNING, over breakfast at the Dead Horse Diner on Main Street, he told her about the permit.

Day remembered that time in the winter when he and Shep had come into the office together, talking about running the Selway, about applying for a permit. Who would Nick take down the river now? She asked him.

Nick didn't know. Bob couldn't go; he still slurred his words, spoke little, and his coordination wasn't good. "I'll find someone."

Day could see that he'd never considered her. She should be thankful. Instead, she was worried. What if he met a woman who wanted to go? No. Nick had made a commitment to her now. But...

Last night was the first night in a week she'd slept in a bed. Day should have slept well. Instead, she'd awoken in the middle of the night, trying to find him. In her distress, she would have traded her bed for the naked ground if he had lain beside her.

He liked it that I came on the Maze trip. He said so.

"Nick, I could go with you."

"Down the Selway?" His voice cracked. "White water makes you throw up."

"It's been a long time since...well, since I've tried it." With her fork she stabbed a piece of cantaloupe in her fruit cup. "It's mostly habit now. Not going, I mean."

He didn't believe her. She'd gone white. The real Day sat before him, dressed in a shimmery emerald sleeveless dress and lime high-heeled pumps, her hair up in a French twist like Grace Kelly. This elegant woman was telling him that she was dying for a trip down the loneliest, most rugged river in the west.

She's changing, Nick reminded himself. *We really had some good times in the Maze. Maybe she wants to try the river again.*

If so, he wanted to be there for her. But the Selway wasn't the place to start. There were gentler rivers. Like the San Juan. A San Juan trip could serve a dual purpose. The basket in his trailer had come from a pit house on the cliffs above the San Juan River corridor, and the easiest way to reach the area was by boat.

He could put back the basket.

"What about trying the San Juan first?" he said. "We could go in April, before things get busy at Rapid Riggers. I think I can get a permit."

The San Juan was the first river Day had ever rowed, with her father and Grace. No big rapids. Nick was sweet to suggest it. He'd probably be bored out of his mind. *But maybe with his help,* Day told herself, *I can really get over this fear.*

She realized that she did want to defeat her fear. And not to win Nick's admiration or the respect of her employees or even to feel that she'd won her father's posthumous approval.

But simply because she was tired of being scared.

WHEN THEY ARRIVED at the rehabilitation facility in Grand Junction later that morning, Bob was in the common area watching TV. Both felt a familiar shock seeing their friend. Despite the number of times they'd visited him since his accident, the difference from the Bob they had known still made them sad. Although he wore the same shaggy hair and beard that he had in his river days—and though he'd largely recovered from the physical injuries of the crash— his facial expressions and manner and motion had all been altered by brain damage.

Seeing them, Bob squinted, looking for a moment as though he didn't know who they were. "Oh, hi."

Nick sat down beside him and hugged him. "How're you doing?"

"I need to work." Obviously it was foremost in his mind; often he had trouble articulating thoughts.

As she took an adjacent seat, Day caught what he'd said and wanted to reassure him. "We miss you at Rapid Riggers."

Before either she or Nick could mention the possibility of his living above the river office, Bob said, "I can row now."

Shit, thought Nick. Taking people into the wilderness required sound judgment, split-second reflexes, a dozen things Bob lacked—and might never have again. That his friend had once possessed those qualities but no longer did made Nick angry and upset.

He could see Day wondering how to fix things. Afraid of what she might say to Bob, that she might make him hope, Nick cut in. "You can't row yet, Bob. But there's stuff to do, and... We want you around. In fact, we had an idea."

While Nick spoke to him, Day noticed that Bob seemed to grow even more despondent. Wondering if he'd rather talk to Nick alone, she said, "I'm going to find the ladies' room."

Bob watched her leave. "Can I come home now?"

"Soon," Nick said. "We're going to take you out on visits for a while, then see if they'll let you come home."

His friend swallowed and shut his eyes, and he was crying. "I'm all messed up."

Nick reached for the other man and embraced him, held him while he cried. "A couple of months ago you couldn't eat by yourself, Bob. It can take years to get better." He wanted to promise they'd climb mountains, row rivers together again. But all he could say with certainty was "We're going to be with you."

THEY TOOK BOB OUT for another drive around the cliffs and buttes of Colorado National Monument. Later, when they'd returned him to the facility and left him, Nick was subdued. Wanting to put his friend's pain out of his mind—and settle some things with Day—he said, "Let's go to Aspen."

"Aspen? We can't afford to breathe in Aspen, let alone eat."

"Sure we can. It's your birthday."

She agreed they should go to Aspen, and as he drove her Porsche toward Glenwood Springs, he said, "You know, that night at the Marble Quarry was something I'll never forget."

"Me, neither."

"I'm glad you're trying some of the things I like to do, Day."

"So am I." She meant it. If only she was a better athlete. The challenges were growing more difficult. The Selway...

It would be a triumph if she could ever accompany him down that river.

In Glenwood, they grabbed a quick sandwich, then continued up the mountain. The aspens and other trees had not yet begun the greening of spring, and they saw cars with skis on the roof going both ways on the road. In Aspen Nick parked outside the elegant Hotel Jerome. It had begun to snow, and he zipped his guide shell and helped Day button her navy wool spring coat. They walked up the street arm in arm and ducked in the first store they saw, which sold nothing but Christmas ornaments.

Then, at the same instant, they both spotted an ornament of a yellow-and-gray raft, exactly like the Rapid Riggers boats. Nick said, "We'd better get this," and took it to the counter.

When he handed Day the package, she said, "For me?"

"Actually, this is our first jointly owned Christmas-tree ornament. What do you think about that?"

"Sometimes I make it a point not to think, Nick." *Do you have a fever, or what?* Day tried to forget it.

They browsed till five, then found the Thai restaurant a shopkeeper had recommended for dinner. Over wine, Nick handed Day a small gift-wrapped box. "Happy birthday. From just me."

"No others *is* a good rule." She peeled off the tape, unfolded the wrapping paper. In the box was a thick silver ring on a black satin cord. A movable knob on the outside of the ring could be slid along the metal to correspond with letters representing the months of the year. A card was attached to the cord. Reading it, Day learned that the ring was an Aquitaine, an instrument for telling time using the sun. Eleanor of Aquitaine had given one to her lover, Henry II, so that when he was out hunting he would know when to leave to meet with her.

"You set the knob to the month, then turn it toward the sun, and the sun shines through the hole. You can read the hour inside."

"Thank you, Nick." Day hung it around her neck. "I love it."

His eyes never left hers. "Maybe now isn't the time to talk about this—in light of what's going on with Bob. But I want to live with you, Day."

He *had* been serious about the Christmas ornament. When she could speak, she asked, "Where?"

"We could get a bigger trailer. On my land." It didn't matter how he'd bought the land, Nick reasoned. It was his. She never had to know anything more.

"I have a house," Day pointed out.

"If we rented it or sold it, we could build one of our own on the river."

"That's a big commitment."

"I know."

Day sipped her wine. She really needed to think. Was it Dr. Joyce Brothers who'd said you should never live with a man you wanted to marry?

Not ready to answer, she changed the topic. "Nick, what do you think about asking Susan if she knows some way to look for Kelly? She's linked with an adoption-reunion service on the Internet. There are a lot of resources like that."

"I've checked all the adoption-reunion listings I know. Not the Internet, but . . ." He grimaced. "People list themselves if they want to be found. Kelly hasn't. She knew who she was. She wouldn't forget that. She was seven."

"She might have forgotten."

"Then I won't be able to find her, will I?"

"Can I try? Can I talk to Susan?"

Nick considered. He'd told Day. Could he stand for his other friends to know? "I guess."

After dinner, they walked in the snow to a bookstore and coffeehouse. Nick examined climbing magazines, then browsed through the bargain books. Discovering a volume called *Arthurian Legend,* he flipped through it and admired color plates, pictures from old manuscripts, photos of England, text from various Arthurian stories. He selected a copy of the book, took it to the counter and bought it, then hunted for Day. She was upstairs in the architecture section. When she saw him, she closed a book she'd been reading.

"Oh, you're ready? Let me pay for this book. I'll just be a minute."

He waited while she paid, and when she joined him, he nodded to the coffee bar in the back of the store. "Want to get something?"

"Sure."

They ordered cappuccinos and apple cobbler. Nick gave her his paper bag, passing it over the table. "I got you this."

She flushed, smiling. "You already got me something."

"It's still your birthday, isn't it?"

"Well, it's not yours, but I bought this for you." Day handed him a hardbound volume.

Nick read the cover. Gustav Stickley's *Craftsman Homes.*

"He was like you," she explained. "He loved simplicity and the outdoors. These homes were built in the early part of the century, and he made outdoor sleeping rooms with fireplaces, things like that. The book has house plans in it.''

"Really?'' Was she considering what he'd suggested, building a house together? His misgivings about the land and how it was bought resurfaced. Nick squelched them. He'd tell her everything in maybe five years. When he could say it was that long since he'd stolen anything.

They examined the books together, then set them aside and sipped their coffee.

"You never answered me," he said. "You want to discuss it?''

"Well, Bob's not a problem. I think we feel the same way about him, Nick.'' That they would care for him as long as he needed it. "I'm thinking of logistics. You know, it would be easier if you wanted to move into my house. And if Bob came there, too, it might be simpler. If he can live on his own later, the river office is a good option.''

"This is something we can discuss with Susan. She sees him even more than I do. But sure, I don't mind moving into your house for a while. I'd want us to figure out something else eventually.'' The place on the river. If he returned the artifacts to where he'd found them, he would feel at peace with it.

Day said with significance, "Yes, I hope we do figure out *something else.*''

Marriage. Nick smiled at her from his eyes. "For now, why don't you give me back my house key?''

HE HEADED BACK to Salt Lake City early the next morning with the plan that Day would take the train to see him the following weekend. She did, and they made love on the mattress on the floor of his room, near the stack of his textbooks. They hiked in the foothills of the Wasatch Mountains and went to a film festival and ate Greek food.

The following weekend he visited Moab without telling her.

Nick drove directly to his trailer to pick up two of the three artifacts. The other one, the basket, he'd found on the Navajo side of the San Juan River. He would return it when he went down the river with Day.

In his trailer he transferred the double mug to a smaller cardboard box, padding it with newspaper, and tucked the coyote effigy, carefully wrapped in an old bandanna, beside it. Then he took the Mesa Verde black-on-white bowl from the box. He'd found it in an alcove near Grand Gulch. He'd rappelled to the place from above, then to the canyon floor with a full pack.

Now the memory made him sick. For years he'd ignored what he was told, that the archaeological record, learning the history, was the most important part. He'd believed that the "moki" diggers were the experts when it came to exploring ruins. That the artifacts were what mattered.

The bowl *was* beautiful. He stood up to carry it to the couch, and without warning, a section broke free from one side and fell to the peeling linoleum floor, where it shattered into dust.

The quiet accused him.

Nick was incredulous. What had happened? There had been no cracks in the bowl. Heartsore, he squatted to gather the pieces.

What should he do with them?

It would be faster to take the double mug back to New Mexico without making the other stop.

Uncertain of anything except that he'd been destructive, that his life was some form of destruction, he opened another cabinet under the loft and placed the potsherds inside.

THAT NIGHT, Grace stopped by the river office and coaxed Day to join her downtown for pizza and beer. Zac was out of town, on a modeling job, and she didn't feel like cooking.

While they sat outside the pub eating, Day filled her in on Bob—and confessed that Nick was going to move in.

Grace seemed pleased. "He's really changing. When we were in the Maze, he said he's going to try to work with the Moab ambulance next winter."

Traffic passed on the street behind Day. A horn honked in the spring night. "Yes. I guess we're both changing. I'm going down the San Juan with him."

Grace lifted her eyebrows and swallowed a piece of pizza. "I guess you and Zac will both be facing your river nemesis. He's going on the Cataract trip with the Japanese businessman."

Day knew how Nick felt about that trip. Zac's mental-health problems troubled him. Sitting back in her plastic chair, she asked, "Are you sure he can spare time from the hotel?"

"For this, yes. It's important, Day. He needs to believe in himself." Grace's mouth tightened, and she dropped her gaze to her plate.

"Is something wrong?"

"We're just having a little disagreement." Briefly she cast her eyes at the other tables. They were all occupied by strangers, tourists in cycling togs, and the ambient noise lent privacy to their conversation. "I want a baby," she said.

Day saw the implications. Zachary's mental illness was not chronic, but he perceived it as a flaw. A genetic flaw. Without being told, she understood her sister's hope, that perhaps the Cataract Canyon trip could restore Zac's faith in himself.

Grace thrust her head forward, peering past Day at Main Street. "Wasn't that Nick's truck?"

Day looked in time to see a blue '57 Chevy stop for a light farther down the street. The sinking sun glared on the windshield, and it was impossible to see the driver. But Day saw the equipment box in the bed. It looked exactly like

Nick's truck. It couldn't be; he'd said he was busy this weekend and made it sound like he had to study, work on the ambulance. "He's in Salt Lake."

Grace started asking about Bob, volunteering that he could live at the River Inn, but Day couldn't forget the truck. When she got home, she called Nick in Salt Lake.

His roommate Jack answered. "He's not there? He said he was going down south. I thought he meant to see you."

The moment swiftly became awkward as they both began to wonder what Nick *was* doing.

And if he was seeing someone else.

New Mexico

THERE WERE TENTS on the canyon floor, and as soon as Nick saw their shapes in the darkness, he gazed up the rock wall at the alcove ruin. Moonlight shone on string stretched between wooden stakes.

Archaeologists.

They were digging the ruin where he'd found the double mug.

Instinctively he backtracked the trail through the canyon, wanting to distance himself from the dig. He walked for almost a mile before he felt safe to sit down and think.

Parking his pack against a boulder, he listened to the mosquitoes and the frogs. It was one in the morning.

Nick tried to remember everything about his first visit to the ruin, but it was four years back. What else had he taken? An olla... Yes, everything from the site had been beautifully made, Pueblo III. But there hadn't been much. After a while he'd found only sherds.

But if archaeologists were digging, they were trying to learn something, and what he knew might be valuable.

He kept a notepad and pen in the first-aid kit from his pack. Uneasily he switched on his headlamp, keeping the beam softer than was useful. Under the strain of fear, he started to write a note. It took so long that he lay down on the boulder. He drew pictures, a map. It mattered where things were found, and he tried to recall everything.

The note took two sheets of paper. When he was done, he left his pack; carrying the double mug and the note, he wove back through the canyon.

He wouldn't risk going up to the alcove. There was no reason to put the mug back where he'd found it. They would move it, anyhow. And he might be seen.

So instead, silently he crept toward the nearest tent and set the mug in the sand outside the fly, holding down the note. Stealing away, he jogged, then ran back up the canyon, his heart pounding.

Never in his life had he felt so afraid of being caught.

Because never had he had so much to lose.

NICK WASN'T SEEING someone else. Day didn't believe he would do that. She didn't understand why he'd come through Moab without trying to see her, but by Saturday morning she was convinced it was his truck she and Grace had noticed. Maybe he'd gone backpacking. But if so, why hadn't he invited her? Was he running?

The strangeness of it all reminded Day about his sister. They really ought to try to find Kelly. It was bound to help Nick.

At work that morning, after Leah and a guide named Joe had left on a four-wheel-drive trip with a dozen passengers, Day found Susan in the office. "Susan, I've wanted to ask you about something. Nick said it was all right with him." Quietly Day confided what Nick had told her.

Susan bit her lip, and her eyes watered. She dried them with a paper towel. "I'll help any way I can. Have you gotten on the Net?"

"Not yet. But I think that's worth trying. Nick said he's listed with all the adoption-reunion services he knows about—but not that one. How do you get on?"

"I'll help. There's a bulletin board where you leave messages." She squinted suddenly, as though at a recollection, then shook her head.

"What?"

"Nothing. I don't even want to say it. Because I know what it's like to get your hopes up and be disappointed."

"What?"

"I think there was a message for a Nick a few months ago. Oh, come on, Day. It's a common name."

"Well, let me talk to him tonight and see what kind of message he wants to leave. Then maybe you can help me?"

"Sure."

"Thank you, Susan." Day hugged her.

"Hey, don't muss my Mohawk. He was what you were crying about on Christmas, wasn't he?"

Pride kept Day silent.

"A little bird told me you two were moving in together."

"Grace is not a little bird, she's a parrot."

Susan said, "I'm really pleased, Day. I love you both. I hope it lasts."

A heaviness clasped Day's heart. Nick's relationships had an average duration of six months.

New Mexico

"SHIT," SAID JOHN FRAZIER, handing the double mug to Theresa, the artist, for her to draw. "I hate these guys. He thinks he's an archaeologist."

Rory studied the note, the drawn map. "He's repentant," she pointed out. "He's sorry. See? He said so."

The others gave her a look of disgust.

Theresa studied the mug, then made a face at the drawings of the other artifacts he'd taken.

"He's not much of an artist, either," grumbled John. "Cretin."

Rory was ashamed of the conversation. Their pot hunter had felt enough pain for what he'd done to return an object he'd stolen four years earlier and to try to detail everything else he'd taken.

But he *was* ignorant, focused exclusively on artifacts. If he'd seen anything else, he hadn't found it noteworthy. There was no bringing back the history he'd destroyed.

And his note was no help at all.

CHAPTER THIRTEEN

NICK RETURNED the coyote effigy to the burial cave without encountering the Navajo tribal police or anyone else and arrived back in Salt Lake late Sunday night. Free of the artifacts—all but the pot he'd broken and the basket he would return on the San Juan trip—he told himself that nothing stood between him and Day now. Until he found the note his roommate Jack had left on his door. *Day called.*

She knew he'd gone somewhere. Imagining what she must be thinking, Nick picked up the phone and called her.

"Hi," she said. "I saw your truck in town Friday night."

No condemnation in her voice. Just resignation and curiosity.

"I went backpacking. Down south."

"Why didn't you tell me?"

Nick couldn't answer right away.

On the other end of the phone Day felt his hesitation. "Did you go with someone else?"

"No."

His answer was a breath, a flat denial. But his discomposure was evident.

Nick clutched the receiver, knowing he should lie. Say something about needing to be alone, by himself.

He couldn't lie to Day. All he could do was stand there, holding the phone.

She said nothing, and finally he told her, "I'm through with school Friday. I'll be home for good. I thought I'd bring Bob to spend the night. In your guest room?"

"Our guest room?"

He felt such relief he could have cried. She wasn't going to question him. She had accepted his unexplained trip. "Our guest room," he said. "Is it okay?"

"Sure, if you don't mind sharing the house with a couple of dogs. I promised I'd take Coupon and Ninochka. Zac's modeling in L.A., and Grace is going with him. They're going to some movie premiere."

Nick remembered *Kah-Puh-Rats*, the movie Zac had been filming when he became psychotic in Cataract Canyon. It was out on video now, but one viewing had been enough for all of them. No one liked to remember when Zac was sick.

"Bob will like seeing the dogs," Nick agreed. "And I'll like seeing you. I love you."

"I love you, too, Nick." In Moab Day felt her own relief. He hadn't been escaping her; he'd just needed some space. Maybe if they ever found his sister, he would need less.

WHEN HE DROVE into the Rapid Riggers lot on Friday, it was four o'clock, and the sun was sinking, coloring the river and Carl Orson's Santa Fe-style building on the opposite bank. A circus of flags and banners waved from beams in the adobe, and Carl's row of orange-and-blue rafts was impossible to ignore. Even Bob found his voice to say, "Oh, my God. When did that happen?"

The spontaneous response made Nick laugh. But looking around Rapid Riggers made him frown. The four new rafts and those he'd painted that winter sat on trailers in the yard, but the row of Suburbans had a used and abused look, and the whole outfit appeared vaguely untidy.

"While you were sleeping," said Nick. "Want to get out or go right over to the house?"

Before Bob could answer, the Porsche turned into the lot.

"I'll get out." Bob's legs had recovered from the accident. His primary difficulty with walking was balance, and the solution was practice and concentration.

Nick walked around the hood to stand near his friend, but his eyes smiled at Day, emerging from the Porsche. She was brighter than the other colors of spring in a yellow stretch-knit dress and black-patent leather boots.

As the dogs tumbled after her, Nick said, "Hi, Ninochka. Hi, Coupon, you little stinkpot." When Day came over, he hugged her. "I love you."

She clung to him, kissed his mouth, a lipstick kiss, then turned to Bob and embraced him. "Hi, you. I'm glad you're here. Susan's on a four-wheel-drive trip, but she's coming over for dinner."

"Good," Bob said.

Coupon wriggled around his sneakers, and Bob carefully bent down and picked him up. As he straightened, he grabbed Nick's arm, catching his balance.

Nick smiled encouragingly, and he and Day both watched Coupon kiss Bob's face. Day didn't think Coupon was the ugliest dog in the world anymore. Zachary had damned good taste, and so did his dogs.

She told Bob and Nick, "You should see the River Inn. It's about ready for the grand opening."

"Wish *we* were." Nick grimaced at the river outfit and caught Day's eye.

They needed to talk. If he was in for the long haul with her, the same was true with Rapid Riggers. And they'd done things her way long enough.

SUSAN BROUGHT VEGETABLES from her garden for dinner, and together she and Day and Nick made spring rolls and a vegetable stir-fry. The four of them ate on Day's back patio, and it was decided that Susan would drive Bob to Grand Junction the next day. She visited with them till ten, when Bob said he was tired and had a headache and went to bed.

Nick locked up the house and joined Day in the bedroom, and they moved together in the dark, desire heightened by their recent separation. As they kissed, Day felt all the tender magic she'd always known with Nick. Commitment carried it further. They couldn't prevent the bed's rhythmic rocking, but Day pressed her mouth to his shoulder, muffling the cries she wanted to make. His hands held her through the emotion and physical release of orgasm, and Day had never felt more certain of his love.

His friend sleeping in the next room reassured her that Nick was done running. That he had grown into a man who would stay.

Afterward, fitting her tightly against him, cradling her with his whole body, he said, "Day, we need new vehicles."

It was the last thing she'd expected him to say. She realized they'd never really reached an agreement about new equipment—just a temporary compromise. Nick was back now, and his ideas about how to run the outfit hadn't changed.

"Nick, it's such a risk," she said at last. They already had one loan out. "Payments on the kind of money you're talking about could put us under."

That wasn't going to happen. "Is that all?" he asked. He held her close.

Day knew what he was saying.

They had each other.

Giving up, she said, "Oh, get your frigging loan."

"I thought you'd see it my way."

Day wriggled out of his arms. "I almost forgot. I have something for you." Naked, she went to her chest of drawers. Returning to the bed, she switched on the bedside lamp and handed him the gift-wrapped box.

It looked like a clothing box, and there was a bulging envelope taped on top. He opened it. After the word "Congratulations!" she had stuck a Life Saver candy. Nick kissed her. He hadn't thought his becoming certified as a paramedic mattered to anyone but him.

Smiling, he unwrapped the box and opened it.

She'd made him some paramedic pants, with pockets for all his supplies.

BOB LEFT THE NEXT DAY at noon, and on Monday Nick began teaching the annual Moab classes in advanced first aid and wilderness medicine and CPR. They were attended by guides throughout the canyonlands, and even Grace and Zac signed up. They would be using the Rapid Riggers river permits to guide canoe trips from the inn. Day needed to renew her certifications in order to drive passengers to the put-in.

Nick and Day rode bicycles to the community center, which was on a ridge overlooking town. But as soon as they entered the room where the class would be taught, they separated, so that he could prepare to teach and meet with the other instructor. When Zac and Grace and Fast Susan came in, Day sat with them in the back row, drinking the bad coffee provided and listening to other guides and outfitters exchange stories.

Nick opened the class. "Welcome to advanced first aid and wilderness medicine. I'm Nick Colter of Rapid Riggers River and Jeep Expeditions. I'm a paramedic. This is Lorraine Gates of River Legends. We'll be instructing this class. Please sign the sheet that's going around the room, so we'll know you're here."

He explained that most first-aid classes were designed for urban environments where hospitals were minutes away.

"In the wilderness, you can find yourself with an emergency situation when you're *days* from help. So in this class we teach what we call second aid, which helps you care for injured people until they can reach the definitive care of a medical team."

That morning they reviewed the ABCs of rescue. Airway, Breathing and Circulation. Day had taken the course many times before, so the concepts were familiar, but she paid keen attention. One horrible day in Cataract Canyon had forever affected the way she viewed first aid and CPR.

At noon when they broke for lunch, Nick got away from the questioning students to eat with her. They'd packed their lunches together that morning, and they ate them outside in a covered pavilion above the Moab Valley. Nick was wearing his sunglasses, with a cotton keeper strap attached.

The sight transfixed Day. She forced herself to think of other things and eventually remembered her talk with Susan. She told Nick how Susan had said he could post a message for Kelly on the Internet. "It can say anything. You probably want to do something straightforward like 'Kelly, I'm looking for you.' You could have a question, too. Something no one else could answer."

Nick frowned over the sandwich he was eating. Setting it down, he reached for Day's notebook and pen, which she was using to take first-aid notes. He wrote, "Kelly—I am looking for you. What is the name of the—"

He stopped. What if the Internet turned up nothing, too? He'd been through this before, trying to find her. The disappointment was intense, affected him for weeks. He put down the pen. "Let's not do this."

"Nick." Day looked away from the strap holding his sunglasses.

"She's not going to be on the Internet."

As he resumed eating, she read what he'd written. "What's the name of the *what?* Come on, Nick. Let's just try."

He drank some more water. "The mouse."

Day tipped her head sideways, interested. "What mouse?"

"I made up stories about him. He was a thief and a chief. He took care of the other mice." If Kelly was alive and if she could remember anything about their childhood, she would remember the name of that mouse.

He gazed down at the streets of Moab. "We never ate the mice."

Day closed her eyes. She had to find that woman. For Nick. And for Kelly, wherever she was.

WHEN THE WEEK of first-aid and CPR classes was over, Bob came to Moab for another overnight visit, and this time Susan suggested that the two of them stay upstairs at the Rapid Riggers office. It seemed to work well, and on Sunday, Nick asked Bob to help him with some simple work on the back porch. Untangling old lines, checking to see if they were frayed.

Having his friend there working gave Nick more peace than he'd known since the accident, and he was eager for Bob to leave the rehab center and come back to Rapid Riggers. It looked like that could happen soon. Susan and Bob both said they'd been very comfortable upstairs.

To give Bob a sense of his value to the outfit, Nick talked to him about the new vehicles and rental mountain bikes he wanted to buy. Bob surprised him by saying, "You should wait till July to, you know, go to the bank. Then, you have...money."

Nick caught his drift. In July the outfit would appear fiscally robust. It sounded like wisdom, and he met Bob's eyes and said, "Yeah, I think you're right. Thanks."

Susan drove Bob back to Grand Junction that afternoon, and when she returned, it was with the news that he could move home the following weekend. She and Day and Nick talked about it in the reception room while Leah and Joe reorganized the kitchen for the upcoming season.

Nick asked, "Are you really going to be okay, Susan?"

"No problem."

"Upstairs is okay?"

"We love it. I'm going to make curtains this week."

"I see." Nick smothered a grin. "None of us asked *how* was last night."

Susan patted his cheek affectionately. "You have a dirty one-track mind. And it's a good mind, too."

They embraced. "It was really great to have him back today, huh?"

Susan said, "It was the best."

NICK AND DAY rode their bikes to work the following morning, and as he unlocked the office door, Nick told her, "I need a swamper for that Cataract Canyon trip. I'm not sure who to ask."

A swamper helped with unloading gear from the raft, setting up the Groover—the toilet—washing dishes, et cetera.

"Can't Zac do that?"

He wheeled his bicycle inside, and she rolled hers after it. As they leaned them against opposite walls and removed their helmets, Nick said, "Another pair of hands would be good." He didn't want to come out and say Zac's mental health worried him. The first time he'd mentioned it had been enough.

Day wished he trusted Zachary more—in many ways—but it couldn't be helped. She stepped behind the counter to consult the schedule. "Susan's running Westwater that week, and Joe has a Needles trip."

"What about Leah? I can let her row some, see how she does in Cataract before we give her any passengers of her own."

Day's heart clenched. Not Leah. She wasn't ready for that. To hide her insecurity, she went into the kitchen and began making coffee.

Nothing in the way Nick had spoken should make her afraid. He wouldn't sleep with another woman. *But why didn't he ask me?* Maybe because she was needed in the office.

Or because it was Cataract.

Day abandoned the coffee and returned to the reception counter, where Nick was flipping through the logbook. "Nick, why don't you take me?"

THE SAN JUAN came first.

They left early Wednesday morning. The put-in was just three hours from Moab. They drove there in Nick's truck and were rigging the raft by nine. By ten, they had the boat in the water, after watching three others launch.

Day didn't even seem to notice the extra ammo can Nick tied into the raft, the can that contained a 1500-year-old basket, the last artifact in his possession. Nick had known she wouldn't. She had other things on her mind. The river.

Trying to rid herself of just that worry, Day coated herself with sunscreen, picked up *Tales from the Thousand and One Nights,* which she was reading, and settled into the raft. The water raced by, carrying the new spring snowmelt from the San Juan Mountains. They wouldn't see white water until tomorrow, and the most difficult rapids on the river were only class II, but already her stomach was swimming. She'd skipped breakfast.

As Nick shoved them away from the shore and stepped over gear on the way to his seat, Day studied the mud banks, the low slickrock that would grow to towering sandstone cliffs. "I love it down here. Moab's getting so crowded. But here there's nothing."

Nick fitted the oars in the oarlocks. "True."

The edge in his voice reminded her that he'd lived down in this area before he'd come to Moab. "Nick, where was that shack?"

The shack? The rhythm of the oars possessed him. It was a rhythm that had saved him, a rhythm Sam Sutter had taught him. "Outside Covenant. Why?"

"Maybe it would help you to see it now."

Nick had never thought to go back. He wasn't sure the shack was even standing—or how he'd feel about seeing it if it was. "I don't know if I could find it."

The subject burned away in the peace of the morning, under the sun evaporating water droplets from the raft. Spotting a beaver paddling on the far side of the river, Nick nudged Day and pointed.

She laid aside her book to watch the coffee-and-cream water and the banks passing like a slow movie, to follow Nick's sun-browned arms as he rowed by the green cottonwoods on Sand Island.

"This was the first river my dad ever took me on," she said. "I was about six. I loved it. We had a big mud fight. Him and Grace and me."

Nick knew what those family trips were like. In high school Sam had brought him along and never stopped him from climbing as high as he wanted on the cliffs along the river corridors. From the Colorado, they'd hiked up Horse and Jasper canyons. Day had groaned under her pack, and she and Grace had sunbathed on the rocks while he and their father explored.

"Do you remember the first time I kissed you?" he asked.

"Yes." It had been in the Doll's House above Spanish Bottom. Day had been sixteen and had wanted to stay down on the river beach, but her father had insisted she hike to the rim. At the top she'd found an isolated rock and collapsed in the shade until Nick found her.

"It was the first time anyone kissed me with his tongue. Remember when my dad found us?"

"He didn't buy the line about you having something in your eye."

They both laughed. For the most part, Sam had always let them be, as though he'd known he couldn't keep them apart if he tried. But as the years passed, he'd said how he felt about Nick's treatment of his daughter.

One remark, the last thing he'd said on the subject before his death, would stay with Nick forever.

Aware of the memory, living with it, Nick shipped the oars and crawled back in the raft to lie beside her against the dry bags and let the river carry them. Taking off Day's sunglasses and setting them aside, he kissed her beneath her Rapid Riggers hat. Then he unfastened her life vest and unbuttoned her blouse. "Remember the first time I did this?"

"Yes." Beneath her hat brim, she watched his fingers, his brown hands.

In his mind Nick saw the basket in the ammo can. By nightfall it would be gone, and he would be free.

He slid his hand into her blouse, cupped her breast over her bikini top. Her tremulous response excited him. In love with her, he asked, "Will you marry me, Day?"

The disbelief in her eyes turned rapidly to joy. She nodded and pressed her head against his throat. Yet even as he held her and knew that he was the luckiest man alive, Nick thought of the basket.

Day had forgiven him ten years of indecision. Of callousness. Of confusion. Of other women.

But pot hunting was a felony. And he wasn't sure she would forgive that.

"DID YOU GET a permit?"

"I knew you'd ask that."

Day continued to eye him suspiciously. Nick's moral development did not always extend to getting the right permits, and he'd just eddied out on the Navajo-reservation side of the river.

He grinned. "So the way I see it is that I rowed, so you should pitch the tent and set up the Groover."

"All right." Uncomplaining, she loosened the knots on the webbing that secured the dry bags.

While she set up their outdoor bathroom behind some tamarisk, Nick carefully moved the basket from the ammo can to his day pack. The pit house where he'd found it was a half hour away, a climb up a nontrail on the side of the canyon.

When Day emerged from the brush, Nick said, "I want to go up to a ruin I remember. I think it would be a hard climb for you."

Day trusted his judgment on that. "I'll stay here and read."

"I'll be back in, say, an hour and a half."

"Have fun."

Up on the mesa top, a half hour later, he found the pit house.

The sight shouldn't have shocked him. It was just as he'd left it.

Gutted.

Nauseated, he remembered how he'd found it, when the floor was smooth, when the sand had covered all but the rim of that single basket. There had been others, too, and an ancient twig figure, which he'd kept for a time, then sold for four thousand dollars.

Now there was a gaping hole in the floor.

He remembered the tents in New Mexico. *They're doing the same thing.* To excavate a site, whether haphazardly or methodically, was to destroy it. Even archaeologists admitted that.

Nick wished he'd left this ruin as it was. He wished he could be discovering it for the first time now, with maturity, and that he could go down to Day and bring her back here. They would touch nothing.

As the sun turned the slickrock and sand into mounds of copper and gold, he put the basket in the earth and carefully buried it, and used his boots to scrape the dirt back into the hole.

He had expected the act to make him feel free. But as he left the pit house and began walking back toward the canyon where he'd left Day, he knew he would never be free of what he'd done.

And maybe that was as it should be.

"WHAT'S WRONG?" she asked him in the tent that night.

Nick shrugged in the dark. His conscience had never manifested itself in his body before. But tonight he couldn't make love. "I don't know. Nervous about getting married." It was close to the truth. He hugged her naked body. "Just lie close to me for a while."

She did.

Outside, frogs sang in the tamarisk and the river whispered as it slid by.

After a minute he asked her, "How do you want to get married?"

Day gave herself the advice she would offer any woman given the chance to make an honest man of Nick Colter. "Soon. Like at the courthouse on the way home."

She was transparent and candid. He loved her for that. And for loving him so much.

"Truly?"

She nodded.

His body responded to her love. "Okay." He pressed against her. "I think I can do this now."

"I'm noticing." She moved up onto her knees.

"I can definitely do this."

When she felt the muscles of his thighs behind hers, it excited her more. Feeling that excitement, Nick did all he could to take her higher. He kept his mind blank of all but her, until he came inside her. Then, however, the guilt assaulted him, and he knew why he didn't feel free.

The mug and the basket and the fetish were gone.

But other artifacts had been sold.

And the life he was bringing to Day had been bought on those gains.

THE NEXT MORNING, Day met her first rapid of the trip.

"Doing okay?" he asked as the sound of the white water grew louder.

"Sure." Just a little rapid. Class I +.

"This one's nothing. Four-Foot Rapid."

Nick rowed into the white water, and Day hung on. The bouncing of the boat and the spray of the water made her stomach feel as it had when she'd rappelled. Then, suddenly, it was over. It had only been a riffle.

Nick shipped the oars and climbed to the back of the raft where she sat. "You know what I think?"

"What?" She tried to look as if going through the riffle had cured her fears.

"I think you should row."

Day knew he was right.

She rowed Eight-Foot Rapid and the Upper Narrows, and the feel of the oars was something she remembered from long before. She had liked rowing once. Now, guiding the raft in the current gave her a sense of power, of competence, of all she could do. She'd been born beside a river, descended from river people. She was Sam Sutter's daughter.

And Nick's kind of woman.

There on the San Juan, she was her own kind of woman, too. Day liked that very much.

As they left the Upper Narrows, her limbs and posture felt strong, straight energized. Resting on the oars, she gazed downstream toward Ledge Rapid. "Do you want to row?"

She was watching the white water, her fingers still wrapped around the oar handles. Pleased with what he saw, Nick lay back on the dry bags and made the ultimate sacrifice. Yawning, he said, "And you thought I was just taking a little break."

AS THEY DERIGGED that night, he said, "Maybe we'll have you on the Selway yet."

Her stomach flipflopped, but she replied, "Who knows?" Fear returned. Cataract. She'd played in Class II white water today. That was nothing.

"Day?"

How could he pick up on things so easily?

"Just leave that stuff. Sit down with me." They lay together on the sand, and he cradled her against his chest. "What gets to you most about that accident?"

"The screaming." She told him something she'd never said. "He was wearing his glasses held on with that kind of keeper strap, like you wear. They were twisted sideways on his face, and he couldn't move them, though his hands were free. I never knew why. Whenever I see those keeper straps, it all comes back."

Nick knew about things like that. Whenever he saw his guide shell with the hood inside out, it reminded him of the mountain biker's body beneath the Portal Trail. He saw everything all over again.

"You don't *have* to go, Day."

It surprised her that she didn't see Leah and Shep in her mind.

She didn't even see her father.

Just herself.

"I think I do."

TWO NIGHTS LATER they camped at the take-out, and in the morning they loaded the truck. Tying the boat into the back, Nick said, "Want to get married?"

Day was trying to hoist the cooler into the truck bed. "Today?"

"Don't try to lift that. I'll get it. Yes, today. Want to?"

"Yes!"

"We don't have rings. What do you think? Trading post?"

"You are so cheap." They'd buy silver Hopi wedding bands. Day loved the idea. "Yes, trading post."

It was early, but there was a trading post near Lake Powell, and they stopped there and found matching silver bands with the signs for water and for thunder and lightning etched on them.

"Give us a minute," Nick told the man behind the counter and drew her away.

"We could go to Salt Lake, Day. Get you a diamond. I'll buy anything for you. Tell me what you want."

"You. And Hopi wedding bands." Her charm bracelet was silver, too. And the Aquitaine he'd given her for her birthday. No other jewelry mattered.

Nick went back to the counter and bought their wedding bands for forty dollars.

"IF ANYONE HAD ever told me I was going to get married in Blanding, Utah..." Nick muttered as they approached the courthouse in the dry desert heat.

"Or that you were going to get married at all."

They paused outside the brick building, and her blue eyes asked if he was sure. All around him was the edgy feeling that came from the town, this part of southeastern Utah, this land where cattle and mining and old values were king, where a man could dig up pots because the government was his, and government land was his, too. Where people dis-

ciplined their children without interference. *Do as you see
fit.*

In slow small steps he was rising above his childhood. By
some miracle he'd found a friend who loved him, who had
been willing to wait for him to make that climb. He embraced her. "How many of my babies do you want to
have?"

"Six?"

The clerk who issued their license was young and pretty.
"Just get off the river?"

"Yes."

"I saw your boat in your truck bed." She notarized the
document and handed it to Nick.

He said, "We need someone to marry us now."

"Let me see who I can dig up."

She found the mayor. Beaming at the prospect of fulfill-
ing such a happy function, he collected the clerk and a
court reporter as witnesses. In his dry little office that
smelled of Utah dust, the mayor said, "Do you, Day, take
Nicholas to be your lawfully wedded husband, to have and
to hold from this day forward...?"

"I do."

"Do you Nicholas...?"

"I do."

They exchanged rings, and Day watched his hand slide
hers on her finger and knew she would never take it off. She
put the other ring on his hand and silently bound him to be
faithful, to be hers forever.

"By the power invested in me by the state of Utah, I
pronounce you husband and wife. You may kiss the bride."

Nick did, then thanked the mayor and gave him a ten-
dollar bill for officiating. After signing another document, they left, and when they were outside the courthouse and down the steps, he and Day grabbed each other.
In her dusty wraparound cotton miniskirt, she jumped up
on him and wrapped her legs around his waist and her arms

around his neck, and he carried her to the truck and held
her against it and took her mouth, amazed that she was his
wife.

And he her husband.

The courthouse window opened, and the clerk and the
court reporter whistled enthusiastically and blew on a toy
horn.

NICK DIDN'T HEAD straight home.

Without explaining, he turned toward Covenant on the
small eastward highway, and he watched the dirt roads, the
ranch roads, the roads to nowhere.

Day knew he wasn't going back to Moab. She knew
where he was going, and she said nothing, but moved over
on the bench seat and buckled herself in beside him. She
studied the desert outside and felt his bare leg against hers
and gazed down at her ring. They were married. She was
married to Nick Colter and wanted to sing in triumph.

Rolling lines of sagebrush and slickrock outcroppings,
humps of pinkish-brown sandstone, poked up from the
desert, giving texture to the land. The country was familiar to Nick. His chest tight, as though someone larger than
him had twisted one arm behind his back, he kept a vigi-
lant eye out for landmarks, not even certain what he
sought.

Then, out of the mix of red sand and light green sage,
rose a rock that was all black on one side, covered with a
patina of desert varnish. There was a picture cut in it, a
petroglyph, and the petroglyph had been blasted away with
a rifle.

Awareness took hold. A mile beyond that place a double track led away through deep sand. Nick's father had
made him lay boards and rocks on that road for their truck.
He was scared, anxious, but he switched on the signal and
spun off the highway onto the track, and the landscape
spoke to him through the opaque memory of childhood. It

was like a river where your foot disappeared when you dipped it in. But he knew the rocks.

He had hidden among them. *Nick! You'll be sorrier if I have to find you!*

He had always been found and dragged, screaming . . . That was how his arm had been broken. When his father took him to the doctor two weeks later, after the other cuts and bruises had healed, they'd had to break his arm again.

There was sweat on his upper lip. Day saw the set of his jaw, the strange expression in his eyes as he guided the truck over the sandy ruts. The road was getting worse. Anyone would turn around. Except Nick, today.

"We don't want to get stuck."

"You can say that again." He steered around a miniature gorge in the road.

Dust had settled all over the windshield, like the dust on his father's truck. The air was dry and ovenlike, though this was only April. He remembered July. Sweating, sticking to the seat, butt sore.

Day watched the odometer. *We're going to get stuck. I know it.*

She knew better than to ask him to stop. He had committed himself now. Yet the way he looked—angry and scared—dug a pit of misgiving inside her.

What he'd been through was hideous. Facing where it had happened could put him in a mental hospital.

Too late to say that maybe this wasn't a good idea, after all.

"Do you want me to drive?" she asked.

"No."

"Is it far?"

"I don't know."

They had come miles already on this nowhere road. If they had a flat . . .

"Be careful, okay?" They still had two full five-gallon water jugs. They even had a can of gasoline. But she hadn't brought real hiking shoes, just high-top sneakers for the river.

He didn't answer.

The miles rolled on. It was approaching three o'clock, the spring sunshine slanting down on the desert. The land was desolate, dry and dusty, but in the distance Day could see the mixture of pines and red rock and rising land that meant forest.

Nick glowered at the road, driving too fast. The truck bounced, and Day would have hit her head on the roof if not for her seat belt. The cab was like an oven, but whenever she opened the windows dust plumed in.

They were miles from anywhere.

No wonder he was allowed to be treated like that. No one knew he existed.

Even now, rumor said, polygamists excommunicated by the Mormons hid out among these sandstone monoliths, blending into the landscape that gave freedom.

The road petered out in a parched setting that reminded Day of the ghost town of Cisco on the way to Grand Junction from Moab. But there were just two buildings here, both uranium-era, both falling apart.

A wooden door banged open on the larger of the two, a one-room shack.

Nick braked hard in the sand, a scream building inside him.

He wanted to make himself small, to hide under the steering wheel of the truck....

He had done that. He had hidden there.

No one inside, Nick. You're big now.

Zachary had gone mad in Cataract Canyon. What if this made him insane?

He barely noticed Day beside him, slender and fair and still. He forgot her. He opened the door and got out, and the heat scorched him. They had sweated beneath the house. He'd had fevers there. Infected sores.

We should have died.

In the dust lay the curved shape of a rotted ax handle, and he picked it up. Beside it, a scorpion raised its tail. Hearing the truck door slam, Nick glanced behind him, but it was just Day. He forgot her again.

There was still glass in one of the windowpanes, and when he reached the building, he swung the ax handle against the glass with all his might. The window broke, and so did the ax handle, and he remembered how much strength there was in a grown man's arm. He searched until he found a talus-size boulder with a centipede crawling on it. He hurled it against the shack, denting the wall. He kicked the swinging door and went inside.

Nothing there but a broken table that looked like it had been stolen from a hotel a long time before.

But there was still a trap in the floor. The cover was gone now, and he could smell everything. It smelled the same. It reeked.

A shadow blocked the light from the door and he jumped.

"It's just me."

She looked scared, reminding him of Kelly. Kelly, with her funny face and funny voice.

His throat choked, Nick pushed past her. Outside, he found a four-by-four post, two feet long, and knocked the black ants off it. Circling the shack revealed another whole windowpane, and Nick slammed the post through it, breaking the wood surrounding the glass.

Day backed away from the door of the cabin and sat on the front bumper of his truck. She wrapped her arms around herself and watched him throw his strength at the building, his hair flying wild, his face contorted.

Why did I suggest we come here?

But it had to be a good thing, because such pain had to have reason.

He went inside the shell of a building, and she heard him hitting the walls with that four-by-four. She heard him scream and stood up, poised to do something. She didn't know what.

Ants crawled on her legs, and she brushed them away.

The four-by-four smashed against the door, and a man's cry of rage flew out into the desert, into the empty space.

Day clutched herself, imagining a child screaming with no one to help. Who would hear? This had become surreal. It was their wedding day, and he'd come here. She did not want to imagine what was in his mind.

But finally the sounds from the shelter changed, softened, went away.

She crossed the white salt-covered mud toward the door he'd broken. "Nick. It's Day. Don't throw anything at me."

He sat against the wall, his face dirty and tear-streaked, his head in his arms. When she came in, he sprang up and pulled her toward a square gap in the floorboards. "Smell that? Ever tried to sleep in an outhouse? We should have died."

The floor beneath the hole was dirt, and any smell was faint. But to Nick it must be strong.

He snatched up the four-by-four again, banged it dully against the door. "I remember more things. I remember things. I shouldn't have come here."

"I'm sorry."

Outside, he threw the post as far as he could. Then he saw his truck and he went to it, climbed into the back. There had to be something, something he could use.

Emerging from the shack, Day stared at the other structure, a smaller stone shed with no door. Nick had told her things about that building. She was glad it seemed to have escaped his attention so far.

He jumped out of the truck bed, then reached inside and pulled out the spare gas can.

"Nick." She hurried toward him, to head him off as he walked toward the shack. "You could start a brushfire."

"It's April. And I don't care if I burn down the whole state of Utah."

"I'm going to take the truck. I'm going to go get the fire people. Don't do this."

"There's sand everywhere. Nothing to burn."

"Sparks. Sagebrush."

"It rained last week."

"It won't make it better, Nick."

"That's what you think." He walked by her, and she watched him douse the walls of the building with gasoline.

Day shuddered.

The water in the truck. Should they wet the ground? Which way was the wind blowing?

Flame lit up the wall.

Nick stepped back, then walked purposefully back to the truck. In a moment he passed her again, carrying one of the five-gallon water jugs. His black hair hung loose and tangled around his face, and his T-shirt was stuck to his body with sweat.

Day sat on the bumper of the truck, and the heat from the blaze reached her even there. Within ten minutes, the building burned and fell in on itself, and soon only the tin roof lay black and smoldering on the ground.

No sirens came.

Nick poured water on the hot ashes, which sizzled and sparked at him, and then, leaving the heat, the remains of the blaze, he regarded the small stone shed.

There was no sledgehammer among the tools in his truck, no way he could take down this place. He crept toward it, toward the vacant hole of the door. Crumbling brick. It was brick, and he saw a gaping hole in the brick that he remembered.

Tears fell out of his eyes, but he didn't notice them. He went back to his truck and got in. Vaguely he noticed that

Day had found one of his shovels and was shoveling sand onto the hot coals, wiping sweat from her bright red face.

But when he started the engine, she paused in her shoveling and watched.

As he drove slowly and deliberately toward the brick building, Day reflected that flames from the shack had shot twenty feet in the air, and no one had come.

The wall of the little stone building caved, and through the windshield Nick saw the color of the wall inside. He backed up his truck, and he ran it against another wall, knowing he was wrecking the chrome bumper and that the blue paint was being scraped and the hood dented by the falling bricks.

He didn't care.

When all that was left were low broken walls and broken wood from the workbench inside, when all was turned to rubble, he switched off the ignition and got out of the truck. Walking toward the ruin he'd made, he found another ax handle on the ground. He flung it toward the smoldering ashes, and then he went to Day.

His face was smoke-grayed, his eyes red, his clothes filthy.

"You're right," he said. "It doesn't help."

CHAPTER FOURTEEN

THEY STAYED LATE at the place, until the last embers were extinguished, then drove all night to reach Moab. Day was asleep beside him, and Nick avoided the house where they lived together and took her to his trailer, instead.

His eyes were wide awake, alert with memory. He hadn't stopped thinking, hadn't been able to slow his heart, since he'd set eyes on the shack. The walls he'd burned still lived in his mind, and though the trapdoor was gone, he still knew what the underside looked like, how no light came from around the edges or from anywhere. He had knocked down the walls of the stone building, the springhouse with no spring, but he still felt what had been done to him there. He felt too dirty, too foul inside, to go to Day's house. But he wanted her with him.

At the old Dewey Bridge, he steered the truck down the sand road. Day's head was on his shoulder, and he swayed with the bumps, so that she wouldn't fall away from him.

He parked under the cottonwoods. "Day."

Stirring, she pressed her face to his neck, even though he could smell how he stank. It was how fear smelled.

When she opened her eyes and saw where they were, he said, "I'll turn on the hot-water heater. If you want to sleep more, you can get in my bed."

Day blinked at the trailer, looking confused. She was his wife, but Nick felt as though he'd abducted her. What else would bring his bride here? She'd come only once before, to drop something off. But Nick had loved it, as he'd loved her visiting his caves.

He explained nothing. She was his. That was enough.

Inside the trailer, he stood on the ladder of the loft to check that the sheets were clean, that everything was okay. He pulled back the sheets for her, then stepped down to the floor and let her climb up. She moved wearily, and he followed her, to tuck the sheets around her.

"I'm so dirty," she said. She smelled like the fire, too.

"You'll be clean again."

Day turned her cheek against the pillow and curled up in a ball, chilled. He kissed her, and then she felt him slipping away, going down the ladder. The sound of him lighting the pilot on the hot-water heater was reassuring. The sound of the door shutting behind him as he went outside was not.

In a moment she heard water running and remembered that he had built an outdoor shower stall for the trailer. Nick would love a Craftsman home, she thought. It wouldn't be bad to build one here, in this wild land by the river. Day sat up and peered through the long flat window and saw him take off his clothes outside the wooden stall. Cold water wouldn't stop him. He seemed less vulnerable here than he had beside that shack, smashing things, out of control.

As the sound of splattering water made a hailstorm outside, she lay down, telling herself things would be normal soon.

The trailer was cool. It was spring, and Nick hadn't bothered to light the wood stove, but without it the sheet and single blanket on the bed weren't enough covering. Day knew she couldn't sleep unless she was warmer.

It was almost dawn, growing light, when she climbed down from the bunk and opened the nearest door. Towels, sheets. No blankets. As the shower outside went off, she ducked beneath the loft to open other cabinets. One held a drill, hammer, tools. Another had shelves, and she crouched to peer back in them for a blanket.

The door opened behind her, and cold air rushed in.

"Nick, do you have any more blankets?"

She started to close the cabinet, then opened the door again, to squint at an object on the bottom shelf.

Pausing beside the towel closet—he'd forgotten a towel—Nick watched her remove the broken bowl from the cabinet.

"What's this?"

"Mesa Verde black-on-white."

"Where did you find it?" She glanced up innocently. "Is there a ruin here?"

On his land. The perfect explanation.

"No."

Day quivered strangely. Why was he so silent? Her eyes floated up his naked body, glistening wet.

He grabbed a towel and came under the loft.

Day touched the sherds.

Here was the cart, Nick saw. *Get in the cart if you want to see the queen.*

If you want the queen.

"I . . ." The words stuck. How could he say it? Any combination of phrases would be equally repulsive to her. He didn't want to pretend that it had only happened once or twice.

He wanted her to know everything.

"I stole it. From BLM land. Three years ago."

"Nick."

He heard the reproach, the disillusionment in her voice.

"I've done a lot of that."

Day's heart folded on itself. What was he saying? "What—like finding things hiking? Taking them? You're not supposed to do that. It's a felony."

"No, Day." *Look at me. Believe your ears.* "I was a pot hunter. I've made a lot of money that way. I've stopped."

I was a pot hunter. Briefly the world changed. She hadn't always known him; he was someone she'd just met, and he was telling her about his unsavory past, something long ago. Then reality overlapped.

He had been a pot hunter. *When?* "What do you mean, a lot of money?" She bit her lip, feeling her face coming apart. "That's gross. You married me and didn't tell me that. What do you mean you've stopped? You mean, like yesterday or something?" Understanding dawned. "Was that what the backpacking trip was about? One last run?"

"I was putting things back."

Day couldn't believe her ears. "What things? Are you telling me you've have stolen pots from public lands and sold them on the black market? How many pieces are we talking about? How many ruins did you loot while you worked as a guide for my father? That's why he left you out of his will, isn't it? I bet he knew!"

"He knew."

She shoved him. Leaping up, she banged her head on the loft and swore. Nick followed her out from under the loft and stood before her, half-wet, a towel around his waist.

This was what she had loved and wanted for ten years. This was what she had pursued, what she had changed herself for. She had made love to him so many times, married him, and now this twisted human being was all hers. He disgusted her. "Did you dig up graves, too?"

"Yes."

"How many ruins, Nick?"

"A hundred. Two hundred. I don't know. You don't count them."

Wasn't he going to deny one single thing?

She gave a loose laugh, on the verge of hysterical. "I've been in love with a career criminal. I *married* a career criminal. What are you, an *idiot?* You can't even sleep with the windows shut. You want to go to jail? You think they'll let you have the windows open, let you sleep outside?"

Nick shrank from her wrath. He was going to the springhouse, dragged there. His father had the ax handle. The scent of the fire filled his nostrils.

"Tell me what my father knew. Tell me what he said to you. Tell me what you've never once told me, and tell me now."

He knew when to obey. He was wild without sleep, and he was afraid. "When I was a kid. I was sixteen. I found a ruin in one of the canyons on the river. You could only get there by boat or by a long hike from the Amasa Back. I had the pots in the cave where I was staying, and he saw them. He told me to put them back. I said I would, but I sold them, instead, and he knew. Because I had money. Later he asked me if I still did it, and he said if he ever caught me he'd turn me in. He said he didn't want to see it."

"But he knew."

"Yes."

Day wasn't surprised. Her father had vacillated between bragging about Nick and disempowering him. Even when Nick was twenty-six years old, their best guide, with perfect knowledge of every piece of equipment in the outfit, her father had questioned his judgment about basic things like which life vests should be retired. "You've said you stopped. When did you stop?"

"In January. When I lost you. People change. I've changed."

"You changed kind of late, Nick. You didn't tell me about this."

"I'm telling you now. I made about two hundred thousand dollars altogether. I bought this land, and then—"

"You bought my sister's half of Rapid Riggers." Day wanted to leave and go home, but she didn't even have a car. She was stuck, here in this trailer, with Nick, and she was stuck for good.

He was her husband now.

DAY SHOWERED outside—he'd dismantled the indoor stall. When she emerged from behind the wood partition, Nick was sitting beside the river. Cold, she hurried inside and helped herself to some of his clothes, a pair of shorts with a drawstring and a T-shirt much too large for her. Feeling like a street urchin, she collapsed on the couch and twisted her wedding ring on her finger. Then she went to see the broken pot again. It couldn't be pieced together because some of the sherds had disintegrated to dust.

While she was still examining it, Nick came back in and sat near her on the floor and began talking.

"I had four things that I kept. When I went down to the Four Corners, backpacking, I returned two of them. There were archaeologists digging at one site, and I left a note and told them everything I could remember."

Day was aghast. Did he think that made up for it?

"I took the other thing back on our trip. It was a basket from a ruin on the San Juan."

The San Juan? "You took me down that river to return an artifact you'd stolen?" Not to help her get over her fear of white water. Not to ask her to marry him. "How romantic!"

Nick's stomach hurt. He got up and went to the sink, to make coffee, to pretend she wasn't ridiculing him.

"You're an outfitter." She emerged from under the loft. "And before that you were a river guide. You're supposed to protect the natural resource, not ravage it."

Cut, hurting too much, he shouted at her. "I've stopped!"

"It doesn't matter! You want to build a house on this land! We can't do that. My God, you have the moral development of a five-year-old."

He wanted to hit her. He had never struck another person in his life, and he wanted to hit Day. He rushed past her and went out of the trailer, slamming the door behind him.

The air was socked out of her. *You went too far, Day.*

She'd said what he deserved to hear. She didn't want to think about how much he'd stolen. "I wish I didn't know." Seeing the pot inside the still-open cabinet, Day tried to remember how she had found out.

His voice spoke again in her mind. *I stole it from BLM land.*

He'd told her.

That was the only reason she knew.

HE SAT BESIDE the river while the sun came up. It had taken him twenty-nine years to become a man; it had taken too long. He'd screwed up the one relationship that mattered most to him. He could start all over now.

But not with Day.

She would tell her sister. Especially because of Sam. But nothing would happen to him. Not imprisonment. Not fines. Nothing could be proved. Even if she turned him in—which Nick couldn't imagine—even if he confessed, they would be lenient. The penalty for repeated looting of ruins was up to five years' imprisonment and $100,000 fine, but stiff sentences were rare. Nick had never feared getting caught. He'd never imagined prison, what Day had said—no windows, can't go outside.

She'd called him an idiot. He felt like one.

With the thumb and fingertips of his right hand, he held his wedding ring where it circled his finger, squeezing the metal, holding on. The breeze rippled the river. He wanted to pump up his boat and go. He would float all the way to Cataract, all the way to Glen Canyon Dam, the way he had when he was fourteen and running from people he couldn't see.

The door of the trailer banged. Day strode toward him and stopped halfway. "I want to go home."

He didn't have the courage to tell her that her home was with him. Or to remind her that his was with her.

AT HER HOUSE, as Day unlocked the side door, he yanked the dry bags from the truck bed. He didn't bring them inside. They were red with mud from the river and needed to be washed off. Instead, he emptied them on the porch and brought the clothes into her laundry room, off the kitchen. Then he returned to the truck and retrieved their marriage certificate and license from the glove box.

Day was in the bedroom when he came back in. She was trying to zip up a black sheath with a Peter Pan collar. Nick did it for her, then sat on the bed they'd never bothered to make the morning they'd left for the San Juan. He watched her open her makeup chest and switch on a light on her dressing table.

Clutching the marriage certificate and marriage license, he said, "So do you want to get a..."

She didn't stop lining her lips. She painted her mouth red, then took black-and-white spectator pumps from her closet.

"Do you want an annulment?"

An unspeakable weight fell on her. "I don't even know you anymore, Nick. I always thought you were an environmentalist."

"It doesn't have anything to do with the environment."

"I disagree. What do you think archaeologists have been trying to learn about the Anasazi? Why they left. What they grew. All kinds of things, many of which *are* environmental. Anyhow, I think those things should be left just as people find them, like trees and rocks and petroglyphs, and... That's what's being practiced now. Conservation archaeology. They don't dig every ruin they know about. They only dig if they believe they can learn something new."

He held the two folded documents. "I asked you a question."

An annulment.

If she said yes, it was over forever between them. Day knew that. But if she said no, would he think it didn't matter?

She opened a drawer in her dresser and found the purse she wanted and transferred the contents from another purse.

"Day?"

"Don't push me."

He stood, clasped her shoulders and made her turn around. "You called me an idiot."

"You did a stupid thing! Two hundred thousand dollars' worth of stupid thing. Leave me alone." She broke away from him and fled the room, and he heard her getting her car keys and the door shutting behind her as she left the house.

SUSAN WAS THERE when she reached the office.

"Hi." Day managed a smile. "Thanks for holding down the fort. Tell me what's happening."

"Booked two Westwater trips and a Cataract trip. I hope the dates work. Mr. Musashi is coming into Grand Junction at three, and Zac's going to pick him up. Now that you're here, if it's all right, I'll leave to go get Bob."

Mr. Musashi. The Japanese gentleman. Day looked at her schedule. Grand opening of the River Inn—tonight. Cataract Canyon—tomorrow. Oh, heavens. Cataract.

And Bob. Bob was coming home today. "Oh, yes," she said. "You can go. Thank you for all you've done."

As she gathered her keys, Susan asked, "How was the river? Ready for the big stuff?"

Day tried to laugh. She was in the big stuff. Over her head in a massive hole.

Dammit, Nick.

When Susan had left, Day got on the computer first thing and went to the Birthright Reunions web site, the way Susan had showed her. Nothing. No response to the message she'd posted on the bulletin board. And no sign of a message like the one Susan had said she'd seen months before, a message for Nick.

Probably someone had answered it. Another Nick.

He had given away his sister.

No wonder he's such a mess.

But his land... Rapid Riggers.

Grace. She had to tell Grace.

Day picked up the phone and dialed the number of the River Inn, then hung up before it rang. Zac and Grace were preparing for the grand opening. She would go there.

THANKFULLY, ZAC HAD GONE for a run.

Sitting with Grace at a table in the Princess Room, while pots simmered and the smells of baking floated out of the restaurant kitchen, Day watched her sister absorb the shock. Everything. Kelly. Their marriage. Pot hunting.

The only thing Day left out was the visit to the shack.

"Where is he?" asked Grace at last.

"I don't know. He didn't seem like he was going to run away. Just like he thought I should accept it now that he's stopped."

Grace readjusted the crocheted tam covering her hair and almost knocked over a tray of filo dough she'd been using to roll miniature spinach pies. "Okay, so, he bought my half of Rapid Riggers with money he got stealing pots."

"Well, he borrowed some of it, but yes, that's the general idea. And he definitely bought his land that way."

Grace sat back. "Well, to be fair, he has made good money at Rapid Riggers. Divide two hundred thousand dollars over ten or fifteen years, and it's sort of like moonlighting. He sure wasn't getting retail for those pots."

"Are you trying to justify him?"

"I'm just pointing out that he's probably made more money from honest sources. He works year-round, always has. Ski patrol in winter, guiding during the river season. He works hard, Day." She winced. "And what you said about his sister... Since he *has* stopped, don't you think you should just forgive him?"

"What about his land? He bought it with that money. Besides, he kept this from me, Grace. He wouldn't have told me if I hadn't found that pot."

"That's not how it sounds to me. If that's true, why didn't he lie to you? He *wanted* to tell you. Look, you knew from the minute you met him that he had problems. For heaven's sake, he couldn't read. So you're surprised? At least it seems like you've hit the bottom of his troubles. Give him a little time."

"He's had a lot of time!"

"Not with you." Grace picked up a piece of filo and dipped a fork into the bowl of filling. "Dad knew, huh? Well, he had those arrowheads. I saw him do an occasional wink-wink nudge-nudge when he said they all came from private land."

Day had never before heard her sister admit that Sam Sutter was less than a holy man. "I can't believe what you're saying. It's like you're saying it's okay. This is a felony. Can you imagine the disgusting people he's dealt with?"

"Like whoever hit him?"

"It's no excuse. Do you know what I've put up with from him?"

Grace's lips tilted slightly as she contemplated her sister. "What?"

"I know what you've put up with. Maybe it's not the pot hunting that's making you mad."

Tears sprang to Day's eyes, and she jerked her head away. What Grace said wasn't true. It wasn't. She hated even the suggestion. Because Grace was intimating that hers wasn't righteous anger over a crime against the common good.

But the bile of jealousy and resentment too long suppressed.

New Mexico

RORY HAD RETURNED to Albuquerque for the weekend, to bring some bones to the lab. When she came home, as soon as she entered her house, she turned on the computer.

She made herself some tea, and while she waited for the water to boil, she checked her e-mail, switched on her printer, ran off notes from friends and colleagues at other universities.

The teakettle whistled, and she went into the kitchen to fix a cup, then returned to her computer. Leaving the tea to brew, she found her way onto the Birthright Reunions home page to scan the bulletin board, the file names.

"To Kelly from Nick."

She'd named the message she'd left long ago "To Nick from Kelly."

This new entry had to be a prank. Some Internet surfer out to twist her mind. Break her heart.

Don't open it. Don't open it. Don't play his game.

She had to.

She double-clicked on the file and read, "KELLY: I AM LOOKING FOR YOU. WHAT IS THE NAME OF THE MOUSE? NICK."

Her heart pounded.

What is the name of the mouse?

No crank had left that message. No crank could possibly know to ask that question. No one could know. No one but him.

There was no e-mail address, and it took her a few frantic minutes to remember how to post a message in the response section.

Shaking, she typed, "NICK: I AM LOOKING FOR YOU, TOO. THE MOUSE IS NAMED ROUSEL. KELLY."

CHAPTER FIFTEEN

NICK SHOWED UP at Rapid Riggers at three, bringing groceries for the Cataract trip. In his faded blue shorts and an equally faded T-shirt, he looked suntanned and sexy, yet Day felt the same revulsion she had that morning.

She knew about pot hunters. She didn't want Nick to have been one.

No one else was in the office, and when Day entered the kitchen, he asked without looking at her, "Are you still coming tomorrow? If you're not, I have to find someone else."

Because of Zac.

Day almost seized the opportunity. So what if he took Leah?

But Nick wasn't why she'd decided to go down Cataract Canyon in the first place. It was for her.

"Yes. I'm coming."

"When's Bob supposed to show up here?"

"Anytime. Susan left at nine."

Nick said nothing more to Day. She returned to work on the computer, confirming the reservations Susan had made that morning, and soon Susan's VW bus wheeled into the lot. Day heard the screen door bang and saw Nick go down the porch steps.

From the window she watched him open Bob's door, embrace his friend, grab his bag and walk slowly beside him to the office. Ready to be leaned on if Bob should lose his balance.

It made her anger seem unreasonable.

It made her recall what Grace had said.

NICK DISAPPEARED at five, and a half hour later, Day prepared to shut off the computer and go home. Susan said, "Wait, don't. Have you checked Birthright?"

"This morning. But if you want to get on the Net, feel free." Day's mind was still on business. "While you're on there, would you please check that German tour web page? I can't find it, and the guy who writes it said he was going to mention Rapid Riggers. I'd like to see it."

"Sure. I'll do that right away. Bob's upstairs sleeping. We're going to stop by the party for a little while—till he gets tired."

The grand opening of the River Inn. Full circle from New Year's Eve.

Susan and Day exchanged weary looks. It had been a long few months, and Bob had long years of recovery ahead.

Day said, "Grace and Zac will be really glad to see him. She called and asked if he'd be coming."

"Good." Susan took her seat at the computer. "You know, we could have our own web page, Day."

"The thought never crossed my mind. I guess that could be useful. Want to look into it?"

"Sure. I can do that now."

Day drove home alone and found Nick's truck gone. She showered and changed into her dress for the party. The ivory Grecian-style sleeveless gown looked like a 1920s flapper dress, and Day wore a long string of pearls with it. When she was dressed, she looked down at her wedding ring, the simple band of silver etched with Hopi symbols, and impulsively went to her room to exchange the pearls for her Aquitaine. Then she opened her jewelry box and took out her charm bracelet.

Symbol of the years. Love and pain.

Grace had said, *Maybe it's not the pot hunting that's making you mad.*

Day's hand shook as she fastened on the bracelet.

Where was Nick?

She poured herself some Courvoisier, settled on the blue leather couch and waited, remembering the night of the solstice, when he'd come here—and left.

He didn't want a relationship with you, Day. Now you know why. He tried to keep it from happening.

She sipped her drink, recalling the way Nick had walked Bob from the car to the office. Nick, who'd saved Bob's life. *Oh, Nick, you know how to be good.*

She went to the telephone and dialed the number at his trailer. It rang four times, and then his machine switched on. After his message she said, "Nick, it's Day. I was just wondering if... are we going to this thing together? I'm going to leave at seven, unless you call me."

As she hung up the phone, her front door opened and he came in, wearing his suit.

They both froze, and then he shut the door.

Neither spoke.

He looked nice.

Forgive him, Day.

I can't. She retreated into the living room to pick up the purse she'd laid on top of the television.

Wandering over to the breakfast bar, Nick ignored her. She had hurt him, and he rebelled from telling her what he'd done that morning, how he had tried to make amends. He *hadn't* done it for her.

He'd done it for himself. He could start over with or without her.

"Did you talk to Grace today?" he asked at last.

"Yes." Day knew what he was wondering. "She knows everything. But don't worry. She considers it a misdemeanor. A lot of people do."

Nick caught the breath of hauteur. Without emotion he said, "I guess we should go to that party. Whose car do you want to take?"

Before she could answer, the phone rang.

Nick picked it up. "Hello?"

"Nick, it's Susan. I was just on-line with that adoption reunion network. Somebody answered that message Day and I posted."

The kitchen clock ticked beside his ear.

"Nick?"

"Yeah."

"Do you want to hear it?"

Day was just across the room. He wanted to protect himself. From her. Glad she couldn't hear Susan's end of the phone conversation—but also longing for the old Day, his best friend—he said, "Yes."

"She says, 'Nick: I am looking for you, too. The name of the mouse is Rousel. Kelly.'"

Rousel.

"Nick? Are you there?"

"Yeah. Thanks...Susan. Thanks a lot." Day was playing with her purse, but he knew she was listening.

"Is that the name of the mouse?"

"Yes."

"She left an e-mail address. Do you want me to post a message back to her?" Susan's voice brimmed with excitement, and Nick knew she could feel joy for him because she would give anything to see her daughter again.

He remembered Day that morning, how she had looked at him when she found out that he'd stolen pots.

A terrible thought came to him.

What if his sister rejected him, too?

"Um . . . not right now. Thanks, though, Susan. Thanks a lot."

As he set the receiver in its cradle, Day's eyes regarded him sharply. "What was that about?"

"Nothing. Let's go to this party."

THEY TOOK the Porsche, and it was a tense and silent ride. When they reached the River Inn, the lot and drive were so packed they had to park back out on the road, but Nick said, "I'll drive you to the door."

"Thanks." When she stepped out under the cotton-woods in front of the hotel, there were people milling on the screened porch, and someone whistled wildly.

"They're here!"

As Day climbed the steps, Fast Susan pushed open the screen door and embraced her. Her Mohawk was perfectly spiked, the ends tipped with silver to match her dress. "The newlyweds! Grace just told me. Where's Nick going?"

"To park." Day thought she'd throw up. "Where's Bob?"

"Resting in the parlor. He really wants to see you guys."

Lew emerged from the door of the old kitchen. "Here comes the bride!" he sang. "All dressed in white!"

Silver letters were strung along the side of the house, inside the screened porch. CONGRATULATIONS, NICK AND DAY. And underneath was a hand-painted banner. WELCOME BACK, BOB. WE LOVE YOU.

Zachary hurried outside to hug Day and kiss her cheek. Pip was behind him as he said, "You look beautiful. Where's your husband so I can congratulate him?"

"Parking." She could feel sweat gathering under her makeup.

"Hello, Day." Pip's smile was both wistful and forgiving. "Nick's a lucky man."

"Thank you." She needed to get inside before Nick came, before people started banging glasses or demanding that they dance or . . . She tried to ease through the men toward the door, smiling at everybody, glowing. Acting.

Susan was at her elbow. "Did you stop at Rapid Riggers and leave a message for Kelly?"

Kelly.

Day blinked at her as they squeezed inside. "What are you talking about?"

"Nick's sister." Susan's brows drew together. Her friend, in a slow baffled voice, said, "He didn't tell you. We found his sister."

AFTER SUFFERING kisses that were worse than nothing and holding Day through a slow dance to "Moon River," Nick retired to the parlor with Bob.

It wasn't the haven he'd hoped for.

His friend said, "I'm really happy you married her. Once, when my car needed a new transmission, she lent me five hundred dollars. Said I could pay it back whenever."

"I thought you had memory problems," said Nick, not wanting to know about Day's good deeds.

"What do you call it? Short-term?"

Nick wasn't sure whether or not it was a joke. Bob seemed almost like a shadow of his old self.

Bob said, "She's better-looking than . . ." He crunched up his forehead.

"Than anybody. That's what you meant to say, isn't it?"

Bob smiled. "Right."

Nick let his friend have his happiness. He played the part for Bob. And fought the horrible numbing hurt all through him.

He wasn't glad he'd married Day. Not without telling her the truth first. It *had* been an abduction.

He'd stolen her choices.

Because he'd been afraid that if she knew everything, she wouldn't choose him.

ZACHARY INTRODUCED Day to Mr. Musashi, who seemed to be pleased with his surroundings at the River Inn.

It wasn't true that their Japanese visitor knew no English. He knew "hello," "goodbye," "please," "thank you," "yes," and "no." Day bowed to him and used Zachary's services as a translator to extend her wishes for a pleasant vacation and Cataract Canyon trip. The wealthy businessman beamed at her and nodded many times.

At least the trip can be a success, she thought. She was good at hiding her anger toward Nick. She'd had practice.

At last, tired of the crowd, she slipped off her shoes and stockings and walked down to the river in the twilight. But before she arrived at the water the door of the screened porch creaked.

It was Nick. From under the giant cottonwood, he said, "I'm ready to leave whenever you are."

His voice was cold.

When Day started toward him, he turned away. "I'll go get the car."

Nick had parked in a turnout almost a quarter mile from the inn. Reaching the Porsche, he swore and began madly yanking off the tin cans tied to the bumper and hurling them into the tamarisk. But the strings were tight and he cut himself, and finally he rested his arms on the roof, above the window painted with JUST MARRIED, and caught his breath.

I didn't want it to be like this, Day. I just wanted you to keep loving me.

Instead, he'd given her what she wanted and more. His whole heart and all his trust.

And she hated him.

THE CAR WAS LIKE a morbid joke. When Nick pulled up beside the cottonwood tree, Day gazed stupidly at the words on the window before she made herself walk to the passenger door and open it.

Buckling her seat belt, she ignored the obvious, the rancor between them. "You didn't tell me about your sister."

The minute Nick saw Susan, he knew Day had been told. Susan had said, *That's a pretty big one to keep from your new wife, Nick. What's wrong?*

He would let Day or Grace tell her that.

"Aren't you going to answer her?"

"I don't know."

The words were clipped. Day knew what they meant. *Don't talk to me; I can't stand the sound of your voice; I can't stand your presence.*

Day tried to picture Nick's sister. She would be about twenty-three. Maybe she looked a little like Nick. Perhaps she still had a cleft lip and palate. Perhaps not.

But whoever she was, she had been scanning that bulletin board at the Birthright web site for one reason. To find her brother.

"Nick, you need to answer. Think about *her*. She is probably *sitting* at her computer waiting for you to answer. You owe her an answer."

"She knows I'm alive. I know she's alive. That's enough."

Enough for a woman who'd been molested by her father at seven, then given away by the only person she trusted? "You can't be serious. She needs you." *You need each other.*

The miles fell away in silence until he turned onto the highway. Just before the Rapid Riggers lot, he flipped on his right turn signal.

Day let herself breathe.

Through the windshield, under the porch railings, Nick could see the sign in the office window. NEXT TRIP: 9 A.M. The sign referred to the Daily.

But his next trip was at nine in the morning, too. Cataract Canyon, with Day.

They would be gone for four days.

It was a long time for Kelly to wait. Little Kelly, whose eyes had been so changed after that terrible day, after the sounds he'd heard from upstairs.

She needs you.

"What am I going to say?" At least Day was talking to him.

"Just tell her where you live and what you do and ask her if you can see her."

Nick wasn't sure he wanted to see her.

She needs you.

He grasped the door handle.

In the office, Day turned on the light, sat down and booted up her computer. "Let's look at her message first." She got on-line, went to the Birthright web site, called up the bulletin board. "There it is."

As she double-clicked on the file, Nick peered over her shoulder.

The message came up, and seeing it was twice the shock of hearing the words Susan had spoken on the phone.

"THE MOUSE IS NAMED ROUSEL."

On a message pad, Day noted Kelly's e-mail address, then logged off and set up to type an e-mail letter. She looked at Nick expectantly.

Hot, sweating, smelling things that weren't in the room, he loosened his tie. *What if she doesn't like me? What if she hates that I stole pots?* What if she said the things Day had said? *That's gross. You idiot.*

Day saw his face. A hard place inside her cracked, and the warmth that was her love for him crept through. *He's so scared.*

She typed, "KELLY: I'M AN OUTFITTER AND A PARAMEDIC, AND I LIVE IN MOAB." She added the Rapid Riggers e-mail address and signed the message, "NICK."

He nudged her aside, and she watched him slowly find the right keys. He deleted the part about what he did for a living.

Feeling close to tears and unsure why, Day gazed up at his face. Why had he done that?

But he'd already turned his back.

She knew his heart, and her own heart ached. At the moment, to himself, he wasn't an outfitter and a paramedic.

He was scum.

She remembered reading that a knight's heart must be hard and resilient, yet soft and pliable as hot wax. Right now Nick's heart was hurt, and she loved him too much to want to do anything but fix it.

She forgave him then.

She forgave everything.

AS NICK REMOVED his tie and hung his jacket in the closet, he heard her in the bathroom, running the water, brushing her teeth. When they'd come inside, she looked up at him and met his eyes, and for that minute things had felt almost right. She had said, "Shall we go to bed?"

He flicked off the light, took off the rest of his clothes and propped the French doors open. When he turned around, Day was there. Naked.

The long hellish hours fell away, and there was just a curtain of night and tenderness. In her bed, in her fine cotton sheets, he felt her body, her skin against him. "I love you."

"I love you, Nick. I love you so much."

Nothing else mattered, none of the other steps he was taking to make things right. The only thing that could help was her love for him and his for her. He worshiped her with his mouth and his tongue and his penis, trying to please her, glad when she cried out in the night. And when he had given her everything and could only hold her, she nudged him onto his stomach. She lay beside him and stroked his legs and rubbed her cheek and her lips against his lower back, where he knew she was kissing his scars.

He shuddered as she tried to unhurt him.

And pieces of the pain fell away.

FROM THE INNER OFFICE, Day could hear Nick in the next room talking to Joe. In twenty minutes the guide would drive them to the put-in at the River Inn, hauling the raft; then, with another shuttle driver and a second car, he'd take the vehicle and trailer down to Hite Marina. But Day had time to check her e-mail first.

Kelly had answered.

Her message made Day protective, so fearful of Nick's being hurt that she contemplated destroying what his sister had written.

She could not.

Day switched on her printer and listened to it hum, warming up, then printed the letter. Taking it from the printer, she went out to the reception area and handed it to Nick.

He knew what it was and took it into the kitchen, to read in privacy.

Dear Nick,
I would love to come to Moab and see you. I can come

in May. Till then I am field supervisor on an archaeological dig in New Mexico. Since I was adopted, I
have been known by the name Rory Abbot. My parents let me pick my name, and I wanted to be called
Aurora, like Sleeping Beauty. The Disney version was
the first movie I ever saw. Please keep writing to me.
I've also enclosed my post-office-box address, in case
you would rather write a real letter.

Your sister,
Rory

Day had followed him into the kitchen. "Nick."

"I know." He pushed back into the reception area,
folded the e-mail and tucked it in his personal ammo can,
the waterproof can in which he kept his sunglasses and
camera while on the river. He doubted he would answer.
His sister would never accept him.

He was cursed.

And she was an archaeologist.

OUTSIDE THE RIVER INN, Day cooled herself in the shade
of a giant cottonwood, while Nick, with Zac translating,
gave Mr. Musashi a basic river-safety lecture. Don't drink
the water in the river, this is how your life vest should fit,
this is the Groover. Welcome to the wilderness.

A park-service ranger stopped by and checked Nick's
boatman's license, first-aid kit and the life vests. Then
Grace came outside in a white lawn dress—attired as the
hostess of the inn—to see them all off.

"Do you have everything you need, Mr. Musashi?"

He held out his camera to her and said something to Zac.
He wanted to pose with Zac and Nick while Grace took a
picture. After that he took a picture of Grace and one of
Day.

At last they launched.

Day found a place in the back of the raft and opened *Tales from the Thousand and One Nights*. She was trying to learn the story of Aladdin, to retell to the children at the library. Day had developed a sudden fascination with urchin thieves who make good.

Mr. Musashi tapped her shoulder and held out his million-dollar Japanese camera. Gesturing, he asked her to take a picture of him with the river in the background.

Day obliged, then settled back to watch Nick row, almost grateful for the turmoil of her thoughts, the revelations of the past few days. They stole her mind from the inevitable.

That the river flowed down.

She had set out for Cataract Canyon, and there was no graceful way to turn back.

THEY CAMPED that night just inside Canyonlands National Park at Little Bridge Canyon. Because Day was the swamper, it was her job to help derig for the night. She helped Mr. Musashi pitch his tent, then arranged the bathroom, then helped Nick slice vegetables for dinner. It was hot and dirty work, work she hated.

It was work Nick had done for years.

She should get used to it. To river trips and backpacking trips and climbing vertical rockfaces. To roaring white water.

And the truth was, she would be proud of herself if she went down the Selway.

It was only this trip, this trip that made her tense, scared. A wreck inside.

While Day stood working at the table, Zachary bent past her, retrieving a soda from the cooler for Mr. Musashi. As he straightened up, he stopped, looking curiously at the Aquitaine that dangled from the cord around her neck. Day had tucked it inside her life vest on the river, but now it hung down in front of the blouse she wore over her bikini. "What is that?"

Nick lit the Dutch oven beside them.

"It's an Aquitaine," she said. "It tells time when you turn it toward the sun. Eleanor of Aquitaine gave one to Henry II so that he'd know when to meet her for trysts."

Zachary smiled. "Henry met quite a *few* people for trysts. It became a source of discord between them. But that's a remarkable instrument you have. Let me see how it works."

Lifting his eyes from the fire, Nick watched Zac point the Aquitaine toward the sun. Leave it to Zachary Key to know that detail. *Quite a few people*... Nick had just read the card that came with the piece and thought it sounded romantic. Now he felt stupid, but he just shrugged at Day.

She said, "You did good."

Zachary winced. "Sorry, friends. I didn't think."

"You think too much," said Nick with a smile of forgiveness.

As Zachary hurried away with Mr. Musashi's soda, Day tried out her Aquitaine, holding it up to the sun. "I love this thing. It says it's five o'clock."

"Let me see." Nick left the fire and stood beside her.

Day watched his brown fingers on the ring.

Then his fingers were touching her face, and he said, "No others."

"I know."

THAT NIGHT, Nick observed Zachary closely. He was relaxed and confident, making their passenger feel happy and at ease.

Good.

The year before, Grace had flipped a raft in a keeper hole in Cataract. Her husband had saved her life and lost his own mind. He had climbed on a cliff above the river, then borrowed a dory and set out for the Big Drop with no life vest. Nick had feared for his life. And Grace's, when she followed.

Zac seemed steady now, and Nick counted on his staying that way. He'd wanted a swamper along to help if Zac got out of hand, and Day was good in a crisis. But she was meeting a demon of her own on this trip.

The screaming, she'd said.

Last thing before they turned in, Zac helped him put out the camp fire, and the two of them ended up sitting together in the dark. Zac told him about Eton, not just about learning Japanese, but about going to school in uniforms designed in another century, about answering to bells, about customs from the time of George III. In spite of himself, Nick was interested. Especially when Zac said, "Eton was fine. But when I *first* went to school . . . it was different. I was seven. My mother had overdosed on pills the night before. But I was a little man and off to school I went."

Nick glanced at him in the dark. He was surprised. That it had happened. Also that Zac had told him. The last seemed brave.

Just hours earlier, Nick had resented Zachary's Oxford education, resented his knowing some trivia about Eleanor of Aquitaine and Henry II, while Nick wasn't even completely sure when they'd been alive. But Zac had been in low places, too. Not just when he was a kid, either. As a man, he had become ill—psychotic—in front of an entire film crew and his own wife.

Low places.

Almost as low as the space under the shack. As low as eating bugs and listening to your father molest your little sister.

The bridge to other people, to Day and Grace and Zac, to Susan and Bob, seemed less long, less far.

ON THE AFTERNOON they reached Cataract Canyon, they could hear the rapids from a long way off. For Day, the sound and the thousand-foot cliffs were familiar as a recurrent nightmare. As the cathedral world floated by, she wondered, *Why am I here?*

Near the riverbank a sign warned of dangerous rapids approaching. Foam stretched wide across the river. It was the stew of Brown Betty Rapid, named for the ill-fated kitchen boat of an 1889 Colorado River expedition. Before the raft hit the white water, Nick pulled off to river right, to the beach at Spanish Bottom.

Day was derigging when Nick's shadow fell over her on the hot sand. "You can do that later. Let's go look at the white water."

Mr. Musashi and Zac accompanied them to the edge of the beach and up a trail in the boulders. Day, in her high-top sneakers, found it a scramble. Nick grabbed her hand and helped her up to the boulder from where they could see the class-III rapids below.

It was in Capsize Rapid, almost ten miles downstream, that Jim Antonio had died. But the power of the river spoke here, calling so loudly that Day couldn't hear Nick's voice unless he yelled to her. Contemplating the water tumbling through the cataract, she wanted to turn back, even to call a helicopter to take her out of the canyon.

And after dinner that night she threw up.

While she bathed her face in the river, Nick said, "Want to talk?"

"I want it to be over."

"It will be."

Day bit her tongue, knowing he would laugh if she told him about her premonition, a premonition she knew was totally irrational.

Nick hugged her. "Sometimes Cataract makes *me* scared enough to want to throw up. It's okay. I won't let anything happen to you, Day."

She gave him the smile that showed her courage. "There's no one I trust more than you."

Nick felt a goose walk over his grave.

The sound of the cataract was getting to him, too.

IN THE MORNING Day helped clean up after breakfast and rig the raft, then listened while Nick, with Zac translating for Mr. Musashi, reviewed the use of throw bags—and how to swim a rapid. Afterward they all climbed into the boat, and Zachary shoved them away from shore.

In the white water, Day surrendered to the bouncing sensation of the raft. She threw her weight to whatever side of the raft Nick indicated, to keep them from flipping. Water washed over the tubes, soaking her.

Her adrenaline raced. Her stomach rose and plummeted.

And the trepidation, the tension, stayed. The white water roared around her, too often larger than the raft, and she knew in her heart that she was surviving, not rejoicing. She searched for the kind of strength she'd felt on the San Juan. It eluded her. This river was too big, too big for her. And Day realized the truth.

I'm never going to love big white water again.

She counted rapids. Day knew she'd be counting till the end, till they reached Lake Powell and the water had calmed.

They stopped for lunch before Mile-Long Rapid, and Day lathered on more sunscreen and helped Nick with the dishes, then raided his ammo can to read the river guide.

Capsize was in Mile-Long Rapid, but it was only rated III +. Farther on lay the Big Drop, class-IV white water.

It's almost over. By tonight you'll have done it, Day. And after that, you'll be able to face anything.

They packed up and pushed the boat away from the shore.

Mile-Long Rapid.

She held on, moved where Nick directed, endured the plunging of her stomach. As they passed out of the foam into smoother water before another rapid, Nick rested on the oars, letting them drag in the water.

He was wearing his sunglasses and she hers, but Day knew he was gazing right at her. He said, "That was it."

"What?" Her throat was tight, and her head ached from the sun.

"Capsize."

Relief flooded her veins. She hadn't even recognized the rapid. She'd been too busy punching tubes, helping to keep the raft right.

Nick leaned forward at the oars and kissed her mouth.

Day strove to make her smile natural, enthusiastic.

They were over the worst.

The next rapid was Been Hurt. They navigated it without incident, and afterward Nick stopped to scout. They had reached the Big Drop.

Day did not accompany him and Zac and Mr. Musashi up onto the boulders to look at the white water and assess the hazards. Instead, she read the guidebook. This rapid, Satan's Seat, was the second to last in the canyon. Its principal feature was a big keeper called Little Niagara. After Satan's Seat came Satan's Gut.

She knew these places, had visited them in another lifetime.

Almost over. Oh, God, will he want me to make this trip again?

And if he asked, would she go?

The men returned to the boat, and Nick spun the raft out into the flow, easily heading onto the tongue.

He's done this a million times.

The boat hurtled forward, sliding down into a trough like a roller-coaster car, then rising back up. Icy water crashed over Day's head, and the fingers of her right hand clung to the webbing that held the dry bags in place, while the fingers of her left found a D-ring in the tube.

As water showered again, Day had the split-second impression of a long projectile shooting up from the river. With the sight came impact, a blunt point plunging into the side of her ribcage, knocking the wind out of her, stabbing her, doubling her over. She lost her handholds and grasped the raft frame, instead, but she couldn't sit upright.

Nick made a wild grab for the oar that had jerked from his grasp. He locked his fingers around the handle, and as the raft poured down the tongue between Little Niagara and the hole on the opposite side, he jabbed the oar back in the oarlock. Wondering what had popped the oar, he made for the beach on river right to get his bearings and scout the next rapid, Satan's Gut.

Day leaned forward, gripping the raft frame, as the white water lessened to bouncing waves of foam.

When he eddied out, Day was the logical person to jump out with the bow line and hold the raft. Fighting pain from the oar's striking her, she sat up and stepped into the water. Then she realized she'd forgotten the bow line. She bent over to grab it.

The motion brought agony. Hardly daring to breathe, able only to take shallow quick breaths, Day shut her eyes and held on to the raft as the others got out. Nick began hauling the boat to safety, and she let go and straightened up, catching her breath.

God, that hurts.

Staring vacantly at the white water, at a massive boulder hiding part of Satan's Gut, she wished the rapids were over.

"Day? Coming?"

They were going to scout the rapid. Nick had removed his sunglasses, and his eyes invited her to come. For some reason she was afraid to be alone. Afraid to be apart from him. She nodded and started to walk, until she had to cough. The piercing stitches in her chest made her stop.

"Day?" Nick watched her cough again, deeply. "Are you okay?"

"Yeah. The oar hit me. I'm just getting my wind." She tried to breathe and clutched the area around her life vest.

The oar hit her? Instant replay—the force with which the oar had popped free of the oarlock and shot out of his hand.

"Why don't you sit down?" he suggested. He led her a short distance from shore to a place against a large smooth boulder.

She sat down gingerly, white-faced, and coughed again. In pain.

Scaring him.

Zachary had followed them across the sand, and Nick asked, "Zac, could you please get the first-aid kit?"

"Sure."

Day heard Mr. Musashi say something in Japanese and Zac reply.

"Day, try not to cough right now. When I take this vest off, you can support the place that hurts with your hands." Nick unfastened her life vest, watching her face, and she barely noticed him holding her wrist, glancing at his watch. Nick. Nick would take care of her.

She wasn't bleeding, but when he unbuttoned her shirt, exposing her bikini top, he saw the bruise. Just below and to the side of her left breast.

"It's right here." She started to point, then coughed again, fiercely, clutching her side.

Nick contained his emotions. "I think you've cracked a rib. I'm going to tape it up for you." Her cough sounded ominous, and he kept his gravest fear to himself.

I think you've punctured a lung.

CHAPTER SIXTEEN

NICK TOOK ZAC ASIDE. "Get out the signal mirror and give it to Mr. Musashi. Explain that we're trying to get the attention of an aircraft. Then clear the beach and lay out everything you can find that's bright-colored. Life vests, anything we've got, in a big X."

A year ago others had done the same thing—so that a chopper would come and get Zac.

Zachary asked, "What's happening?"

"I think she broke a rib and it may have lacerated her lung. When you've done the other stuff, bring a couple sleeping bags and an air mattress over. You can get ours out of my dry bag."

Zachary nodded, and Nick thought, *Keep it together, Zac. Don't let me down now.* Returning to Day, he took off his life vest, dropped to his knees in front of her and smiled. "Doing okay?"

She nodded. He knew she was frightened. So was he.

Taking a roll of two-inch wide adhesive tape from the ammo can that held first-aid supplies, Nick asked, "So, have you ever wondered why, when birds fly in a V, one side of the V is longer than the other?"

Day squinted at him, trying to breathe normally. "Why?"

"Because there are more birds on that side."

She started to laugh, but it hurt. "Don't do that again."

As he ripped pieces of tape, he tried to forget it was Day, the person he loved most in the world. Right now, he was all she had. *Maybe the cough is a throwback to her smoking.*

He didn't think so. He'd never carried oxygen on a river trip, didn't know anyone who did. He wished he had it now. "Okay, go ahead and put your left arm on your head. When I tape this, tell me if it hurts worse."

She nodded and lifted her arm above her head. She felt scared. There was no reason, but her fear made it hard to breathe. "It hurts a lot."

"Broken ribs are painful. Here?"

"Yes." She coughed, had to take her hand off her head. She felt like she was dying. "God." When she could, she lifted her arm again.

"Okay, I want you to take a deep breath and let out all the air."

Day did as he said.

He taped her ribs. "Okay?"

She took a breath and nodded, then carefully lowered her arm. Nick found his blood-pressure cuff and stethoscope, while behind him, Zac pulled Day's sleeping bag out of its stuff sack and inflated her air mattress.

Beyond Nick and Zac, Mr. Musashi flashed a signal mirror toward the sky. As Nick assessed her vital signs, Day said, "I have to go out in the helicopter?"

"I knew you didn't want to run that last rapid." He wrote something down, then reached for her hand again.

Day saw him squeezing her fingernail. "Is everything normal?"

"About what you'd expect. Let's have you lie down on the side that's hurt." Her body weight would exert counterpressure on the hole in her lung and help keep air from filling her chest cavity—air that would prevent her lung's expanding and make it harder for her to breathe.

Nick helped her lie down on the mattress, registering her every wince, and tucked his life vest beneath her feet. "Okay?"

She nodded.

He pushed a lock of hair off her cheek. Her skin was cool. *Come on, we need an airplane.* What he heard was an outboard motor. A J-rig, with three large inflatable pontoons, was bounding through the rapids.

Nick got up, waved his left arm at the J-rig, a sign that they had an emergency.

The boatman saw him and turned. Wild West River Expeditions out of Green River. There were seven passengers on board.

Nick waded into the water, grabbed the bow line.

"What's up?" Letting the motor idle, the boatman came toward Nick on the center pontoon. Beneath his visor, his sunglasses reflected Nick's face, and his beard was silty, as though he'd enjoyed a mud fight earlier that day.

"I'm Nick Colter, with Rapid Riggers in Moab, and I'm a paramedic. This woman suffered a compression trauma from an oar handle. She has a chest injury, broken rib and suspected lacerated lung. We need a chopper and oxygen."

From the air mattress where she lay, Day gazed at the life vests arranged in the sand. Why did Nick want a helicopter? He'd taped her up, and Satan's Gut was the last rapid.

The coughing returned, hard, and she saw blood on her hand.

"Nick?" She tried to sit up.

The Wild West boatman gunned his outboard and turned the J-rig into the current.

Nick jogged back to Day, seeing blood on her fingers. He handed her a triangular bandage to wipe up the blood. "You need to lie down, Day."

She moved gingerly.

Nick rearranged the life vest beneath her feet, covered her with a sleeping bag and monitored her breathing. Her lips were already faintly blue.

"Could I have some water?"

He shook his head, smiling at her, meeting her eyes. *Oh, God, Day, hang on.* What was she doing on this trip? She should be back at the office, putting on lipstick, tormenting Daily boatmen with her stockings and heels. It was his fault she was here.

She whispered, "What's wrong with me?"

"I'm not sure, but we're taking good care of you." A nightmare, to be saying these things to Day. These were the things you said when you didn't want the patient to know she might die. Day needed oxygen. It could be hours before a helicopter got here. "Are you allergic to any medications, Day? Any medical problems we should know about?"

"No." As he checked her vital signs again, she coughed, and more blood came up. The pain was worse. "I feel dizzy." Her breath felt too fast, and she couldn't get enough air.

Nick didn't take his eyes from her. Her blood pressure was falling. If she started going into shock, they were in trouble. It would be harder for her to breathe on her back. *Go, Wild West!* There was no telling when the J-rig would reach a radio or phone.

She could die. He wanted to say things to her, to tell her to hang on, that he needed her. But revealing his fear would frighten her.

Nick held her hand, tried to keep a clear head. Knowing he should check her vitals again soon, he spent the interim calming her. "So I was looking through the book I gave you for your birthday. There are lots of pictures of England. I never knew there were real places those stories were supposed to have happened. Like the castle where Arthur was born. I want to take you there.''

His calluses, the texture of his skin, soothed her. She barely heard his words. Only felt his hand. Did he know how bad she felt? *Don't complain. He knows.*

"I was thinking, too, about a house. We could build it behind Rapid Riggers. Our land reaches from the river to River Inn Road. Day, tell me how you're feeling.'' Though her shallow breaths told him plenty.

She tried to answer and coughed, hard, fading beyond white to blue and gray with pain.

God, where's an airplane?

Two rafts pulled over. Current Adventure Tours. Lew was one of the guides. He talked to Zac, then came over. "How're you doing, May-Day? Anything I can do, Nick?''

The twin engines of a small aircraft rumbled above. Nick closed his eyes. "Just make sure they see us." Thank God.

Mr. Musashi and the two Current Adventures guides flashed signal mirrors at the plane, and the aircraft tipped its wings as it passed over the beach.

Fifteen minutes, at least, till a helicopter landed. Nick asked her, "Okay?''

"Yes.''

"A plane just flew over. We'll have a helicopter soon.''

She'd always been brave. She knew him well enough to understand that something bad was happening now. But he couldn't talk about it. And he had to focus every minute.

Time dragged as he watched her condition deteriorate. He saw signs of air beneath her skin. When he touched it, he felt a crackling sensation beneath his fingers, like Rice Krispies. Subcutaneous emphysema. A certain sign she'd injured an air-containing part of her respiratory tract.

"Nick?'' She spoke suddenly, as though she'd just awoken in the dark.

"What is it?''

"Oh. Nothing."

He smoothed her hair back from her lackluster eyes. Her skin was cold and clammy, and when he touched his fingers to her carotid artery, her pulse was weak.

She was going into shock.

Her eyes were shut, and he said, "Day? Are you okay?"

She nodded.

"Stay with me. All right? I love you." He wouldn't say that again. Anyone could hear that catch in his voice. Which meant she could. He monitored her breaths. Fast but too shallow.

Day struggled for air. She couldn't think where she was or what was happening. Zac's voice asked, "What can we do, Nick?"

"Tell Lew to clear the beach so the chopper can land. I'm going to start rescue breathing. I want you to monitor her pulse. Day, are you okay?"

"Yes." She coughed. "I can't breathe."

"Day, we should have a helicopter here pretty soon. Can you roll onto your back?"

She tried, painfully easing down on the air mattress. "I can't breathe, Nick."

"I know. I'm going to give you some breaths."

She was afraid. *I'm dying.*

He tilted her head back and lifted her chin. Day felt his mouth cover hers, a tight seal, felt his breath going into her. She coughed. "Nick..." Hands soothed her. She heard him counting.

Tears squeezed out of her eyes, and she shifted, trying to get comfortable.

"Relax, Day."

She didn't know who spoke. She lost what was going on around her and only felt the pain and his mouth again and the breath that wasn't hers. Time suspended. Then everything was black.

"Day, are you okay?"

She did not respond.

"Do you have a pulse, Zac?" He glanced at his watch. *He didn't even have an oral airway with him.*

"Yes. It's weak."

But it was there. *Hang on, Day.* If her heart stopped beating, they were in trouble. With her cracked rib, chest compressions could tear her up inside. Nick didn't feel the sweat streaming off him or the sand beneath his knees as he counted. His ears were tuned to every sound in the air, but there was only the ceaseless pounding of the rapids.

Come on, chopper. "One and two and..."

Minutes later, he heard the distant thrumming of the blades. He kept counting.

"I lost her pulse."

Nick pushed Zac's hand aside and felt for her carotid artery. Nothing. "Give her two rescue breaths and watch her airway. Keep it open." Kneeling beside her, he cleared his mind so he wouldn't think how few people actually survived CPR and how few of them later left the hospital alive. It was a primitive method of lifesaving, the best humans could do, less fail-safe than Na-chu-rú-chu's magic, the singing and gourd-shaking of the Pueblo weaver who had married the Moon. Day's chances had just taken a dive.

Zac gave two rescue breaths while Nick found her sternum and located the proper hand position. *I could kill her. That rib could hit her heart.*

He had no choice. It would take the helicopter too long to land.

"One breath, five compressions," said Nick. He pressed into Day's injured chest, praying her heart to stay sound. "One and two and three and..."

She vomited.

"Roll her on her side." Nick groped for a suction device from the ammo can. He was screwing up.

The black shape of the helicopter passed over him as he continued CPR. His arms and chest grew tired. A gust from the chopper blades blasted him as the craft touched down.

A minute had passed since they'd begun CPR. Nick stopped chest compressions and checked her pulse and breathing. He spun his head and yelled to Lew, who stood twenty yards away directing the helicopter. "No pulse! No respirations!"

Lew yelled what he'd said to the paramedics.

As Nick resumed CPR, shadows swarmed around him. He continued chest compressions, counting, while the paramedics prepared for defibrillation.

"What have we got?" someone asked.

He shot off an answer. "No pulse, no respirations, fractured rib, hemopneumothorax. I popped an oar and it hit her chest. I'm a paramedic." *And she's my wife.*

A female paramedic brought out the paddles. "Stop CPR. Everybody clear!"

Nick recognized the man preparing to intubate Day. These were the same people who had come to get Bob.

"Check a pulse."

Nick got around her other side, knelt close to her.

"No pulse," said the man at her head. "Fire again."

"Clear!"

A paramedic nudged Nick aside.

He stood up as they defibrillated her at 300, then 360 joules of electricity. They were a perfectly orchestrated team.

"No pulse."

He needed to *do* something. To sing. To shake gourds. To bring back his wife, the Moon. *God, Day, come back.*

"Clear!"

Her body jumped with the electricity.

"I have a pulse!"

WHEN THE HELICOPTER was gone, Nick noticed the raft on the shore and remembered Satan's Gut. He remembered Mr. Musashi. He put away the first-aid kit. "Zac, please pack these sleeping bags."

She could die on the way to Grand Junction.

The Current Adventures crew was shoving off, starting down the last rapid of the Big Drop.

Nick tied the first-aid kit into the raft, resecured the dry bag. A mosquito bit his neck, and he hit it haphazardly. He scoured the beach with his eyes. Mr. Musashi stood beside him, putting on his life vest. He looked very sober, and when Zac came near, the man asked him something in Japanese. It looked as though he was asking about Day. Zac answered quietly.

Nick turned away. They were loaded, but before he could step into the raft, Zachary said, "We never scouted."

Nick hadn't scouted the first time, either. When he was fourteen. In the canoe. Each bend in the river had brought something he'd never seen before.

Now he knew these rapids.

But because of what Zac had done for him, for Day, he turned and hiked up onto the boulders and looked at the cataract. And when he came down, it was like the first time.

Since then, he had never felt so alone.

On this trip, there would be no Sam Sutter at the end.

There might be no Day.

IN THE SUPPLY STORE at Hite Marina, Nick waited for the pilot to return from checking his plane, fueling up, whatever he was doing before he could fly Nick to Grand Junction. Day was in surgery there.

Sam Sutter had died in heart surgery.

Nick had gone to the hospital with Day. His last words to Sam were "See you in a few." They'd clasped hands.

Never *I love you*. Neither of them had ever said that.

And when Day had been called to the lawyer's office with Grace...

You were deluded, Nick.

Day thought the pot hunting was why he'd been excluded from the will. Nick doubted it. More and more, he doubted it.

Sam hadn't been able to control him and Day. Had never tried.

But one August morning, six months before he died, he'd said what he thought. Nick couldn't remember what had instigated it. Only the words.

Frankly, sometimes I don't think you're much more than an animal. Someone screwed you up more than I can fix.

Restless, Nick twirled a postcard rack. Zac had left for Moab with Mr. Musashi in the Suburban a shuttle driver had brought. At this rate, he could be in Grand Junction before Nick.

Where was that pilot?

He'd long since gotten over the stupidity of his own expectations regarding the will. But he would never get over wishing Sam had been his father. Had adopted him.

He could have been your father, dumbshit. You could have married Day a long time ago and made him happy. Instead, you made him crazy.

Something he had to live with. Like missing him.

A postcard on the rack caught his eye. A kiva in Grand Gulch Primitive Area.

Abruptly Kelly sprang to mind.

No, not Kelly. Rory.

The archaeologist.

He'd never answered her e-mail. And now she'd been waiting for five days.

There was no fear anymore, no fear of anything except losing Day.

He spun the rack and found a postcard that showed the Maze.

The clerk wandered down the counter. "Need a stamp?"

"Thanks." He gave him some change and borrowed a pen.

Dear Rory—
I have been a moki digger. I'm not now. This is my post-office box.

                                                    Nick

He dug her address out of his dry bag, put a stamp on the card and shoved it through the mail slot a moment before the pilot came inside.

THE VENTILATOR in the intensive care unit made its Darth Vader breaths, a sound Nick never wanted to hear again. Now it was Day instead of Bob behind that mask, Day with a tube in her chest. He'd watched the paramedics insert it on the beach.

Her eyelids flickered at him, then shut, and he held her hand, sometimes pressing his lips to it, while she slept.

When the nurse came to kick him out, he went to the waiting room to find Grace and Zac.

None of them spoke, just drank coffee.

Nobody was sure Day would make it.

Nick finally went to the men's room just to be alone, to hold his arms around himself, to *feel* without people watching. There were so many things he wanted to give her, things it would take his whole life to give, and they might have only minutes.

It wasn't enough.

DAY DIDN'T NOTICE time passing, only the pain and exhaustion, physical and emotional. She knew Nick was there sometimes, holding her hand, and she never wanted him to leave but there was no way to say so. Grace sat with her, too, less frequently. Eventually, a nurse told Day they were weaning her from the ventilator, that she was doing better, and sometime after darkness had come and gone, they removed the tubing and she could talk.

Nick came in right afterward, unshaven. He bent over and gently kissed her, then adjusted her covers. "I love you," he said, looking into her eyes for a long time before he sat down, drawing his chair close.

Day started to cry. Gradually, things had begun returning to focus, and now she remembered. Not just those last moments in Cataract, but everything that had led her there. Her own dreams of what she could be. What she could have.

"Baby..." Nick sounded scared, and his hand touched her head. "Should I get a nurse?"

"No." Her voice barely worked after the hours with that tube in her throat. She closed her eyes, turned her head, surrendered again to the uncomfortable sensations in her body. "I can't be like you want me to be. You should find someone else."

What was she talking about? "What do you mean, Day?" How did she think he wanted her to be?

Tears rolled down her cheeks. She said, "I can't keep up."

Keep up? He held her hand and his own voice broke. "I don't want anyone else. I love you. You don't have to keep up with me." Old scenes came to him. Distant occasions when he'd packed for a trip, taunting, *You could come.* Knowing she wouldn't. Nick almost gagged on the recollections. He had taken other women, instead.

Day was crying.

He knelt beside her bed and kissed the tears on her cheeks. "Shh. Stop. Please. You don't understand. I never wanted you to change for me. I wanted you to be you. I love you. I was so afraid you'd die. All through Satan's Gut I tried to figure out how to hang myself from a boat if you died. I would have given anything for you not to have been there. I knew it was my fault you were, for pushing you."

"No." She jerked her head back and forth through her tears. Frustrated by her voice that wouldn't work, she whispered hoarsely, "I went for me. I didn't want to be scared anymore. I guess I'm not. But I don't like it. I don't like the things you do." Remembering the Marble Quarry, she began crying again. Talking made her tired, made her chest hurt. Still, she had to tell him. "But sometimes I love it. I just want to be with you. But I'm slow, and I'm not a good athlete."

She was sobbing, in a soft choking way, and he could see it was hurting her. "Please, sweetheart. Stop. I just want to be with you, too. Any way. Any place. Even underground. You're like the air. I'd do anything for you. I'm your knight, Day."

Energy waning, Day barely heard. She felt almost hysterical. "I want to be with you so badly. I keep trying to be what you want, but I can't do it. I'm not strong enough."

"You are what I want." How could he convince her? "Day, I *love you.*" He was whispering like her, couldn't make his own voice work.

She shook her head, crying.

He tried to hug her, awkwardly, taking care not to hurt her. He'd spent hours wondering if she would live, and he knew now the size of his love for her. She'd taught him about that kind of love. Could he prove it to her?

He said, "Test me, Day. I want to show you how much I love you. Remember in 'The Knight of the Cart'—that tournament when the queen told Lancelot to do his worst, and he did so badly and was such a coward that everyone laughed at him? That's what I want. I want to do something just because you say so. Something totally unreasonable for you to ask. I won't care if people make fun of me—because it's making you happy."

She tried to wipe her eyes, and he grabbed a tissue and wiped them for her. She looked vulnerable and confused.

Drawing closer, he held her, quiet as a breath. "You can't get rid of me, Day. Even if you reject me, I'll hang on. Whenever I see you, I'll be able to do nothing but stare. I won't be able to take my eyes off you."

Day giggled.

It was good to see her smile under the tearstains. Kissing her face, he said softly, "Please. Test me. Ask for something hard."

Her eyes started watering again. "I've never wanted that. I've never wanted to hurt you in my life."

I never wanted to hurt you, thought Nick. *I didn't know how not to. That's how stupid I was. You don't have a selfish bone in your body. I'm all self.*

"Day, you tell the stories. You know how it is." He spoke low. "It made Lancelot happy to suffer for Guinevere, to do anything for her. He loved to act on the power of his love. Give me that chance."

Looking into his brown eyes, Day understood. "You'll have lots of chances," she said softly.

He put his face against her side, bowing to her, adoring her. "Please, Day."

He did want to be a knight. Touching the head she loved more than any other, Day said, "Give up your Selway launch date."

He hadn't expected that request. It hurt, like someone had torn a chunk out of him—out of who he used to be. But that sacrifice, giving up the chance to run that wild river, giving to *her,* made him feel stronger, his heart bigger. "Thank you."

"And sell your land and give the money away."

He'd already put the place on the market, but his pride had kept him from telling her. He hadn't wanted her to think he'd done it because of her. What an alien concept that seemed now.

"I will."

Weariness swept over her, and she began to feel bad. Talking and crying had taken their toll. Nick saw and called the nurse.

"Having some discomfort?" the nurse asked.

Nick stepped back while Day was given pain medication. When the nurse was gone, he returned to her side, covered her hand with his. Her eyes drifted shut into sleep, but when Nick started to move his hand, they shot open. They were full of tears as she asked one more thing, the thing she would never have to ask again. "Don't leave."

He held her hand. "I won't." He guarded her.

And in the place where Sam Sutter had died, Nick made his own peace with him. Now he was certain he was doing the only thing Sam had ever wanted of him.

To love Day.

A nurse came in a half hour later and said, "She'll be okay if you want to go eat or something. Or clean up."

Nick shook his head. He wouldn't leave till Day said so.

But when she did awake again, she seemed stronger, and she asked, "Where are you staying? You haven't even had a shower."

"Do you want me to take one?"

She smiled. "Every day."

IN THE POST OFFICE, Rory read the postcard again.

A moki digger.

Why had he told her about the digging?

He thinks I'll hate him.

The thought made her sad. The confession was so strange, and it was impossible not to remember another confession, from another pot hunter.

She studied the writing on the postcard, then hurried out to her car and drove to her apartment. The corrugated file envelope in which she kept field notes from the Broken Sandal dig was beside her computer. She had photocopied the note the pot hunter had left, and now she fished it out and compared it to the writing on the postcard.

And then she hurried to pack, to drive to Moab and find him.

In ways she knew she'd never understand, they had been trying to meet again for a long time.

THREE DAYS LATER, Day asked Nick to return to Moab and check on things at Rapid Riggers. He drove home in the Suburban Grace and Zac had brought to Grand Junction for him and reached his trailer just after four o'clock.

When he pulled in, past the realty sign and down his drive, a faded blue Volkswagen station wagon with out-of-state plates sat under the cottonwoods.

Someone was looking at the land.

Nick was glad. He'd gone to the library in Grand Junction, researched, come home and made phone calls until he'd decided where he wanted to give the money, to an organization working to prevent child abuse.

Leaving the Suburban, he saw a woman coming up from the river and waved to her. "Hi. I'm the owner," he said, not wanting to scare her. Did she like the place?

She drew nearer. She had long dark hair.

Her face was like his.

And her car had New Mexico plates.

His eyes started watering for no reason.

She said, "I'm your sister."

"Kel—" Couldn't talk. Could just grab onto her and sob.

RORY HAD NO HARELIP. "I had surgery when I was about nine. They wanted to do it at a particular time, so that it would come out right."

"Obviously it did." The shadows beside the river flickered over a beautiful face. He looked away toward the water, trying to contain his emotions. She was all right. She'd been happy. He hadn't screwed up. He hadn't screwed up this one thing that mattered so much. Mattered—like not puncturing Day's heart with her own rib during CPR.

Both had been risks.

Both times he hadn't known what else to do.

From the cottonwood trunk where she sat, Rory tossed a stick into the current. "I'm mad at them, Nick."

Her parents.

"I'm still mad at them. Maybe I shouldn't be. They've always loved me and I love them. But what a thing to do! My mother is bipolar—manic-depressive. She couldn't adopt through normal channels." She explained that Dr. Levi Black, who had arranged the illegal adoption, had been her adoptive mother's brother.

Rory had grown up in Farmington.

So close. It should have been easy to find her.

The sun disappeared behind the cliffs, and the mosquitoes thickened. They talked, talked until he could ask, "Do you remember why I gave you away?"

"Yes."

A thin word.

"Have you ever talked to anyone about that?"

The movement of her head was negative.

"Things might be better if you...tried to talk to someone." He wasn't good at this. His father had robbed her.

Had raped her. It made him cry. "Don't let it wreck your life."

I needed you, she thought. Seeing him made her know she could talk about it. Because her brother had not lost his life in saving hers. Because she could still know the person who had told her stories about Rousel and made her believe in goodness, not just by speaking but by being. "I'll...do something." She was good at digging. She wouldn't stop now.

Recalling the photocopied note in her purse, Rory brought it out and handed it to him. She told him about the Broken Sandal site and read his dismay when she asked what he'd seen—and told him what they were seeking.

"Feces? You're looking for human feces?"

"To prove that the Anasazi practiced cannibalism. Did you see any?"

"I wouldn't have noticed anything like that. I'm sorry," he added. "But aren't some people upset by that theory, anyhow? Maybe it's better not to know."

Rory dropped her eyes, recalling what she'd just promised she would do. Continue the dig. The dig into what had happened in that shack he'd burned down. The fire had become a lesson to them both that history could not truly be destroyed. "It's always better to know."

She changed the subject then. History was still emerging. *His story.*

"Now tell me how *you* got along, Nick. Who took care of you?"

He thought of Sam Sutter. And of Day.

There was a photo on the kitchen wall at Rapid Riggers, an old man rowing a rubber ducky through Lava Falls in the Grand Canyon. There were friends upstairs. Friends down the road.

There was Day.

And there were stories to tell.

"If you've got time, I'll introduce you to them."

"I have all the time in the world."

NICK STUCK HIS HEAD in the hospital room, then looked back at his sister. "She's sleeping." He tugged on Rory's hand, led her into the room to show her the blond princess dreaming among flowers and balloons, none as bright as she, his true love. His childhood had been made of nights in sequence without days. Each missing day was repaid in this one, in her.

Nick had said something about being "lucky" in Cataract Canyon, but Rory knew that the woman in the bed was breathing because of him. Like her, this man had felt a compulsion to dig in the dirt, to dig up the past. But now the past was behind him, and he saved lives, as he had saved hers.

Rory admired him, and as she had when she was young, she found him to be a candle in a very dark room.

He was bending over the blond woman in the bed, tenderly pulling the covers up to her chin, kissing her lips.

She stirred, and when she opened her eyes, they were the color of the sky, and Rory saw how much her brother's wife loved him. She seemed to have a hard time looking away from him, but when she noticed Rory, the happiness in her eyes appeared to double. She smiled, and Rory felt herself welcomed to a new family.

Nick was kneeling beside the woman he so obviously loved, holding her hand. He said, "Day, this is my sister, Rory. And Rory, this is Day. She took care of me."

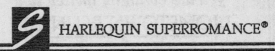

HARLEQUIN SUPERROMANCE®

ANOTHER MAN'S CHILD
by
Tara Taylor Quinn

Marcus Cartwright is rich and handsome. What's more, he's in love with his wife. And Lisa Cartwright adores her husband. *Their marriage, however, is falling apart.*

That's because Marcus can't give Lisa the baby they've always longed for.

So he's decided to give Lisa her freedom—to find and marry someone else. To have her *own* child.

It's a freedom Lisa doesn't want. But she can't convince Marcus of that.

So Lisa decides to take matters into her own hands. She decides to have a baby. And she's not going to tell Marcus until the artificial-insemination procedure is over....

But will Marcus be able to accept Another Man's Child?

Watch for *Another Man's Child* by Tara Taylor Quinn
Available in February 1997
wherever Harlequin books are sold.

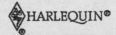

Ring in the New Year with babies, families and romance!

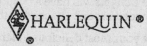

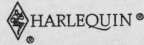

Heartbreak RANCH

Four generations of independent women...
Four heartwarming, romantic stories of the West...
Four incredible authors...

Fern Michaels
Jill Marie Landis
Dorsey Kelley
Chelley Kitzmiller

Saddle up with Heartbreak Ranch, an outstanding
Western collection that will take you on a whirlwind
trip through four generations and the exciting,
romantic adventures of four strong women who
have inherited the ranch from Bella Duprey,
famed Barbary Coast madam.

Available in March,
wherever Harlequin books are sold.

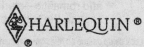

HARLEQUIN ®
®

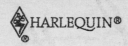
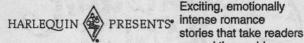

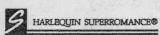